T0286839

THROUGH
The
LIQUOR GLASS

THROUGH
The
LIQUOR GLASS

SARAH FOX

Kensington Publishing Corp.
www.kensingtonbooks.com

KENSINGTON BOOKS are published by

Kensington Publishing Corp.
119 West 40th Street
New York, NY 10018

All Kensington titles, imprints, and distributed lines are available at special quantity discounts for bulk purchases for sales promotion, premiums, fund-raising, educational, or institutional use. Special book excerpts or customized printings can also be created to fit specific needs. For details, write or phone the office of the Kensington Special Sales Manager: Attn. Special Sales Department. Kensington Publishing Corp., 119 West 40th Street, New York, NY 10018. Phone: 1-800-221-2647.

Library of Congress Card Catalogue Number: 2022941325

The K and Teapot logo is a trademark of Kensington Publishing Corp.

ISBN: 978-1-4967-3403-7
First Kensington Hardcover Edition: December 2022

ISBN: 978-1-4967-3405-1 (ebook)

10 9 8 7 6 5 4 3 2 1

Printed in the United States of America

THROUGH

The

LIQUOR GLASS

Chapter 1

When I entered the town hall, I didn't expect to walk into an autumn wonderland. It was as if I'd stepped into another world. Outside, most of the leaves had already fallen from the trees, and the cold bite in the air suggested that winter wasn't far off. Here in the town hall, however, fall was still in full swing, and there was a magical, fairyland quality to it.

A latticework archway curved over the doorway that led from the vestibule to the main room. Yellow and orange sunflowers had been affixed to the arch, along with garlands of fall leaves and white fairy lights. The flowers and leaves were all artificial, but the archway still looked great, and from a couple of feet back, it was hard to tell that the decorations weren't real.

The doorway was only the beginning. In the spacious main room, the decorating committee had gone all out. Strings of orange and white lights stretched across the ceiling and tablecloths in autumn colors covered the folding tables set out along the perimeter of the room. Rustic lanterns filled with micro lights adorned the tables, while bales of straw, pumpkins, and gourds decorated the corners of the room and the spaces between some of the tables.

Although the decor as a whole impressed me, what really drew my eye was the maple tree in the middle of the room. I didn't know for sure what it was made of—papier-mâché, maybe—but it stood at least twice as tall as me, its branches reaching right up to the ceiling. Fake leaves graced the branches, which were also strung with lights.

"Whoa." Booker James stopped short when he entered the room, a pumpkin held in each of his muscular arms. "It's like fall exploded in here."

"I'll take that as a compliment." Mel Costas joined us in the room, gazing around with a satisfied expression.

Mel worked at my literary pub, the Inkwell, but she was also a talented artist and had volunteered to head the decorating committee for our town's first annual food and drink festival, A Taste of Shady Creek.

"It's definitely a compliment," Booker assured her before addressing me. "Where should I put these pumpkins, Sadie?"

I turned in a slow circle, reading the banners hanging from the tables until I spotted the one designated for my pub. "Right over here." I led the way to the table and set down the box I was carrying.

Booker placed a pumpkin at each end of the table. He worked at the Inkwell too, as a chef, and he'd offered to help me transport a few items from the pub to the town hall.

From my box, I unloaded some gourds and a vase holding a bouquet of dried flowers in fall colors. Then I removed a smaller box full of Inkwell fridge magnets and a stack of postcards that featured a photo of the Inkwell on one side and a partial menu on the other, listing some of the literary-themed food and drinks available at the pub. I'd be offering samples of a few drinks at the table, but I wanted festivalgoers to know that they could enjoy a wider variety of options if they stopped by the Inkwell.

Mel expertly arranged everything into a nice display while I tucked the box beneath the table, where it was hidden from view by the tablecloth. The box also held cups and napkins, but I wouldn't need those until the event officially opened the next day.

Voices drew our attention toward the door as several people entered the room.

"Hey, Mel, got a minute?" a woman called out.

"See you guys later," Mel said to me and Booker before jogging across the room.

I surveyed the table. "I think that's it for now."

I glanced Booker's way and realized he wasn't paying any attention to me. He was taking in the sight of the room as a whole, a far-off look in his eyes.

I nudged his arm with my elbow. "Everything okay?"

His attention snapped back to the here and now. "Everything's great. Do you need help with anything else?"

"No, that's all for today," I said. "Thanks for lending me the use of your muscles."

Booker grinned. "Any time. See you at the pub."

He set off out the door. I took a moment to admire all the decorations again and then followed in Booker's footsteps. By the time I got out the front door of the town hall, he was already out of sight.

I still had a couple of hours before I needed to open the pub for the day and I knew exactly how I wanted to spend that free time. I walked across the village green, enjoying the fresh, crisp air and the hint of wood smoke carried by the slight breeze. Although I wasn't eager for the temperature to plummet, as it no doubt would when winter arrived, I found something to enjoy about every season here in Shady Creek, Vermont. Autumn brought stunning colors, evenings cool enough to snuggle up in front of a fire, and the town's annual Autumn Festival. That event had already passed, but now there was A Taste of Shady Creek to look forward to, as well as Halloween, my birthday, and my mom's first visit to my adopted town.

When I arrived at the Village Bean, I waved to the owner,

Nettie Jo Kim, and got in line behind two other customers. While I waited, I noticed that Nettie Jo wasn't her usual relaxed self. She kept darting glances toward the back of the coffee shop while she served the customers at the counter. When it was my turn to place my order, her smile was strained.

"Hey, Sadie," she greeted as she shot another glance across the room. "What can I get you?"

I looked over that way but couldn't tell what kept drawing her attention. There were customers seated over there, but they didn't seem to be doing anything that wasn't expected from customers at a coffee shop.

"Two large lattes, please. One pumpkin spice and one pistachio."

Nettie Jo gave me a more relaxed smile and grabbed two cups, less distracted now. "Got a date with Grayson?"

She knew that my boyfriend loved her pistachio lattes.

"Not exactly," I said. "But I'm going to stop by the brewery."

Grayson owned the Spirit Hill Brewery, located next door to my pub.

I paid for the drinks and then wandered down the counter to wait for them. It didn't take long for Nettie Jo to set them in front of me. I thanked her, and then noticed her dart another glance toward the back of the shop.

"What's going on?" I asked quietly. "You seem . . . uneasy."

She grimaced. "Maybe a little nervous." She discreetly tipped her head toward one of the tables, where a dark-haired woman sat on her own, her attention focused on her phone as she sipped at a hot drink. "That's Dominique Girard," Nettie Jo whispered.

The name didn't ring a bell, and I'd never seen Dominique around town.

"Should I know who she is?" I asked.

"She's a food writer. Pretty well known in New England. These days she writes for *Foodie Fare*."

I'd heard of the magazine, although I'd never read it.

"She's in town for the festival?" I guessed.

Nettie Jo shrugged, her gaze on Dominique. "Most likely. But at the moment she's *right here*."

"And you want to make a good impression." I figured that was a safe assumption.

"I'll say."

A blast of cool air tickled at my skin as someone entered the coffee shop.

"Oh no," Nettie Jo said under her breath, her gaze on the door.

"What is it?" I asked.

A man I recognized but didn't know had just come into the shop, but I couldn't see any reason why that was a cause for concern.

Without answering my question, Nettie Jo scurried along the counter to greet the new customer. "Hi, George," she said with what sounded like false cheeriness. "What can I get you today?"

"A large black coffee," George replied. He was about to say more when he clamped his mouth shut and stared hard at Dominique.

Alarm flashed in Nettie Jo's eyes as George's face flushed.

"Ignore her," Nettie Jo whispered, sounding desperate for George to listen to her.

If he heard, he didn't heed her advice.

Apparently forgetting about his order, he marched over to Dominique's table, his generous cheeks now a worrying shade of red.

"You!" he spluttered. "You dare to set foot in this town?"

Dominique looked up from her phone, her expression one of mild surprise.

"Sorry," she said, completely unruffled. "Do I know you?"

George's face flushed even more. "You're not welcome here!" he bellowed. "You ruined my life and now you think you can waltz back into this town like you own it?"

Dominique remained composed. "I'm simply trying to enjoy a cup of coffee."

Nettie Jo darted out from behind the counter and grabbed George's arm, trying in vain to tug him away from Dominique's table. I was afraid that George was about to have a heart attack or stroke. He really didn't look well. His red cheeks were almost purple now.

"I'm afraid you'll have to leave, George," Nettie Jo said, tugging his arm again.

George shook her off and was about to yell at Dominique again when a woman's voice drew our attention.

"What's going on here?" A tall woman strode into the coffee shop. "George?"

"Oh, thank goodness you're here, Miranda," Nettie Jo said, her relief almost palpable. "Could you please get your husband to leave my other customers alone?"

When Miranda got close enough to see Dominique, her brown eyes hardened. "You!" she seethed.

Nettie Jo's expression of relief vanished. She squared her shoulders. "All right. That's it. George, I won't ask you again. You need to leave." She turned to his wife. "Miranda?"

Miranda glared at Dominique, but she took her husband's arm and guided him toward the door. "Come on, George. It's not worth wasting our time on her."

The two of them stormed out of the coffee shop.

Nettie Jo blew out a breath and looked around her. All eyes were focused on her and Dominique.

"Sorry about that, everyone," Nettie Jo said, attempting to smile. She wasn't very successful.

As the other customers turned back to their drinks and snacks, I edged closer to Nettie Jo and Dominique.

"I'm so sorry," Nettie Jo said to the other woman. "Let me get you a refund for your drink."

"Thank you, but that's not necessary," Dominique assured

her. "I really don't remember that man, but I'm guessing he must be a chef or restaurant owner?"

"Former restaurant owner," Nettie Jo confirmed.

"Ah. I can figure out the rest then. Thank you for defusing the situation."

"It's the least I could do."

Dominique turned back to her phone, so Nettie Jo left her in peace and headed toward the cash register. No one was currently waiting to be served, so I rested an arm on the counter and leaned closer to her.

"What was all that about?" I asked in a low voice.

Nettie Jo sighed as she wiped down the counter. "George Keeler used to own a restaurant here in Shady Creek. Dominique came to town a few years ago and wrote an unflattering review of his establishment. Not long after that, his restaurant went bust."

"Ouch."

Nettie Jo nodded. "As you witnessed, he still harbors a grudge."

A group of three customers bustled into the coffee shop, laughing and chatting.

Nettie Jo cast a nervous glance in Dominique's direction. "Hopefully, today's drama won't give her a bad impression of this place."

"I doubt it will," I said. "You handled the situation well."

The newly arrived customers lined up at the counter, so I let Nettie Jo get back to work. On my way out the door, I crossed my fingers, hoping for Nettie Jo's sake that what I'd said about Dominique would turn out to be true.

Chapter 2

With my drinks in hand, I continued on my way to visit Grayson. After crossing Creekside Road, I followed the long driveway up the hill to the cluster of brewery buildings. Even though it was barely midmorning, the parking lot was already more than half full. I didn't doubt that it would soon be packed.

The Spirit Hill Brewery had enjoyed great success in the time that I'd known Grayson, and the business had prospered even more ever since the brewery was featured on the television show *Craft Nation*. With the food and drink festival about to start, Grayson would be even busier than usual. I hoped I would have a chance to do more than simply hand off his drink to him today. I'd barely seen him so far this week, and when I didn't see him on a daily basis, I missed him terribly. One of the many signs that I was in love.

I stopped in at the main office in case Grayson was working there, but his receptionist directed me to the tasting room, which was located in a building of its own. The spacious tasting room had high ceilings and large windows that offered a beautiful view of the forest. When I arrived in the building, I spotted

Grayson right away. He stood behind one of the tasting counters, chatting with a middle-aged couple. Two of his employees were also busy offering samples of beer to eager customers.

I caught Grayson's eye, and my heart gave a giddy skip when his face lit up at the sight of me. I nodded toward the display of merchandise, letting him know that I'd wander around until he could spare a few minutes. It wasn't long before the middle-aged couple made their way over to the display of beer for sale. Grayson tucked the used glasses out of sight, quickly wiped down the counter, and came over to meet me. He slipped an arm around my waist as we headed for the door.

"Pistachio latte," I said as I handed him his drink.

"My favorite," he said with appreciation.

As soon as we were outside, he tugged me around the corner of the building, out of sight of anyone coming or going from the tasting room.

He brushed his lips against mine. "Also my favorite."

Fortunately, I managed to keep a firm hold on my latte when he gave me another kiss, this one much longer and deeper.

"What have you been up to so far today?" he asked, several blissful moments later.

"Um . . ." It took a second to get my dreamy brain working again. "Not much. But there was some drama at the Village Bean. There's a food writer in town and she and George Keeler got into an argument. Apparently, she wrote a negative review of George's restaurant a few years ago. Not long after, he had to close the restaurant."

"I remember hearing something about that," Grayson said. "It happened before I moved here."

I picked at the edge of the lid on my take-out cup. "I hope the writer doesn't punish Nettie Jo with a negative review of the Village Bean because of George's behavior."

Grayson echoed what I'd said earlier at the coffee shop. "I doubt that would happen."

"What if she comes to the Inkwell? I don't want to end up in the same boat as George, having the place go belly-up because she wrote a negative review."

Grayson pulled me close and gave me a squeeze. "That's not going to happen. Everyone loves the Inkwell and the negative review wasn't what caused George's restaurant to go under."

"It wasn't? I got the sense that he thinks it was."

"Everyone always said that his restaurant would have gone bust, anyway. I'm pretty sure the business was in deep financial trouble long before that review was written."

I digested that information. It eased my nerves, but didn't banish them completely.

I swirled my half-finished latte around in the cup.

"Hey." Grayson tucked my red hair behind my ear. "Is the food writer really what you're worried about?"

"It's not *all* that I'm worried about," I admitted.

He set his latte on a window ledge and pulled me close again. I rested my head on his shoulder.

"Let me guess," he said. "You're nervous about your mom coming to visit."

"A little bit," I confessed. "Or maybe more than a little bit." I sighed. "I really want her to approve of everything."

"Including me?"

I raised my head and smiled, putting a hand to the side of his face. "I honestly don't know how she couldn't approve of you."

"I am quite charming," Grayson said with the grin that always sent butterflies fluttering in my chest.

"You are," I agreed.

"And devastatingly handsome."

"I'm not arguing with you there."

I melted into him as he kissed me.

A burst of laughter startled us apart. A cheery group of tourists had exited the tasting room. I stepped back from Grayson as they reached the corner of the building and came into sight.

"I'd better let you get back to work," I said with reluctance.

"Unfortunately."

Caleb Jollimore, one of Grayson's employees, emerged from the building that housed the brewery's offices.

"Hey, Caleb," Grayson hailed him. "Do you have a minute?"

Caleb altered his path to head our way.

I quickly gave Grayson another kiss and then took a step back. "See you soon?"

"Definitely."

I said a quick hello to Caleb, and then left them to confer about some brewery-related matter as they headed toward the building where the brewing process took place. I'd barely made it halfway across the parking lot when Juliana, the brewery's public relations manager, came rushing out of the main office.

She stopped when she spotted me. "Sadie, have you seen Grayson?"

I pointed at the building over my right shoulder. "He and Caleb just went inside."

"Thank you."

"Is everything okay?" I asked before she could hurry off.

"Great." She glanced around and lowered her voice. "I got word from the tasting room that Phoebe Ramone is here. I'm sure Grayson would want to know."

"Who's Phoebe Ramone?"

"A well-known food critic." Juliana was practically jittery with excited energy. "If we can make a good impression on her, it would be great for the business." She dashed off, calling over her shoulder, "See you, Sadie!"

It seemed I was out of the loop. Before today I hadn't known about Dominique Girard or Phoebe Ramone. Maybe I needed to read more foodie magazines.

On my walk to the Inkwell, I enjoyed the remains of my pumpkin spice latte, savoring the delicious flavor and the fall weather. The forecasters were predicting a series of storms in the near future, but for now the sun was shining and the color of the leaves that remained on the trees seemed even brighter than usual. Although I sometimes felt homesick for Tennessee, where I grew up, I couldn't deny that Vermont was beautiful, especially in the fall. In my opinion, the old stone grist mill that housed my pub and apartment was the most beautiful part of all.

Silence greeted me when I let myself in through the front door of the Inkwell. Puzzled, I glanced at the time on my phone. Booker should have arrived for his shift already. Usually by this time he was busy with prep work in the kitchen, and he almost always sang enthusiastically up until the pub opened. Then he contented himself with humming or singing quietly.

I made my way across the pub and pushed open the swinging door that led to the kitchen.

Booker stood at the prep counter, tossing Red Cabbage of Courage salad in a large bowl.

"Hey," I greeted. "It was so quiet I didn't think you were here. Is everything all right?"

"Sure." Booker flashed me a smile. "I guess I'm thinking instead of singing today."

"Thinking about good things or bad things?" I asked.

"Good. I hope."

I found his response a bit cryptic, and that sparked my curiosity, which wasn't hard to do. Booker didn't seem eager to say anything more on the subject, however, so I left him to his work. I wandered around the main part of the pub, admiring the books I had displayed on the shelf that ran around the room and making sure that everything was ready for the day's customers.

I was straightening books on the shelf when Mel arrived for her bartending shift. Her electric blue and blond hair wasn't quite as short as she usually kept it, and she had it brushed back instead of standing up in spikes.

After she dropped off her jacket in the back, she stationed herself behind the bar, checking to make sure we had clean glasses ready for customers when they arrived. I was still straightening books and occasionally brushing my feather duster along the shelf.

"Everything looks great, Sadie," Mel said.

I stepped back and scrutinized the books. "My mom arrives in a couple of days."

"And you really think she's going to examine every book for microscopic dust particles?"

"No," I admitted with a faint smile. "Not quite."

Mel came out from behind the bar and rested her hands on her hips. "Either she's going to like this place, or she isn't. The alignment of the books on the shelf won't change that."

"You're right." And I knew she was. "But I really *want* her to like it."

"When she sees how happy you are here, she won't be able to help but approve."

I hoped that was true.

My mom had never understood my decision to move to Shady Creek and purchase the pub. She would have preferred it if I'd pursued a more practical profession like dentistry or practicing law. Maybe this visit would help her understand that those paths weren't for me, that I was right where I wanted to be and where I was meant to be.

Only time would tell.

Mel flipped the sign on the door, and our first customers of the day arrived soon after. Getting settled into the rhythm of my workday helped to keep me from dwelling on my mother's impending visit. We were nearly run off our feet during the lunch rush, and even in the middle of the afternoon we had a decent crowd. In the evening, after Mel's shift ended and my other bartender, Damien Keys, took over for her, business picked up again, to the point that I opened up the overflow rooms so there would be enough tables and chairs for everyone.

I was so busy mixing cocktails, taking orders, serving meals, and clearing tables that I barely had a moment to pause for a rest. We were well into the evening, and I was busy mixing three Kiss of the Cider Woman cocktails, when the front door opened and a woman stepped into the pub, bringing a crisp draft of air with her.

My hand tightened around the bottle of dry apple cider I was holding when I realized that the newcomer was Dominique Girard.

A well-known food writer. In my pub.

I reminded myself to keep breathing.

Dominique surveyed the pub from a step or two inside the door. When she spotted a small vacant table by one of the windows, she threaded her way across the room and sat down.

Damien headed straight over to take her order. I wanted to pull him aside and let him know who Dominique was before he approached her, but I didn't have a chance. Not that it mattered. Whether he knew who she was or not, Damien would treat her the same way he treated every other customer, and that gave me no reason to worry.

I delivered the Kiss of the Cider Woman cocktails to the group of women who'd ordered them, and then I returned to the bar. Two other customers asked for pints of beer. While I filled a glass with Sweet Adeline—a beer Grayson made from sweet potatoes and named for his late grandmother—my gaze strayed over to Dominique. Unlike at the coffee shop, where she'd remained focused on her phone most of the time, she appeared to be watching what was going on around her. I hoped she was soaking in the atmosphere and admiring the exposed stone walls and the grist mill's rustic charm. I was so busy wondering if that was the case that I yelped with surprise when beer overflowed the glass I was filling.

Heat rushed to my cheeks. Fortunately, I didn't think anyone had noticed my blunder or my yelp. I quickly cleaned up the mess, pulled another pint, and safely delivered the drinks to the couple at the end of the bar.

I really needed to focus.

I thought I might be able to do just that, until George Keeler walked into the pub.

Chapter 3

George didn't notice Dominique right away, and that gave me a chance to draw Damien aside. Quietly, I told him what had occurred between George and Dominique at the coffee shop that morning. I got him up to speed just in time.

George had taken a seat at a table with some friends, but as I watched, his gaze landed on Dominique and his eyes immediately hardened. A flush crept up his neck to his cheeks. Dread settled in the middle of my chest. I felt certain we were in for a repeat of the morning's drama.

Fortunately, Damien had his eye on George and intercepted him as he got up and took a step toward Dominique's table. Damien put a hand on George's arm and spoke to him quietly. I wasn't sure what he was saying, but it got the desired result. George's face remained flushed, and there was a belligerent set to his jaw, but he turned on his heel and stomped out of the pub.

Everyone else was too busy enjoying themselves to notice what had transpired. That included Dominique. Whereas she was watching the other patrons earlier, she was now focused on her Red Cabbage of Courage salad and her Secret Life of Daiquiris cocktail.

Crisis averted.

My shoulders relaxed with relief.

"What did you say to him?" I asked Damien when he returned to the bar.

"I told him we didn't want any trouble. And I pointed out that if he caused a disturbance and we had to call the cops in, he'd be the one getting in trouble, not Dominique."

"Good thinking," I said. "And thank you."

We very rarely had issues with rowdiness at the Inkwell, but on the couple of occasions when we had, they'd occurred in the evening, when Damien was working. I was always grateful for his presence. Dealing with drunk and combative patrons—usually men—was my least favorite part of the job, and not one that I was great at. Damien and Mel were both far more intimidating than me. Damien, while not particularly bulky, still had a muscular build, with tattoos on his arms. Mel stood a few inches taller than me and was an amateur boxer. Booker was taller than any of us and was a former college football player. I didn't doubt that he could toss someone out of the pub if necessary, but since he worked the afternoon shift, such a situation had never come up. So far.

Relieved that trouble had been stamped out before it could truly ignite, I got back to enjoying my work. I chatted with customers and told tourists about the pub and the inspiration behind the literary-themed food and drinks. When Dominique was nearly finished her salad and her cocktail, I stopped by her table.

"How is everything?" I asked her.

"Great, thanks," she replied with a smile. "You're the owner, right?"

"That's right. Sadie Coleman." I wondered how she knew I was the owner. Maybe she'd done some research before coming to the pub. If that was the case, maybe she was here for work, planning to write about the Inkwell. Nervousness jittered in my stomach.

Her next words helped to put me at ease. "I really like the place you've got here."

I beamed at her. "Thank you so much."

"What inspired you to open a literary-themed pub?"

"My love for books," I said. "I always had a dream of owning my own bookstore one day. Then, when I came to visit my aunt here in Shady Creek, this pub was up for sale. I fell in love with the building as soon as I saw it."

"I can see why," Dominique said. "You can't beat the charm."

My smile brightened further. "It was an ordinary pub at the time, so I decided to make it my own by putting a literary twist on everything." A hint of heat touched my cheeks. I hoped I wasn't rambling.

Fortunately, Dominique didn't seem the least put off. "That's fantastic. I've always loved books too. Now I'm passing my love of reading on to my niece. She wasn't much of a reader at first, but then I introduced her to Nancy Drew and The Baby-Sitters Club. Now she devours books."

"My best friend's daughter got hooked on reading thanks to Nancy Drew," I said. "It's always so great to see that spark lit in a child."

"Definitely," Dominique agreed.

I reminded myself that she was a customer, not there simply to chat.

"Can I get you anything else to eat or drink?" I asked.

"I'd love to try another cocktail." She picked up the menu from where it stood propped up between the salt and pepper shakers. "I'll go with the Count Dracula."

"Perfect for a chilly evening," I said. "I'll get that for you right away."

I took Dominique's empty plate with me and dropped it off in the kitchen before mixing her drink at the bar. I combined blood orange juice with cranberry juice and simple cinnamon syrup. Then I added some coconut rum. As I set down the bottle of rum, my friend Cordelia King perched on a free stool.

"How's it going?" she asked. "Are you all ready for A Taste of Shady Creek?"

"I think so," I replied. "Have you seen the town hall? It looks amazing."

"I've heard that the decorating committee did a great job, but I haven't seen it for myself. I'll stop by the festival at some point, though."

I finished mixing Dominique's drink. "What can I get you?"

"A Milky Way Gargle Blaster and To Be or Nacho Be, please," she requested. "I'm dying for all the cheese and saltiness of the nachos."

Her words made my mouth water and my stomach rumble. I hadn't had any dinner yet.

"I'll have that for you in a minute," I said.

I dropped off Dominique's drink and made sure she was still happy. I glanced over my shoulder as I walked away and saw her taking a picture of her cocktail with her phone. Excitement mixed with flutters of nervousness in my stomach. If she was going to write about the Inkwell, I desperately hoped she was enjoying the food and drinks.

Doing my best to rein in my nervousness, I ducked into the kitchen to place Cordelia's order with Teagan, the chef who worked the evening shift. When I returned to the bar, Cordelia was facing the room, watching a woman who had just walked into the pub.

She turned back to the bar, leaning across it to whisper to me. "Do you know who that is?"

The slim woman had shoulder-length chestnut brown hair with bright red streaks. She wore expensive-looking jeans with a reddish-brown leather jacket, and bright lipstick that contrasted sharply with her pale complexion. I'd never seen her before.

"No clue," I said.

"She tried to get a room at the inn, but we were all booked up." Cordelia and her grandmother ran the Creekside Inn, which was housed in a beautiful Queen Anne up the road from the Inkwell. "Luckily Shady Creek Manor had room for her. But you'll probably want to know what she does for a living." She hesitated, reconsidering. "Or, maybe you'd rather not."

"Now you really have to tell me," I said. "Unless you want me to die of curiosity."

Cordelia smiled at that, no stranger to my curious nature. "She's Phoebe Ramone, a food and restaurant critic."

I recognized her name, having heard it earlier in the day when I was at the brewery. "A Taste of Shady Creek is really drawing in the food writers."

Cordelia nodded. "We've got another writer staying at the inn as well."

"Dominique Girard?" I guessed.

She shook her head. "I don't know her. Our other guest is Nick Perry. He's a travel writer. He's here to write a piece about Shady Creek as a vacation destination."

"Hopefully, all this interest is going to generate some good publicity for the town."

"I'm sure it will," Cordelia said. "And for the Inkwell."

I held up my crossed fingers.

"You've got nothing to worry about," Cordelia assured me. "Anyone who writes about the pub will only have good things to say because this place is fantastic."

"Thank you."

I appreciated Cordelia's confidence and hoped she was right, but I couldn't stop the nervous flutters that swept through me every so often. With both Dominique and Phoebe here at the pub, there was double the pressure to impress. Damien had taken Phoebe's order, so I didn't approach her, instead keeping an eye on her from afar. When Damien delivered a plate of Paradise Lox and a Happily Ever After cocktail to her table, she snapped photos of both, setting off another round of nervous jitters in my stomach. If she didn't like what she ordered, those photos could end up published next to a negative review.

Stay positive, I admonished myself. *She'll love the food and her cocktail.*

I crossed my fingers again.

By the time Phoebe was halfway through her appetizer, I couldn't take it any longer. I wanted to say hello to her and hopefully let her see that the Inkwell was a friendly place. After delivering two drinks to a nearby table, I made sure that my path took me right past Phoebe.

"Good evening," I said as I paused by her table. "I'm the Inkwell's owner, Sadie. How is everything?"

"Great, thank you." She went right back to eating.

I wanted her to be interested in the pub's literary theme, or anything about the Inkwell, but she was clearly more interested in her food than conversation. I didn't want to risk annoying her, so I moved on.

Although disappointed, I tried not to take her reticence personally. She didn't want to chat, but that didn't mean she wasn't enjoying her time at the Inkwell. For all I knew, she was enjoying her food too much to talk. Or, maybe she was busy composing a positive review of the pub in her head as she ate. I definitely wouldn't want to interrupt her thoughts if that was the case.

I spent the next several minutes mixing cocktails for a group of eight tourists who claimed one of the largest tables in the pub. They were food and drink enthusiasts, and had come from Ottawa, Ontario, to take in A Taste of Shady Creek. In addition to checking out the booths at the town hall the next day, they intended to visit all of the businesses involved in the event. They'd already started with a trip to the Spirit Hill Brewery this afternoon.

The next day they'd also be hitting the Five Owls Winery and the local cidery, and the day after that they hoped to check out the Caldwell Cheese Company and the local maple farm and sugar shack. This evening, however, they were relaxing here at the Inkwell.

Two of the tourists had ordered the Poirot cocktail, made from gin and cassis. One had requested the Count Dracula, like Dominique had, and another had asked for the Kiss of the Cider Woman, which featured locally made dry apple cider along with cranberry juice and ginger ale. The remaining members of the group had ordered pints of beer.

Once I had all of their drinks delivered to their table, I headed back toward the bar. Halfway there, I stopped to greet Caleb Jollimore, whom I'd seen earlier in the day at the brewery. He and his younger sister, Alicia, had recently sat down at a small table near the edge of the room.

I asked if they were ready to order, and they both requested pints of beer and burgers with sides of Lord of the Fries. I relayed their food orders to Teagan, and then took them their beers. Once their food was ready, I headed back to their table again.

"You should tell Dominique what her comments did to you," Caleb was saying to his sister as I approached. His low voice rumbled with an undercurrent of anger. "And you can't let her ruin your dreams any longer. You need to start writing again."

Alicia was about to respond, but when she saw me approaching, she snapped her mouth shut. She smiled when I placed her burger and fries in front of her, but the expression didn't reach her blue eyes. I thought maybe she was on the brink of tears. My suspicion grew stronger when she blinked rapidly and angled her face away from me as she tucked her strawberry blond hair behind one ear.

Caleb's smile also seemed halfhearted. Although I was curious about their conversation, I could tell they didn't want me to linger. I left them with their food, but I glanced back over my shoulder as I walked away. A stormy expression passed across Caleb's face as he stared across the room at Dominique.

He clearly didn't like her, and his dislike for the food writer seemed to have something to do with his sister. But how could Dominique have ruined Alicia's dreams?

I had no idea, and I didn't have time to dwell on the question as I had several other food orders to deliver to waiting patrons. When I next had a moment to catch my breath, I cleared away Cordelia's empty dishes. She was no longer seated at the bar, but I hadn't seen her leave. As I was returning from the kitchen, she emerged from the short hallway that led to the washrooms.

"Sadie." She took my arm and spoke quietly. "Phoebe Ramone is in the washroom having a spat with another woman."

"Really?" I said with surprise.

Cordelia nodded, her blue eyes wide. "They're really laying into each other. I'm worried it might turn into a full-blown catfight."

That definitely wasn't good news. The last thing I wanted was to have to toss Phoebe out of the pub or—even worse—call the cops to escort her out. I couldn't imagine Phoebe writing a favorable review of the Inkwell if that happened. It might give Dominique a bad impression of the place too.

Still, I had to think about all my other customers.

Damien was across the room, taking down an order for a group of four. I noticed that Dominique was no longer at her table. Maybe she'd already left the pub.

"Could you let Damien know what's going on?" I asked Cordelia.

She nodded and set off to intercept Damien as he came back toward the bar.

I mustered up my courage and marched toward the women's restroom, hoping I wouldn't find fists flying and blood flowing.

I could hear raised voices before I even got to the door.

"I got the job because I'm a good writer," one woman seethed.

The other woman let out a derisive laugh. "You really expect me to believe that?"

"Jealousy doesn't look good on you, Phoebe."

"I'm not jealous!"

I pushed open the door.

Both women turned toward me. Dominique hadn't left the pub after all. Her eyes shone with fury and Phoebe's expression wasn't much different. She had her hands clenched into fists and her cheeks were flushed.

"Is everything all right in here?" I asked, keeping my voice pleasant.

Dominique shot a glare at Phoebe but then glanced away. "Everything's fine."

Phoebe relaxed her hands, but the tension didn't leave her jaw or shoulders. "Sure," she said. "Everything's great."

The bitterness in her voice didn't match her words.

Dominique brushed her dark hair over her shoulder. "Sorry for any disturbance," she said to me. Then she breezed past me out the door.

Phoebe marched into one of the stalls and slammed the door shut.

I backed out of the washroom. Dominique had already disappeared. Damien stood at the end of the hall. He raised an eyebrow in an unspoken question.

"The situation seems to be under control," I told him. I described Phoebe so he'd know who'd been arguing with Dominique. "Hopefully, they'll stay away from each other for the rest of the evening."

"I'll keep an eye on them," Damien promised.

I intended to do the same.

As it turned out, I didn't have to worry about another altercation between Dominique and Phoebe that evening. Dominique had taken a seat at her table again, but her eyes widened when a blond-haired man walked into the pub. He headed straight for the bar, while Dominique sat frozen, her gaze tracking his every step.

When he perched on a stool at the bar, Dominique jerked into motion, pulling out her wallet and throwing some bills on the table before scurrying out of the Inkwell without looking back.

A line from *Alice's Adventures in Wonderland* came to mind as the door drifted shut behind her: Curiouser and curiouser.

Chapter 4

Thankfully, no further drama played out at the Inkwell that night, and by the next morning I'd pushed it all to the back of my mind. I focused instead on getting ready for A Taste of Shady Creek, which was starting that day. I mixed up several pitchers of cocktails and poured them into large thermoses, which I then tucked into a cooler. The festival was opening at eleven, and I was running the Inkwell's booth for the day and part of the next. Zoe—my part-time employee and Teagan's twin sister—would be stationed at the town hall tomorrow afternoon while Mel worked at the Inkwell and I spent time with my mom, who was due to arrive in Shady Creek the next day.

Every now and then a rush of nervousness skittered through me. I wasn't sure if it had to do with the festival, the food and travel writers who were in town, or my mom's visit. Probably all three. I told myself I was as prepared as I could be for the festival. As for the rest, hopefully everything would turn out well.

Booker showed up for his shift a few minutes early so he could lend a hand with transporting the drink samples over to the town hall. Since I had two heavy coolers to carry, I was grateful for his help. I thought we would take one cooler each, but he insisted on carrying both. I would have struggled to do that myself, but for him it appeared to be no problem.

"Is it all right if I cut my shift short by half an hour this afternoon?" Booker asked as we walked across the corner of the village green. "I already checked with Teagan," he added quickly. "She's okay with coming in a bit early."

"That's fine," I assured him. "Is everything all right?"

Booker had never asked to leave early before.

"I need to get to Rutland before the end of the day, that's all," he said.

Although my curiosity—or nosiness—made me want to ask the reason for his trip, I kept quiet. It really wasn't any of my business. Sometimes I was able to mind my own beeswax.

We reached the town hall at the same time as Helen from the Five Owls Winery, which she owned and operated with her daughter, Katie. Booker and I chatted with Helen on our way into the main room of the town hall. Then we went our separate ways, Helen heading for a table on the opposite side of the room from the one designated for the Inkwell.

Even though I'd already seen all of the decorations, I walked slowly toward my station, giving myself a chance to take in the sight once again. The maple tree in the middle of the room was still my favorite part of the decor. I stopped beneath its branches and gazed up. I hadn't noticed last time, but there was a cute little owl perched on one of the branches and a chipmunk peeking out from a bunch of colorful leaves.

Booker placed the coolers behind the Inkwell's table and then returned to the pub to start his prep work for the day. I set stacks of paper cups out on the table next to some napkins. Then I nudged the fanned display of menus, adjusting one that had gone slightly askew. I didn't have anything else to do but wait for the event to open to the public.

Fortunately, that didn't take long. Alma Potts, who'd helped organize the festival, opened the town hall doors promptly at eleven. A small crowd of eager tourists had congregated on the front steps, waiting to get inside, so the festival got under way immediately. More tourists and several locals showed up soon after, and we quickly had a decent crowd.

For the next day of the festival, I planned to offer a different selection of drink samples, but for today I'd brought Kiss of the Cider Woman, the Evil Stepmother, and The Secret Life of Daiquiris. The Evil Stepmother was made with a sour mix, white grape juice, vodka, and ginger ale, while The Secret Life of Daiquiris featured coconut rum and cream of coconut along with lime juice and mango. I'd also brought a mocktail version of the Evil Stepmother, missing only the vodka.

Everyone who stopped by the Inkwell's table received a fridge magnet and one of the postcards I'd had printed. I had a great time chatting with everyone and was pleased to find that many of the festivalgoers were intrigued by the Inkwell and wanted to know more about the literary theme and how the pub had come to be. Since that was one of my favorite topics to talk about, I had no problem staying engaged with the tourists and other visitors who came by my table.

During a quiet moment, my gaze wandered around the room. I wanted to stop by the other tables at some point. Everyone was offering samples and my mouth watered when I looked over at the Caldwell Cheese booth and the maple farm's table. Grayson's brewery had a booth too, but I knew I wouldn't see him here today. He was in Burlington for a meeting while Juliana, the brewery's head of public relations, took care of things at the town hall.

As I gazed around, movement by the door caught my eye. Dominique peeked around the door frame and surveyed the crowd before entering the room. Her behavior struck me as a tad odd, but maybe she was making sure she had the right place.

Or, I thought, as I recalled the incident at the pub the night before, maybe she was hoping to avoid the man whose presence had sent her running out of the Inkwell. Whoever he was.

Three senior citizens from Pennsylvania came by my table, diverting my attention away from Dominique. The next time I took any notice of her, she had her phone out and was taking photos of the room, including the beautiful fake maple tree. I hoped she was as impressed by the décor as I was.

Unfortunately, I wasn't the only one who'd noticed the food writer. Miranda Keeler stood across the room with her arms crossed over her chest as she glared at an oblivious Dominique. I couldn't see her husband, George, anywhere, and that was a relief. He probably would have caused another scene if he'd shown up. I worried that his wife might do the same, but she turned her back on Dominique and busied herself with entering one of the draws set up on a table near the door. The businesses involved in the festival, including the Inkwell, had donated gift certificates and other prizes that would be given out to lucky winners throughout the event.

Satisfied that Miranda wouldn't stir up any trouble, I returned my attention to the visitors at my table. I stayed focused on chatting and offering drink samples until Dominique's voice rang out across the room.

"Where's my scarf?"

She stood next to the Spirit Hill Brewery's table, her hands on her hips. The leather purse I'd seen on Dominique's arm when she entered the room sat on the corner of the table. As I watched, Dominique said something to Juliana, who shook her head, looking apologetic. There were several people gathered at the booth, checking out Grayson's craft beers, and they quickly drew Juliana's attention away from the food writer.

Dominique studied the room through narrowed eyes. She snatched up her purse and then wandered around, scrutinizing every table and every person present.

When she reached the Inkwell's table, the sharpness in her gaze lessened.

"Sadie, right?" she said to me.

"That's right," I confirmed with a smile. "Is something wrong? Did you lose a scarf?"

"Someone must have swiped it. I left it right on top of my purse while I was taking some pictures. There's no way it could have disappeared on its own."

"I'm sorry to hear that," I said, meaning it. "Would you like me to inform the event's organizers?"

"Please do. I wouldn't bother to make a fuss except that it's a Gucci scarf. Not exactly cheap."

"Hopefully, someone will find it and turn it in to the organizers," I said, although I doubted that would happen.

Dominique was most likely right that the scarf had been stolen. That was a mark against the town, which I hoped wouldn't influence whatever Dominique might write about Shady Creek and its food offerings.

I couldn't see Alma in the room, so I dug out my phone so I could send her a text message.

"Can you describe the scarf for me?" I requested.

"It's black silk with bold-colored flowers on it."

I added that information to the text message. "How long are you in town for?"

"A couple more days. I'm staying at the motel off the highway, if anyone needs to reach me."

I finished composing the message and sent it. "Done."

"Thank you, Sadie," Dominique said. "I know I'm not likely to get it back now, but I appreciate the effort."

"I hope the rest of your stay in town is a positive experience."

"I'm sure it will be." She sent a brief smile my way and then moved on, checking out the other tables in the room.

The next time I had a moment to allow my gaze to wander

away from my booth, I couldn't see her anywhere. I quickly checked online to see what a silk Gucci scarf might cost. My eyes nearly popped out of my head when I saw the price on one.

If Dominique had that much money to spend on an accessory, why would she choose to stay at the local motel? That was the cheapest and most modest of all the accommodation options in town. It was also the farthest from the heart of Shady Creek. Maybe the magazine she worked for was footing the bill and wasn't willing to cover anything more expensive than a basic motel room. That was probably the case, I decided.

Toward the end of the day, Phoebe Ramone showed up at the town hall. Like Dominique, she snapped some photos with her phone before checking out the tables. She started at the Five Owls Winery booth and then moved on to the Caldwell Cheese Company's display. I lost track of her as I chatted with some tourists, and the next time I noticed her she was at the table next to mine, tasting the samples offered by the local cidery.

The man whose arrival at the Inkwell had sent Dominique dashing for the door sidled up next to Phoebe and nudged her with his elbow.

"Fancy meeting you here," he said.

Phoebe's face lit up. "Nick!" She gave him a hug and then hooked her arm through his. "I'm dying to try out Lumière," she said, referring to Shady Creek's fanciest restaurant. "Tell me you'll join me for dinner."

They wound their way through the crowd, heading toward the door. I didn't hear any more of the conversation, but I'd caught enough of it to connect a couple of dots in my head.

I was willing to bet that Nick was Nick Perry, the travel writer staying at the Creekside Inn. However, knowing his name didn't tell me why Dominique had wanted to avoid him. Not that I needed to know, other than to satisfy my curiosity.

Despite that curiosity, I quickly forgot about Nick and Dominique.

A steady stream of people passed through the town hall right up until it closed for the day. I stashed my empty thermoses in my coolers and lugged everything outside. The coolers didn't weigh nearly as much as they did that morning, but I still missed having Booker's help.

I cut across the corner of the village green to make my trip to the Inkwell shorter, and I paused for a break when I was halfway there. Above me, dark clouds rolled in from the north, along with a sweeping, damp breeze that cut through my clothes and chilled me to the bone. That was enough to get me moving again.

Since Zoe and Damien were both working that evening, my plan was to take some time away to visit Grayson. First, however, I served food and drinks through the Inkwell's dinner rush, lightening the load for Damien and Zoe. When the rush tapered off, I texted Grayson to see if he was back from Burlington, but received no response. That probably meant he was still driving, but I hoped he was nearly home, especially since the weather had worsened considerably since I'd returned from the town hall. Rain poured down from the sky, sending rivulets of water running along the Inkwell's windowpanes. I hadn't heard any thunder over the murmur of conversation in the pub, but I thought I saw lightning flash once or twice. The next time I checked my phone, Grayson had sent a reply, letting me know he'd arrived at the brewery and was looking forward to seeing me.

The storm had eased up by then, so I left the pub in the capable hands of my employees and walked up Grayson's long driveway. It was eerie at this hour, with the driveway bordered by woods on both sides. The ominous clouds blocked out the moon, leaving me in near darkness and making me wish I'd decided to drive instead of walk.

A light shone like a friendly beacon up ahead, marking the spot where a branch of the driveway led off to the right, curving through some trees to Grayson's house. His black sports car sat parked in front of the two-story, blue and gray home. Grayson was thinking about trading the car in for something more practical before winter hit, but he hadn't found the time for that yet.

The front door opened before I reached the house, and warm light spilled out into the dark evening. Grayson's white German shepherd, Bowie, bounded down the front steps and hurtled toward me.

"Hey, buddy!" I crouched down to give the dog a hug as his tail wagged furiously.

When I stood up, Grayson pulled me into his arms and greeted me with a kiss that left my mind delightfully hazy.

"Can I cook you dinner?" he asked.

I struggled to order my thoughts enough to respond coherently. "I won't say no to that."

"Is it okay if I check in at the office first?"

"Of course."

Grayson shut Bowie inside the house. Then he took my hand and we walked the rest of the way up the driveway. Rain started to fall again, so we zipped up our jackets and quickened our pace. I'd made the mistake of wearing a jacket that wasn't waterproof. It provided me with some protection from the elements, but that wouldn't last for long.

Fortunately, we didn't have far to walk and we soon neared our destination. The brewery had closed to the public already, and only one car remained in the parking lot. I figured it belonged to one of Grayson's employees.

In the main office, Annalisa, the brewery's receptionist, was standing behind the desk, pulling on her coat. She smiled when we entered the building.

"You're here late," Grayson said to her.

"I needed to catch up on a few things, but it's all taken care of now. How did the meeting go?"

"It went well," he replied. "Did anything come up while I was gone?"

"A woman came by to see you," Annalisa said. "She was very insistent that she needed to talk to you, but she didn't say why and wouldn't leave a message. When I told her you were gone for the whole day, she asked to book a meeting with you for first thing tomorrow morning."

Grayson seemed puzzled by that information. "Did she leave a name?"

Annalisa picked a business card up off her desk and passed it to Grayson. "Dominique Girard."

"She's the one George got riled up about at the Village Bean," I said.

A stormy cloud passed across Grayson's face, darkening his blue eyes. "Dominique Girard is here in Shady Creek?"

There was a hard edge to his voice that I'd never heard before.

Annalisa's eyes widened with worry. "Was I wrong to book the meeting?"

I could tell Grayson was struggling to rein in his emotions.

"No, of course not. It's fine," he said, though the tension in his jaw suggested that everything wasn't fine. He stuffed the business card into his pocket. "Thank you, Annalisa. You can head on home."

Grayson pushed out the door, barely contained fury radiating off of him.

I flashed a quick smile at Annalisa, who still looked worried, and hurried after Grayson. He was storming over to one of the other brewery buildings, moving so fast I had to run in an attempt to catch up to him.

"Grayson!" I called out.

He didn't stop or respond in any way. He wrenched open the door to the next building.

I put a hand on his arm. "Grayson! What's going on?"

He finally stopped and met my gaze. Some of his dark intensity ebbed away, although his jaw remained tense and his eyes didn't lose their storminess.

"I've met Dominique Girard before," he said, still holding the door open.

"I gathered that. But I thought her last visit to Shady Creek was before you lived here."

"It was. I didn't even realize she was the one who wrote that review of George's restaurant."

"Okay, so how do you know her?" I hesitated a split second before asking my next question. "Is she an ex-girlfriend?"

"What?" He seemed taken aback by that question. "No. Nothing like that." He ran a hand through his hair, leaving it more tousled than usual.

Above us, the roiling dark clouds opened up, turning the light rain shower into a downpour.

Grayson put an arm around me and ushered me inside.

"I want to make sure everything is good for the night," he said as the door drifted shut behind us.

He always liked to make a circuit of the brewery before calling it a day.

"I'll explain in a minute," he added.

I followed him through the cavernous room that was home to a giant stainless steel brew kettle, a mash mixer, and other equipment I couldn't name. Grayson gave me a tour several months ago and explained the brewing process, but I'd only managed to remember bits and pieces.

While he did a quick check of all the equipment, I did my best to contain my curiosity. My first thought was that Dominique had written a negative review of the brewery the last time she was in Shady Creek, like she had with George Keeler's restaurant, but clearly that wasn't the case.

At the far end of the room, Grayson opened the door that led to the next part of the building, where big casks of beer were stored. He held the door open for me so I could precede him through it.

When I stepped over the threshold, I froze.

"Grayson . . . ," I said, my voice strangled.

He stepped up next to me and swore at the sight before us.

Dominique lay unmoving on the cement floor, pinned there by a giant oak cask.

Chapter 5

"Is she . . . ?" I couldn't bring myself to finish the question.

Grayson crouched down next to Dominique and placed two fingers against the side of her neck. Her skin had a purple tinge to it and her lips were unnaturally pale. Grayson's grim expression told me what he was about to say before he spoke.

"No pulse."

I placed a hand over my mouth, horrified by the scene before me.

Grayson dug his phone out of the pocket of his jeans. "She's been dead at least a while, I think."

I dropped my hand from my mouth. "How did this happen?" I asked, still in shock. "What was she doing in here?"

"Both good questions," Grayson said as he punched the emergency button on his phone.

I wanted to turn away from the terrible sight before me, but my gaze remained fixed on Dominique. She lay on her stomach, her face turned to the side and her arms and torso pinned down by the big cask. She wore a rain jacket, jeans, and ankle boots.

I stepped closer to her. Blood matted the hair on the back of her head. My first thought was that the falling cask had knocked her over and she'd hit her head on the way down, but I quickly discounted that theory. There was no blood on the shelving unit that the cask had fallen from, and there was nothing else close enough for Dominique to have knocked her head on while toppling over. I couldn't see any blood on the cask either, although there might have been some where it pressed against Dominique's back.

I closed a hand around Grayson's wrist.

"What if this wasn't an accident?" I whispered.

He was listening to the emergency operator, but I knew he heard my words because his gaze sharpened and zeroed in on Dominique's body.

I released his wrist as he inclined his head toward the door we'd entered through moments before.

"We're supposed to wait outside," he said.

That was fine with me. Dominique's body had unnerved me even before I realized she might have been murdered. Now, shivers of unease ran up and down my back. I couldn't wait to get out of there. Even so, I paused when I was partway through the door. I glanced over my shoulder as a breeze tickled my neck. A bank of lights lit up the area where we'd found Dominique, but beyond that the room was all murky darkness. I squinted at the shadows. Past a forklift and several shelving units, an exterior door stood open, allowing the night breeze to flow inside.

I retraced our steps, leading the way out of the building. The rain still poured down and thunder rumbled loudly overhead, so Grayson propped open the front door of the building and we huddled inside where we still had a view of the now-empty parking lot. As soon as Grayson ended his call with the emergency operator, he slipped an arm around me.

"Are you okay?" he asked.

I shivered and nestled closer to him. "Definitely better than Dominique."

I felt his hand tense as it pressed gently against my back. I wished I could feel the warmth of it through my jacket.

"What about you?" I asked. "You knew her."

"We had a history."

I tipped my head back so I could see his face. "But not a romantic one."

"No. Definitely not." He released a heavy sigh. "Sadie, this won't go well for me."

"What do you mean?" I knew he was talking about something beyond the fact that someone had died on the brewery's property. "What kind of history did you have with her?"

He stared out into the stormy night, with one arm still tucked around me. For a moment I thought I'd need to repeat the question, but then he finally spoke.

"It dates back to when I was a private investigator. When I started out, I worked for a man named Lou Shields, a really good guy. I guess you could say he was my mentor. He had a daughter, Samantha. She was in college when Lou passed away from cancer."

Apprehension settled over me, adding to the unease that our unpleasant discovery had left me with. "Did something happen to her?"

Grayson rubbed the back of his neck. "She was killed in a houseboat explosion."

I sucked in a sharp breath. "That's terrible! I'm so sorry, Grayson."

Sirens wailed in the night, drawing closer with every passing second.

"I always suspected that Dominique was behind the explosion," Grayson continued. "But I could never prove it. I never got justice for Sam."

My throat constricted with emotion. I hugged him and continued to hold on to him as two police cruisers pulled into the parking lot. The sight of the police officers climbing out of their vehicles hammered home the meaning behind what Grayson was telling me.

He had a history with Dominique, and not a good one. Now she was lying dead in his brewery. If she'd met with foul play, Grayson could very well end up as a suspect.

That thought was the last straw. Tears sprung to my eyes. I couldn't stop them from escaping to run down my cheeks.

The fact that I knew the two officers who approached us brought me the slightest bit of comfort. I'd met Officers Pamela Rogers and Eldon Howes more than once in the past, and Eldon was dating my best friend, Shontelle. I knew they were both good officers. They wouldn't jump to any conclusions. That helped to stem the flow of my tears.

"Where's the body?" Eldon asked as he and Rogers joined us inside the building, their uniform hats and jackets wet and shimmering from their brief dash from the cruisers to the door.

Grayson pointed to the open door at the other end of the cavernous room. "Through there."

He and I watched as the officers checked out the scene. In under a minute, Officer Rogers had returned to us. I could hear Eldon talking into his radio in the next room, but I couldn't make out his words.

"I'll need to talk to each of you separately," Rogers said to us. "Is there someplace where we can do that?"

"We can go to the brewery offices, or my house," Grayson suggested.

"The offices will do," Rogers said.

It would have been nice to have Bowie's comforting company at Grayson's house, but the offices were much closer. That made them the preferred choice in this weather. Even so, by the time we ran up to the main door of the building and

Grayson got it unlocked, all three of us looked like we'd gone for a swim in the creek that gave the town its name.

Lightning flashed, lighting up the sky, as we hurried out of the pelting rain and into the main office. Officer Rogers asked me to wait in Grayson's office while she talked to him in the reception area. I shut the door behind me and removed my wet jacket, then hung it on the coat stand. Suddenly weary, I dropped into the leather swivel chair behind Grayson's desk.

Questions spun in dizzying circles in my head. I had no answers to go with them, and knowing that added to my weariness, as did my concern for Grayson.

A knock on the door startled me so badly that I jumped right out of the chair. Officer Rogers joined me in the office and asked me several questions about how Grayson and I had discovered the body and what I'd noticed at the time. I made sure to mention the open door at the back of the building, though it turned out she was already aware of that detail.

"Did you know the deceased?" Rogers asked after I'd gone over how we'd found Dominique.

"Not really. I only met her for the first time yesterday." I told her about my brief chat with Dominique at the Inkwell and how I saw her at the town hall during A Taste of Shady Creek. "She's a food writer and critic, apparently," I added. "She didn't tell me that, but I heard it from Nettie Jo Kim at the Village Bean."

"Did Dominique know anyone in town that you're aware of?"

"I'm told this wasn't her first visit to Shady Creek," I said. "That's why Nettie Jo recognized her. And George Keeler wasn't a fan." I quickly summarized what had transpired at the coffee shop. "Dominique also had an argument with another food writer, Phoebe Ramone, at the Inkwell."

After giving her what few details I could about that argument, I added what I'd overheard between Caleb Jollimore and his sister, Alicia. All the while I was wondering if I should mention Grayson's history with Dominique. I didn't want to bring it up, but I was afraid that Rogers might figure out that I was holding something back, especially if Grayson had already talked to her about it. Then again, if Grayson *hadn't* mentioned it and I did, it would look like he was withholding information.

I continued to wrestle with that dilemma while Rogers wrote something in her notebook. Before I could decide what to do, her radio came to life.

"Detective Marquez has arrived," she said after listening to the message coming through her radio. "She might want to speak with you. Could you stay here for the moment?"

"Sure."

She left the office and I stayed standing in the middle of the room. I counted to ten before creeping out into the hall and peeking into the reception area, checking to make sure that Officer Rogers had left. She had, but Grayson was gone too.

I pushed the main door open a crack and peered out into the night. Grayson stood about six feet away, underneath the building's overhang. Officer Rogers stood right there with him.

Fortunately, she had her back to me and I managed to duck inside before she could see me. I stayed by the door, looking out the window. As I watched, Detective Marquez strode across the parking lot, heading toward Grayson and Rogers. I scurried back to Grayson's office, leaving the door ajar. A minute or so later, I heard the outer door open. Then Officer Rogers poked her head into the office.

"Sorry for keeping you waiting, Sadie. You don't need to hang around any longer. Detective Marquez might want to speak with you, but that will likely be tomorrow, not tonight."

"Thank you," I said. "Do you know where Grayson is?"

"Outside, answering some more questions."

I pulled on my jacket and followed her out into the rain. Another police cruiser as well as an unmarked car and an ambulance had joined the initial two cruisers in the parking lot. Light poured out of the building across the way, highlighting the driving rain. I hesitated beneath the overhang, searching for Grayson's familiar figure in the night. Aside from Officer Rogers, the only other people I could see outdoors were two other uniformed officers. They headed around the building, shining powerful flashlights ahead of them.

I contemplated texting Grayson to see where he was, but then I spotted him inside the door to the other building. My jacket didn't have a hood, so I ducked my head against the rain and sprinted across the parking lot.

Grayson saw me coming and stepped outside to meet me beneath the roof's overhang.

"Do they still need you here?" I asked, hoping we could get away to talk privately.

"Marquez wants me close by in case they need access to any other parts of the brewery," Grayson said.

The light shifted as someone moved just inside the door. Grayson glanced that way and put an arm around me, drawing me farther away. The rain pelted us now that we'd left the shelter of the overhang.

"Do you want to go home?" he asked.

"Not really," I said. "I'd rather stay with you."

"There's no point in you freezing out here." He fished a ring of keys from his pocket and slid one free of the metal loop. "How about you wait at my place? Hopefully, I won't be much longer."

I accepted the key with only a hint of reluctance. As much as I wanted to stay with him, the cold rain had soaked my hair and clothes and I couldn't stop shivering. I wanted to ask Grayson what he'd told Officer Rogers, but I feared someone might overhear. Despite the noise of the rain, one of the officers standing inside the door might still be able to make out our words. So, instead, I settled for giving him a quick kiss.

"I'll let Bowie outside," I said. "Don't get too cold."

Grayson grabbed my hand and pulled me back for another, longer kiss. When he released me, the desolation in his eyes frightened me.

A uniformed officer stepped out of the brewery building, leaving me without a chance to ask Grayson what exactly had him so worried.

"Go get out of the rain," he told me as he tucked a wet strand of hair behind my ear.

I nodded and jogged off down the driveway, wishing he were coming with me.

Bowie greeted me enthusiastically, all well in his world. I let him out into the front yard long enough to do what he needed to do and then we both took shelter in the house. In the master bathroom, I peeled off my clothes and climbed into the shower. I stood beneath the hot water until I was no longer shivering. It wasn't so easy to get rid of the chill that ran through me every time I thought of Dominique.

Once dry, I donned one of Grayson's T-shirts and put my sodden clothes into the dryer in the laundry room. We never did have dinner, but I'd lost my appetite, anyway, so I bypassed the kitchen on my way back to the bedroom. I climbed into bed and stared up at the ceiling. A few weeks earlier, Grayson and I had gone on vacation to Nantucket. It was the most romantic and relaxing trip I'd ever been on. Now, here we were, embroiled in what was possibly a murder investigation.

I hoped our Nantucket vacation wouldn't be our last trip together. As soon as that thought ran through my head, I silently scolded myself. Of course it wouldn't be. Grayson hadn't harmed Dominique and the police would realize that. After all, simply suspecting her of a crime in the past didn't make him guilty of killing her. If he'd wanted to take revenge on her, he would have done so years ago.

I decided to believe that the police would view the situation in the same light as I did if they ever found out that Grayson suspected Dominique of killing his mentor's daughter. I didn't see how they could know about that unless he told them, and there wasn't any reason to mention that detail as far as I was concerned. So, at most, the police would know only that Grayson's and Dominique's paths had crossed in the past.

That reasoning allowed me to relax enough that I drifted off to sleep. I didn't know how long I'd been out when a noise woke me. I sat up abruptly, my heart thudding. Faint light glowed down the hall. I relaxed and my heart rate slowed. Grayson was home.

I was about to get up and go find him when I spotted him through the open door. He'd taken off his jacket and shoes and was heading to the bedroom, Bowie at his heels. He stopped in the doorway.

"Sorry," he said. "Did I wake you?"

"I was sleeping lightly, and I wanted to be awake when you got here," I said.

As Bowie curled up in a corner of the room, Grayson sat down on the edge of the bed. I scooted closer and swung my legs over the side of the mattress so I could sit right next to him.

"Are the police still at the brewery?" I asked.

"They'll probably be there all night."

I brushed his damp hair off his forehead. "Are you okay?"

Even with very little light to see by, I couldn't miss his troubled expression.

"I'm fine." He rested a hand on my knee and I drew in a sharp breath at his icy touch. He quickly removed his hand. "Sorry," he said with a hint of a grin. "I guess I'm a bit cold."

I gave him a quick kiss. "Go take a hot shower. We can talk once you're warmed up."

After another kiss, he did as I suggested.

I huddled beneath the blankets as the water turned on in the bathroom. I fully intended to stay awake until I'd had a chance to find out the reason for the troubled look in his eyes. I knew there was something he'd yet to tell me, and it had me worried.

Despite that, my eyelids grew heavy. I decided it wouldn't hurt to close them for a few minutes. My mind grew hazy.

When I opened my eyes, I blinked with confusion. Daylight seeped through the cracks in the curtains. Rolling over, I saw that Grayson's side of the bed had been slept in, but was now empty.

Somehow, I'd slept right through until morning.

Still groggy, I climbed out of bed and made a quick trip to the bathroom to brush my teeth. When I returned to the bedroom, Grayson appeared in the doorway, fully dressed in jeans and a blue Spirit Hill Brewery T-shirt.

"You should have woken me last night," I said as I tucked my messy hair behind my ear.

He joined me over by the bed. "I didn't have the heart. You looked so peaceful."

I stepped up close to him, slipping my arms around him. "And you look good."

He grinned and ran a finger down the side of my face. "So do you."

I easily could have become carried away with the direction we were going, but something still wasn't quite right in his eyes.

"What is it?" I asked. "Are you really okay?"

His face grew more serious. "I am." He took both my hands in his. "But, Sadie, things could get bad for me."

"I've been thinking about that," I said. "I doubt you have a strong enough motive to be considered a serious suspect if Dominique was murdered. The police won't know that you think she killed Samantha."

He gave my hands a gentle squeeze. "But they will."

"How? Did you tell them?"

"No. Maybe I'd seem less guilty if I had, but I wanted to buy myself some time."

"Time?" I echoed, not sure what he meant.

"I didn't want them to arrest me on the spot."

"They wouldn't have done that." My confidence wavered. "Would they?"

"They might have." Grayson scrubbed a hand down his face. "Because a few months after Samantha died, the police arrested me for harassing Dominique. The charges were dropped, but there's an official record, Sadie. As soon as Detective Marquez finds out about that, I'm going to be her prime suspect."

Chapter 6

"No." I didn't want to believe that the situation was as dire as Grayson thought. "You could have sought revenge on Dominique years ago if you were so inclined. Why wait until now? That doesn't make any sense."

"The police might think that all my old feelings were brought back to the surface when Dominique showed up here in Shady Creek."

I didn't like how plausible that sounded.

"But why would she come to the brewery in the first place?" I asked. "She obviously knew you blamed her, so why would she want to talk to you?"

"I wish I knew. Maybe *she* wanted revenge."

"By writing a negative review of the brewery?"

He shrugged. "Could be."

"Whatever you do, don't suggest that to the cops," I said. "If they think Dominique threatened to write something negative about the brewery, that makes your motive even stronger."

"I don't think they'll need me to suggest it. They'll connect the dots on their own."

"But the dots don't go together."

"It looks like they do," Grayson said. "And that's all that will matter."

I let out a groan of frustration and dropped down onto the edge of the bed.

"Hey." Grayson sat beside me and put an arm around my waist. "I'll figure something out. I'm not spending the rest of my days locked up in jail when I could be here with you."

I put a hand to his face, grazing my thumb over the stubble on his jaw. "I definitely want you here with me." I shoved aside my frustration, wanting to be proactive. "So let's figure this out."

"Maybe you should let me do that."

I pulled back from him. "Why? I've helped unravel mysteries in the past."

Grayson tugged me closer again. "I know, but you've got the festival and the pub to deal with, and your mom is arriving today."

I let out another groan, this time dropping my forehead to Grayson's shoulder. "She's going to freak out when she hears that there was a murder in Shady Creek last night."

He stroked a hand down my hair. "And I'm guessing it will be a strike against me that it happened at my brewery, even if the cops don't end up arresting me."

This day was definitely not off to a good start.

As soon as I had that thought, a wave of guilt hit me. At least we were here, alive. Dominique didn't get to experience this day, or any others in the future.

"Let me worry about my mom." I didn't add that I could do that well enough for the both of us. I glanced at the bedside clock. "And I've got a couple of hours before I need to get ready for the festival, so let's make the most of that time and get you out of this mess before you're truly in it."

Grayson seemed on board with that plan. "I left a message for Jason last night and he texted me a while ago. He's already at the office, getting the brewery's surveillance footage from yesterday. He turned a copy over to the police last night and he's bringing the footage over here so we can take a look."

"Great idea." I wished I'd thought of the security cameras. "I bet the footage will show that you didn't kill Dominique. It might even show us who did."

"Maybe," Grayson said. "But there aren't any cameras inside the buildings, only on the outside."

"But the killer had to get in and out. If there *was* a killer. Could it have been an accident?" I was still holding out some hope for that, I realized.

"I don't think so," Grayson said. "That cask wouldn't have rolled off the shelf on its own. Someone must have hot-wired the forklift and used it to dislodge the cask."

That's what I'd figured. Each cask sat in a metal cradle on the shelf. That, combined with the weight of the cask, would have made it extremely difficult to move without the help of a fork-lift.

"While we're waiting for Jason, I'll make us some breakfast." Grayson kissed my forehead before standing up. "I took your clothes out of the dryer when I got home last night." He nodded at the carefully folded pile of clothes sitting on top of the trunk at the foot of the bed.

"Thank you," I said. "That was sweet."

Grayson grinned and pulled me to my feet before kissing me on the lips. "So are you."

I would have liked to follow that up with another kiss, but he was already on his way to the kitchen. That was probably for the best. We couldn't afford to get distracted with all that was at stake. We'd have plenty of time for kisses once the present situation was cleared up.

I dressed quickly and ran my fingers through my hair, tidying it as best I could. Then I followed the delicious smells wafting from the kitchen.

Someone knocked on the front door as I passed by it. Bowie gave a deep woof and came running.

For one frightening moment I thought it might be the police at the door, here to arrest Grayson. Then I remembered that Jason was supposed to be on his way over. A quick check through the peephole confirmed that it was indeed Grayson's best friend and head of security at the Spirit Hill Brewery.

"I've got it," I called to Grayson.

Maybe he'd already assumed that was the case. I didn't see how he could have missed the loud knock, but he hadn't emerged from the kitchen.

"Morning, Jason," I greeted when I opened the door. "I'm hoping you've got good news for us."

He gave Bowie a pat. "I wish that were the case."

My hopes crashed as he stepped into the house. "But surely the footage must show that Grayson wasn't at the scene of the crime when Dominique was killed."

"What I saw on the video doesn't necessarily prove anything one way or the other, but . . ."

He trailed off when Grayson appeared in the doorway that led to the kitchen.

"But what?" I asked.

"Hey, Jase," Grayson said. "You'd better come take a look at something."

The grim edge to Grayson's voice sent my anxiety spiking skyward.

I shut and locked the front door and then hurried after Jason, whose long strides had already taken him into the kitchen. Bowie had taken off ahead of us both.

"What's going on?" I asked with trepidation, barely noticing the omelets sitting on two plates on the granite countertop.

The guys stood with their backs to me, facing the kitchen

sink. I couldn't see why they were staring in that direction until Grayson stepped off to the side.

The cupboard under the sink stood open.

My first thought was that there was a leaky pipe. No big deal considering what else we had going on.

But then I saw the wrench lying beneath the pipes.

A wrench with blood on it.

Chapter 7

"Please tell me that isn't what I think it might be," I said, my voice pitched slightly higher than normal. "Grayson?" I prodded when he didn't respond.

"I wish I could," he said eventually, his turbulent gaze still fixed on the wrench. "The killer must have used it to hit Dominique in the head before crushing her with the cask."

"You didn't touch it, did you?" Jason asked.

"Of course not." Grayson scrubbed a hand down his face. "But it's one of the faucet wrenches from the brewery. It's probably got my fingerprints all over it."

"How do you know it's from the brewery?" I asked, denial wrestling to keep its place in my head.

"It's got *SHB* engraved on the handle," Grayson said. "I did that with all the tools."

"I don't need to tell you that this isn't good," Jason said.

"No you don't."

I pressed my fingers to my eyes, my mind spinning in a dizzying whirl. "Hold on." I dropped my hands. "It's your wrench and you left it in your house. What's the big deal? It can't be the murder weapon. That must be someone else's blood. Even if you had killed Dominique—which you didn't, of course—you never would have been dumb enough to leave the murder weapon in your own house."

"I didn't leave it there," Grayson said.

"Then how did it get there?"

Grayson glanced at me but then his gaze skittered away, landing on the door that led to his backyard. "Last night when I came in, I went to let Bowie out one last time. I found the back door open a crack. The lock had been jimmied."

"What?" Sudden images of a black-clad intruder creeping through the house while I slept sent my heart racing.

Bowie must have picked up on my distress. He whined and nudged my leg. I rested a hand on his head.

"You didn't hear anything last night before I came home?" Grayson asked me.

"No, but I fell asleep."

"Bowie would have reacted if someone came in the house. If he kept quiet, then the wrench was planted before you got here."

I nearly sagged with relief. A thought struck me. "But how would anyone get in with Bowie here?" I glanced down at the dog as I stroked the fur on his head.

"Jason brought him home just before you got here," Grayson said.

"I had him for the day while Grayson was in Burlington," Jason added.

"So the wrench was planted right after Dominique was killed," I said, thinking out loud. My anxiety spiked again. "Grayson, someone's trying to frame you for what happened."

Nobody disagreed with me.

"Aside from us three, who else in Shady Creek knows about your history with Dominique?" Jason asked.

"Nobody, as far as I know." Grayson gave it some more thought. "Maybe Dominique told someone?"

"None of this makes any sense." I could feel myself sliding toward despair.

"We can't worry about that now." Jason handed Grayson a thumb drive. "That's the surveillance footage, but before we get to that we need to make a decision about the wrench."

All three of us stared at the blood-smeared tool.

"If we touch it, we'll be tampering with evidence," I said. "But if we don't . . ."

"The cops will find it if they search the house," Jason finished for me.

"And the way things are going, that's probably going to happen." Grayson crossed his arms over his chest.

"Can we prove that someone broke in and left it?" I had to ask the question, even though I didn't anticipate a good response.

"A few scratches around the lock won't be enough," Jason said, confirming what I already knew.

Grayson frowned at the wrench. "We have to report it."

My fear was growing stronger with every passing second. "We also need to find out who really killed Dominique. Quickly." I looked to Grayson. "What can you tell me about her?"

"I can tell you plenty about her from eight years ago, but nothing from more recent years," he said. "I had to back off or end up in jail, so I've tried to move on."

"What about her business card?" I asked. "Was there anything on it other than her name and phone number?"

Grayson put a hand to his back pocket. "It'll still be in the jeans I was wearing yesterday."

He left the kitchen and I turned my back on the wrench. I couldn't bear to look at it any longer. Instead, I focused on the omelets and picked up one of the plates.

"Hungry?" I asked Jason.

"You're not going to eat it?"

I handed him the plate. "I've lost my appetite." My stomach sat like a lump of lead in my abdomen.

Jason apparently didn't have the same problem. He also didn't seem to care that the eggs were likely cold. He took a seat at the kitchen table and dug in.

Even with my back to what was likely the murder weapon, I was keenly aware of its presence. It was almost as if it were emitting a palpable and dangerous energy.

I turned and nudged the cupboard door shut with my foot, blocking the wrench from sight. That helped, but not much.

Grayson reappeared, and right away I noticed the tense set of his jaw.

"What's wrong?" I asked, not sure I could handle any more bad news, especially since I hadn't had a cup of coffee yet.

He handed me the business card. "I never looked at the back of it."

The front of the card listed Dominique's name, the magazine she worked for, and her phone number and e-mail address. I flipped it over.

On the back of the card, handwritten in blue ink, were the words "I need to talk to you about Samantha."

"Why would she write that?" I stared at the card, my mind spinning as I tried to come up with an answer to my own question. "If she wanted to confess to killing Samantha, why not go to the cops? Why come to you?"

"Good question," Grayson said.

Jason set down his knife and fork. He'd already demolished the entire omelet. "Maybe she could prove that she *didn't* do it."

Grayson rubbed his jaw. "Again, why come to me instead of the police?"

Jason shrugged. "Maybe she couldn't prove it yet. Maybe she needed your help to put the pieces together."

"Up until yesterday, I would have dismissed that possibility," Grayson said. "But now . . . I don't know."

"Okay." I tried pulling my thoughts together. I was still distracted by the bloody wrench beneath the kitchen sink, even though I couldn't see it. "So whatever the reason she wanted to talk to you, it had something to do with Samantha."

"And probably Samantha's death," Grayson added.

"Could that have anything to do with Dominique's murder?" I asked.

"At this point, just about anything is possible." Grayson checked the remaining omelet. "It's not too cold," he said to me. "Do you want it? Or I can make you another one."

"No thank you." I pressed a hand to my stomach. "I don't think I can handle anything but coffee."

Grayson grabbed a mug and filled it with freshly brewed coffee before handing it to me. He took the omelet and joined Jason at the table. I drew in a deep breath of coffee-scented steam and sat down next to Grayson.

"Why did you think Dominique killed Samantha?" I asked as I added cream and sugar to my coffee. "Did they know each other?"

"The two of them were close friends but they had a nasty falling-out shortly before the explosion. Something to do with a guy, but that's all I could ever find out about it. And when I talked to Dominique after the explosion, she claimed to know nothing about what happened, but I knew she was lying. I couldn't prove it, though." Even now, years later, the memory added an undercurrent of frustration and regret to his words.

I gave his hand a squeeze. "You said you could tell me a lot about Dominique from eight years ago. Maybe we should start there. What did you learn from tailing her?"

Grayson cut into his omelet. "The places she went, who she hung out with. I took photographs of people she interacted with. I've still got it all in a file folder in my study."

"That might not be so good," Jason said.

I finished his thought. "Because the cops might find it." I turned to Grayson. "Maybe you should give it to me. That way I can study it and the police won't find it."

"Unless they decide to search your place," Grayson said.

"They have no reason to do that."

"Yet," Grayson corrected me. "They know you're my girlfriend. If I become the number one suspect, the police might dig through your life in search of more evidence against me."

"Maybe." I didn't like to think about that happening. "But it's worth the risk. If they find the folder in my possession, I'll tell them that I was researching Dominique, not trying to hide it. Detective Marquez knows I can't keep out of a mystery."

Grayson set his fork on his empty plate. "Okay, maybe. Let's deal with the security footage first." He looked to Jason. "What have you got?"

"Laptop?" Jason asked.

"On the coffee table."

Jason disappeared into the living room. I cleared away the empty plates, needing something to do. By the time I returned to the table, Jason was sitting down again, with Grayson's laptop in front of him. He plugged in the thumb drive he'd brought with him.

"There's nothing of interest until about forty-five minutes before you found the body." Jason turned the laptop so Grayson and I could see the screen, which was split in two. One side showed the front entrance to the building where we'd found Dominique's body, and the other side showed the back door.

As we watched the screen, the front door opened and a man dressed in coveralls stepped outside.

"Caleb," Grayson said. "Leaving for the day, judging by the time code."

He ducked his head against the driving rain and ran off screen in the direction of the parking lot.

Jason fast-forwarded another couple of minutes and then let the footage play at normal speed again. A shadowy figure appeared at the edge of the screen and darted toward the door Caleb had exited earlier. The figure paused in the glow cast by the security lights and pushed back the hood of her jacket.

"Dominique," I said.

If I hadn't known who to expect, I might not have been able to identify her. It was hard to see much beyond the fact that she was a slim woman with long hair.

She slipped inside the building and out of sight.

Another shadow darted toward the door, reaching it seconds after it latched behind Dominique. The second person didn't push back their hood. They disappeared inside without giving us a good view of their face.

"Who is that?" I asked. "The killer?"

"Must be," Jason said. "There's nothing more until this."

He fast-forwarded the footage on the other side of the screen until the back door of the building flew open. A dark figure shot out of it. We barely got a glimpse of the person before they ran off screen.

"No one else goes in or out until you and Sadie arrive," Jason said.

"Then whoever followed Dominique inside must be the killer," I concluded. "But why did Dominique go in that building in the first place?"

"She probably figured I wouldn't want to talk to her and wouldn't show for the meeting she booked with Annalisa," Grayson said.

Jason followed that line of thought. "So she decided to ambush you when you got back to the brewery?"

Grayson nodded. "Probably."

"But someone ambushed her instead." I pushed my mug of coffee aside as a wave of nausea washed over me. The feeling intensified when I thought about Dominique's family and their terrible loss. She'd mentioned a niece who loved reading. Now that poor girl would never see her aunt again.

"Can you go back to the point when the killer goes into the building?" Grayson requested.

I was relieved that he'd interrupted my melancholy thoughts.

Jason rewound the footage and then paused it at the moment

when the killer stepped into the pool of light outside the door, right before slipping inside.

"That's the best view I can get," he said.

I fought back a growing sense of frustration. "We can't even tell if it's a man or a woman."

Whoever it was, they had the hood of their black rain jacket pulled up over their head. The footage had never once offered a glimpse of the person's face.

"And it could be me," Grayson pointed out.

"But it's not," I said.

"No, but we can't prove that it isn't. And that rain jacket . . ."

He didn't need to finish his sentence. I could do it for him. "It looks similar to yours."

Grayson had a black rain jacket. He was wearing it when we found Dominique. Just days before, while taking Bowie for a walk after a rain shower, I'd pointed out to Grayson that it wasn't a great color for visibility in poor weather. Little did I know at the time that it could also implicate him in a murder.

"What do we do now?" I couldn't keep a hint of despair out of my voice.

Grayson took my hand. "Sadie, you should go."

"No way," I protested. "I can't walk away when you're in trouble."

"Jason and I will take care of things, but as soon as I tell the cops about the wrench, they'll be on the doorstep."

"What exactly are you planning to do?" I didn't think I was going to like the answer to my question.

"It's better if you don't know."

My heart sank. "Don't do this. Don't shut me out."

"I'll give you guys a minute," Jason said, already getting up from his seat at the table.

"We'll figure this out together," I said to Grayson once we were alone.

He squeezed my hand. "We will. But we're going to report

the wrench, and I don't want you to be here when the police show up. I also don't want you to know what I'm going to do next, because then you won't have to worry about telling the police anything but the truth."

"I want to be here by your side no matter what happens."

Grayson kissed me and skimmed his thumb back and forth over my knuckles. "That means more to me than you can ever know. But I really don't want the police to suspect you of being an accessory after the fact or anything else. Please do this for me."

I didn't like what he was asking, but I could see in his eyes how important it was to him. "I'm not going to stop looking into this," I said. "Not until your name is cleared."

"And I won't ask you to. I only ask that you be careful and that you let me take these first steps on my own."

I still wasn't quite ready to concede. "I don't like it."

"I know. I'm sorry."

My mind looped back to something he'd said earlier. "What about that file on Dominique?"

"I'll get it for you." He left the kitchen and returned less than a minute later with a manila envelope.

As Grayson handed it to me, I fought back tears, determined not to cry. I hugged the envelope to my chest. "You should have a lawyer."

"I've got one I use for business matters, but I'll talk to a criminal one before the end of the day." He tucked my hair behind my ear, and the gesture almost made me lose the battle against the threat of tears.

"Promise you'll be careful?" I asked, my voice little more than a whisper.

"I promise."

I still didn't want to walk away, but I finally relented. I stood up and took hold of Grayson's hand. "Let me know what happens?"

"I will."

He pulled me in close for a lingering kiss.

When I walked away a few moments later, I couldn't bear to look back.

Instead of putting my jacket on, I draped it over one arm, using it to hide the envelope Grayson had given me. I was overly aware of every movement I made, and I hoped I didn't appear unnatural in any way. The last thing I wanted to do was draw attention to myself and what I had hidden beneath my jacket.

When I reached the footbridge that led to the Inkwell, I let out a sigh of relief. I was almost safely home with the file.

My relief didn't last long. When I glanced back down the road toward the brewery, my stomach gave a nauseating lurch. Two police cars and an unmarked vehicle turned off Creekside Road and headed up Grayson's driveway.

Chapter 8

I stood frozen on the footbridge, panic holding me in a tight grip.

I didn't think enough time had passed for the police to be responding to a call from Grayson about the bloody wrench. Maybe the cops were simply heading back to look at the scene of the crime again. I hoped that was the case, but I had a terrible feeling that it wasn't. More likely, trouble was swiftly headed Grayson's way.

That thought was enough to get me moving. I whipped out my phone and then hesitated. I wanted to warn Grayson, but I didn't want anyone to look at our text messages later and conclude that we knew we had a reason to be worried.

The police are heading up to the brewery, I wrote. **More crime scene work, maybe? I hope you can reopen soon.**

I sent the message, knowing Grayson would realize it was a warning.

With that done, I ran around the old gristmill and unlocked the back door. I charged up the stairs to my apartment and tucked the manila envelope out of sight in the storage compartment of the rustic coffee table Damien had made for me.

"Hi, Wimsey!" I called out to my snoozing cat. "See you later!"

He cracked open one eye as I rushed out of the apartment but made no move to leave his perch on the back of the couch. I paused outside the back door long enough to lock it, and then I was off running again. I didn't slow my pace until I was halfway up the brewery's driveway, and then only because of a painful stitch in my side. Pushing through the pain, I kept going at a brisk walk and soon reached the branch of the driveway that led to Grayson's house.

Even though I knew what to expect, my heart plummeted when I spotted the police vehicles parked out in front of the house. As I'd feared, they were interested in my boyfriend this time, not the crime scene.

Whether Grayson had a chance to report the wrench or not, the police would have it in their possession soon. Detective Marquez already stood on the front porch with a uniformed officer at her side. Two other uniformed officers stood at the base of the wide steps. The door was open, but Grayson wasn't the one standing there conversing with Marquez. Jason was the one doing the talking.

As I approached the house, Detective Marquez handed a piece of paper to Jason. He glanced at it and then stepped aside so the police could go inside.

My heart drummed a frantic beat in my chest. They really were going to search the house.

For a second, I felt so light-headed I thought I might pass out. I rested a hand on the trunk of one of the trees that lined the driveway, leaning my weight against it.

Jason was still talking to Detective Marquez, in the foyer now. I drew in a deep breath and approached the house, wanting to know what they were saying. I didn't get close enough to eavesdrop. Officer Pamela Rogers put up a hand to stop me.

"Sorry, Sadie," she said. "I'm going to have to ask you to stop there."

It seemed Jason's conversation with the detective was over, anyway. He called to Bowie and then came out of the house with the dog's leash in hand. The white German shepherd trotted down the steps behind him.

Jason clipped the leash onto Bowie's collar and continued on in my direction.

"Walk with us," he said, slowing but not stopping when he reached me.

I glanced at the house again. All but one officer had disappeared inside. The other stood stationed by the front door.

I swallowed back another wave of panic and fell into step with Jason, walking quickly to match his much longer strides. Bowie wagged his tail and gazed up at me.

"Where's Grayson?" I asked in a hushed voice as I gave Bowie a pat on the head.

"I don't know." Jason didn't bother to lower his voice.

"What do you mean you don't know?" I whispered.

I shot another glance over my shoulder. We were far enough away now that the officer by the front door wouldn't be able to overhear us.

"Me not knowing was part of the plan," Jason said. "Grayson took off as soon as he got your text. He didn't have a chance to call the police about the wrench. He figured if he stayed and told them in person, he'd be arrested on the spot. We agreed that I'd wait for the cops and tell them I was there because he'd asked me to take Bowie for a walk."

"So when will he be back?" I asked.

Jason sent a sidelong glance my way before speaking again. "Once his name is cleared. Until then, he's in hiding."

I stopped in my tracks. Jason kept walking. I jogged to catch up with him again.

"So they'll find the wrench and think Grayson was trying to hide it?"

Jason's only response was a brief nod.

"He'll be a wanted man. A fugitive." A wave of nausea and light-headedness hit me so hard that I almost stumbled.

Jason put a hand to my elbow. "Are you okay?" he asked with concern.

I'd probably gone as pale as a ghost.

I nodded. He removed his hand from my elbow and I wrapped my arms around my stomach.

"Where is he hiding?" I asked, not wanting to accept that Jason couldn't tell me.

"I really don't know. He thought it was best that way."

"So you wouldn't have to lie?" I guessed, since that was the reason Grayson had given for keeping me in the dark.

"He's looking out for both of us."

"But I want to look out for *him*, and I know you do too," I said.

They'd been best friends since they'd met in their early teens.

"And we will," Jason said. "By doing whatever we can for him in his absence."

"What about Bowie?" I asked, looking at Grayson's beloved dog.

"I'll take care of him," Jason assured me.

I was silent for a minute or so as I came to terms with everything. "Okay," I said eventually. "Grayson's gone." Just saying those words hurt. "So what do we do now?"

"I think you know the answer to that."

He was right. I did know.

We were going to prove that Grayson was innocent.

To do that, we needed to find the real killer.

*   *   *

I parted ways with Jason and Bowie at the foot of the brewery's driveway. I didn't want to think about the police searching Grayson's house and finding the wrench, but I couldn't stop myself from doing so. I also couldn't keep myself from worrying about Grayson. Where would he stay? How would he get food? When would I see him again? All those questions made my heart ache. What I needed to do was distract myself by immersing myself in the challenge of finding Dominique's killer.

Unfortunately, I couldn't do that right away. I needed to be at the town hall in less than an hour and I still had sample cocktails to mix before the food and drink festival started for the day. I considered whether I could skim through the contents of Grayson's file on Dominique while I got ready for the festival, but I quickly dismissed that idea. Most likely, I'd end up spilling the drinks on the folder or I'd make a mistake while mixing the cocktails and mocktails.

Despite the swirling of anxious thoughts in my head, I managed to get the drinks ready and loaded into the coolers with a few minutes to spare. I dashed upstairs to my apartment and shoved the manila envelope into an old messenger bag that I dug out of my closet. I probably wouldn't have time to peek inside the envelope during the festival, but I wanted it with me in case things got slow at some point. Otherwise, I'd be kicking myself for not taking it along.

Of course, if I did have a chance to look at the information Grayson had collected, I'd have to do so without anyone knowing what I was reading. That probably meant I should have left it at home, but I decided to stick with my plan. Even if I didn't have time to look at the information, having it close at hand made me feel a little bit better, whether that made sense or not.

Like the day before, Booker showed up a few minutes before his shift was set to start and helped me transport the drink sam-

ples over to the town hall. He didn't comment on the presence
of the messenger bag I had with me, and for that I was glad. I
didn't feel like talking about Grayson's predicament at the moment. I needed some time to come to grips with it myself first.

Once I had the drink samples set out on the table and
Booker had returned to the Inkwell, I studied the scene around
me. The other business owners were slowly filing into the
room and heading for their booths. The doors wouldn't open
to the public for another ten minutes and no one was paying me
any attention, so I figured this might be the best opportunity I
had to sneak a peek at Grayson's file.

I carefully eased the folder out of the manila envelope. A
couple of photographs slipped free and flitted to the floor. I
quickly snatched them up. One showed a younger Dominique
entering what looked like a bank. The other showed her talking
with two twentysomething women. One had a backpack and
the other a messenger bag. Dominique held a couple of books
in her arms. Judging by the buildings in the background, I
thought the photo had been taken on a college campus.

I tucked the photos back into the file folder and carefully
flipped through the rest of the contents. Aside from a small pile
of photographs, the folder held a thin notebook, a couple of
newspaper clippings, and printouts of a few documents. I
scanned the top document. It looked like it was the ownership
information for a houseboat. It was probably safe to bet it was
the houseboat that had exploded and killed Samantha.

I focused on the notebook next. I flipped through the pages,
which were full of notations written with blue ink. Grayson's
surveillance log, I concluded, recognizing his handwriting. At
the top of each page was a date, with times and notes written
below. I quickly leafed through the pages again. Grayson had
kept close tabs on Dominique over the course of two or three
weeks.

A sudden sense of hopelessness hit me like a punch to the

stomach. Grayson had watched Dominique so carefully, had investigated the explosion as thoroughly as he could, and yet he hadn't been able to prove Dominique's connection to Samantha's death.

My investigation into Dominique's murder couldn't end up like that. If I failed, Grayson would either end up in jail or have to remain a fugitive indefinitely.

Determination quickly moved in to replace my hopelessness. One way or another, I had to clear Grayson's name.

I wouldn't give up until I did.

Chapter 9

When I glanced up from the folder I had open on my lap, I realized that the town hall was busier than before. Someone must have opened the doors to the public, because the first few tourists had already wandered into the room. I stuffed the folder and its contents back into the envelope and tucked it away in my messenger bag for safekeeping.

I smiled and greeted my first visitors of the day. Once they'd sampled the drinks and we'd chatted for a few minutes, they moved on to the cidery's table. I leaned forward so I could see past two women who'd stopped to chat with each other. A young woman sat behind the Spirit Hill Brewery's table. I knew her name was Elizabeth and that she worked at the brewery in some capacity, but I didn't know her any better than that. It didn't surprise me that Juliana wasn't running the booth today. As the brewery's head of public relations, she must have had her hands full dealing with the double catastrophe of having someone murdered on the brewery's premises and having the owner suspected of being the killer.

Hopefully, the media didn't yet know about that last part. But if it wasn't public knowledge, it would be soon.

I checked my phone and couldn't stop myself from feeling a pang of disappointment when I saw that I had no text messages from Grayson, even though I knew it was silly to expect otherwise. Of course he couldn't text me while he was a fugitive. If he so much as turned his phone on, the police might be able to track him down. Even if he'd had a burner phone, the police knew about my relationship with him and I didn't want anything in my phone records to give him away.

Knowing that I wouldn't hear from Grayson didn't stop me from checking my phone several times over the next hour. I was tempted to text Jason to ask if he had any news, but that was something I should ask in person. Again, I didn't want anything in my phone records that I wouldn't want the police to see.

After checking my phone for the umpteenth time, I set the device aside and got a pleasant surprise when I saw my aunt Gilda coming my way. She wore a cozy shawl in fall colors that complemented her auburn hair, which she wore tied back in a fancy knot.

"Morning, hon," she said when she reached my table. "This place looks wonderful."

"It really does," I agreed. "Mel and the others did a fantastic job."

Everyone seemed to appreciate the decorations. Dominique, Phoebe, and I weren't the only ones who'd taken photos of the beautiful maple tree in the middle of the room.

Aunt Gilda's face grew serious. "I heard about what happened at the brewery."

That wasn't unexpected. News always traveled fast in Shady Creek.

"Is it true that you were there when the poor woman was found?" she asked.

"Unfortunately," I said. "Grayson and I found her together." I eyed a group of tourists headed our way. "I'll tell you more later."

She seemed to understand. She wandered over to the neighboring table while I entertained the tourists for the next few minutes. After they'd sampled all the available drinks and had each taken a menu, they wandered over to the Caldwell Cheese Company's booth. Once they were gone, Aunt Gilda returned to my table.

"Excited about this afternoon?" she asked.

"As much as I can be after what happened at the brewery," I replied. A rush of uncertainty made me second-guess my response. "I think."

Aunt Gilda gave me an appraising look. "You're not still nervous, are you?"

"A little," I confessed, although that was probably an understatement. "It's so important to me that she likes the Inkwell and even more important that she likes Grayson."

"I've told you before and I'll tell you again that there's no need to worry."

I wished that were the case. Aunt Gilda may have heard about Dominique dying at the brewery, but it didn't sound as though she knew about Grayson's unfortunate situation. How could I introduce my mom to my boyfriend when he was on the run from the police?

How was I going to explain his absence?

For a second, I was tempted to go into hiding myself. The only reason I didn't give in to that temptation was that it would make it harder for me to help Grayson.

"I'll do my best not to worry," I said, even though I knew that was likely a lost cause.

"Are you staying here until the festival ends for the day?" Aunt Gilda asked.

"No." I glanced at the time on my phone. "Zoe should be here any moment to relieve me."

"Did I hear my name?" Zoe appeared by the table, a smile on her face.

"It's like I summoned you magically," I said.

Mild alarm flashed across her face. "Am I late?"

"Definitely not," I assured her. "In fact, you're a few minutes early."

I made sure Zoe didn't have any questions, and then I left her to look after the booth.

I walked out of the town hall with Aunt Gilda. She'd taken a short break from work, but needed to get back to her hair salon, which was located across the village green. I tucked my arm through hers as we made our way down the steps of the town hall.

"Are you all right?" she asked with concern. "I don't know how you keep managing to come across dead bodies."

"It's definitely not on purpose," I assured her. "And I'm okay, but I'm worried about Grayson."

As succinctly as possible, I told her about the fact that the police suspected Grayson and had searched his house. I left out the part about the wrench under his kitchen sink and the fact that he'd gone into hiding. What I did share was plenty enough to shock Aunt Gilda.

"How could they possibly suspect Grayson?" she asked.

I appreciated how indignant she sounded.

"They had a history."

Again, I kept the story as brief as possible. We'd already reached the other side of the village green and would have to go our separate ways soon.

"An explosion," Aunt Gilda echoed when I was done. "What a terrible way to lose someone you know."

"It must have been awful," I agreed. "And Grayson still feels guilty for not getting justice for Samantha. He hasn't said that, exactly, but I can tell."

Gilda shook her head in sympathy. "Surely the police can't arrest him. I don't doubt for a second that he's innocent, so how could the police have enough evidence to make a real case against him?"

My knees shook as we stopped at the edge of Sycamore

Street and waited for two cars to drive by. "I sure hope they don't arrest him," I said, dancing around the subject of incriminating evidence. "But I don't know if he'll be able to join us tonight."

Grayson was supposed to have dinner with my mom, Aunt Gilda, and me on my mom's first evening in Shady Creek.

"That's understandable," Gilda said.

I hoped my mom would think so too.

"Maybe he can join us for a meal later in the week," she added.

"Fingers crossed." I released my aunt's arm now that we were standing outside her salon. "Despite my worries and everything going on with Grayson, I really am glad that mom's coming to visit."

Gilda patted my arm. "I know you are. I'm glad she's coming too. I think a lot of what feels to you like disapproval is actually worry. It'll be good for her to come and see for herself how settled and happy you are here."

"I think so too. And thank you for putting her up at your place."

I would have had my mom stay with me in the spare bedroom of my cozy apartment, but she'd expressed reservations about sleeping above the pub. She'd likely go to bed while the Inkwell was still open, and even though I'd assured her that I didn't run a rowdy establishment, the potential for noise concerned her. Aunt Gilda, my late dad's sister, was happy to offer up her spare bedroom. Gilda's apartment was located above her hair salon, where noise at night definitely wasn't an issue.

Aunt Gilda headed into her salon and I cut across the corner of the village green to get to the Inkwell. I stood back from the old gristmill, scrutinizing my fall and Halloween decorations with a critical eye. Pumpkins and gourds sat on bales of straw, and the Sherlock Holmes scarecrow that Mel had made the year before stood sentinel on the lawn. In recent days, I'd added a few gauzy ghosts to the maple trees, and they fluttered and swayed in the light breeze.

I thought the gristmill looked postcard perfect as always, but would my mom think so?

I remembered that I'd promised Aunt Gilda I'd try not to worry about such things. It would have been easier to keep that promise if the murder hadn't happened. My mom would freak out if she knew I'd found a dead body. I hoped she wouldn't hold the police investigation against Grayson.

"Stop worrying," I admonished myself out loud. "Everything's going to be fine."

Not for Dominique, though.

I tried my best to push that sad thought aside, but I couldn't quite banish the cloud of melancholy that had followed me around since finding Dominique at the brewery. The cloud had only darkened since the discovery of the wrench in Grayson's house.

The real clouds overhead were growing darker too. It looked as though more rain was on its way. Maybe even another thunderstorm.

I heard the sound of a car pulling into the Inkwell's parking lot. I spun around as hope bubbled up inside me. Disappointment and wariness quickly popped those bubbles. I should have known that it wouldn't be my mom arriving. I wasn't expecting her for a couple of hours yet.

My heart plummeted when the driver climbed out of the silver sedan.

Detective Marquez.

Chapter 10

"I hope I haven't caught you at a bad time," Detective Marquez said when she reached me.

"Not exactly." I glanced toward the pub's front door. "I just got back from the town hall and I was about to get to work."

"Are you able to take some time away?" Marquez asked. "I'd like to ask you some questions at the station."

I nearly gulped with apprehension, but managed to hide any signs of fear. At least, I hoped I'd succeeded at that. "I have to check with my staff. I'm not sure how busy the pub is at the moment."

"I'll wait." She stood her ground, and it was clear that she wasn't going anywhere until I checked in with Mel and Booker.

"I'll be right back," I said, relieved that my voice sounded steady because I felt anything but.

At least the detective didn't follow me into the pub. Customers occupied several tables and a couple of stools at the bar, and I didn't want to be the topic of the day's gossip. If the customers saw me leave with Marquez, the speculation would probably begin before I even got out the door.

I hurried behind the bar, where Mel was in the process of filling pint glasses with beer.

"How's everything here?" I asked.

"So far so good," she said. "How are things at the festival?"

"Fine." I waited as Mel delivered the pints to two men sitting at the end of the bar.

"What's wrong?" she asked as she passed by me on the way to the kitchen.

I followed on her heels. "Is it that obvious?"

"You look like you're about to break some bad news," Mel said by way of reply as she pushed open the swinging door.

Booker looked up from the grill, where hamburger patties sizzled away. "There's more bad news?"

I'd shared the basics about Dominique's murder with them via text message. They'd probably heard about it through the local grapevine too.

Mel hooked a thumb over her shoulder at me. "Ask Sadie."

"I do have bad news," I said. "The police searched Grayson's house this morning."

"In connection with the murder?" Mel asked.

"Unfortunately. It seems he's the prime suspect. As far as I know, anyway."

Booker shook his head as he flipped one of the burgers. "They're barking up the wrong tree."

I appreciated the fact that he didn't doubt that even for a second.

"And at the moment they're sniffing around *this* tree," I said, pointing to myself.

Mel set down the platter of nachos she'd just picked up. "As in they want to search the pub?"

"No," I said quickly, but then I reconsidered my answer. "At least, I don't think so. Detective Marquez wants me to go to the station with her to answer some questions."

"Should one of us come with you?" Booker asked as he plated a burger.

"I don't think that's necessary," I said, although having company would have been nice. "Besides, I need you guys here."

Mel scrutinized me with her blue eyes. "Do you need a lawyer?"

The mere thought sent a quiver of anxiety through me. "I doubt it. I'm pretty sure it's just some standard questions. I found the body with Grayson, after all."

"And you're the prime suspect's girlfriend," Mel added. "How much trouble is Grayson in?"

My face fell and, to my dismay, my eyes filled with tears.

"Hey." Booker wiped his hands on a towel and put an arm around me. "Is it really that bad?"

I nodded as I tried to get my emotions back under control. "I think someone's trying to frame him."

"What can we do to help?" Mel asked.

I smiled as the tears in my eyes subsided. "For the moment, hold down the fort? Hopefully, I won't be gone long."

"We'll be fine here," Booker assured me, and Mel nodded in agreement.

"Thank you." I drew in a deep breath and forced myself to walk out of the kitchen as if nothing were wrong.

I pretended to be cheerful and exchanged greetings with a few of the locals scattered about the pub, but I didn't stop to chat.

Outside, I found Detective Marquez over by her car, talking to someone on her cell phone. As I walked in her direction, she ended the call and slipped her phone into the pocket of her suit jacket.

"Can I give you a lift?" she asked, already opening the passenger door of her sedan.

"I'd like to follow in my own car, if that's okay," I said. "I need to get back to work as soon as possible."

For a terrifying split second, I was afraid she'd take me into custody and stuff me into the backseat of her car with my hands cuffed. Thankfully, she simply nodded her agreement.

I hurried over to my old white Toyota and climbed into the driver's seat. Detective Marquez didn't pull out of the lot until I had my engine turned on.

I drove across town to the police station with white knuckles. When I parked and released the steering wheel, my fingers were sore from gripping it so tightly.

Detective Marquez waited by the back door of the station, so I couldn't linger in my car, gathering up my courage. I'd have to make do with whatever courage I already had. That didn't feel like much.

When I reached the door, Marquez held it open for me. I stepped inside and found myself in a hallway with off-white walls and gray linoleum flooring. I'd been to the police station before, but never in this back corridor. The detective led me along the hall and stopped outside an open door on the left.

"We can talk in here," she said, gesturing for me to precede her into the room.

Inside, the walls were the same off-white as in the hallway, but there was gray carpeting rather than linoleum. A table sat in the middle of the room with four chairs tucked beneath it. In one corner, a camcorder was attached to a tripod. The room was otherwise empty.

"Detective," a man said from the hallway, out of my line of sight, "we're finished over at the motel."

"Thank you, Hanson," Marquez said before following me into the room.

"Were you searching Dominique's motel room?" I asked.

"Take a seat," she said, ignoring my question.

I pulled out a chair and sank into it. I figured I was probably right, but I didn't have a chance to think about what the police might have found there. Marquez had shut the door and was taking the seat across from me. She set a notebook and pen on the table in front of her.

"I'll be recording our conversation," she told me. "It's standard procedure."

I tried not to fidget as she used a small remote control to turn on the camera. She stated our names and the date and then got down to business.

"I'd like to go over the events of last evening to start," she said.

She got me to explain how Grayson and I had found Dominique and what we'd done between the time of the discovery to the moment when the first officers arrived on the scene. That was straightforward enough. I simply repeated what I'd told Officer Rogers the night before.

"How long were you with Mr. Blake before you found the body?" Marquez asked.

"I'm not sure, exactly, but I'd say around ten or fifteen minutes."

I realized that she was trying to figure out whether Grayson had had the opportunity to commit the murder. What had Jason said? There was a gap of about forty-five minutes between the time when the killer ran from the brewery and when Grayson and I discovered the body.

"It could have been a bit longer," I added, wishing I could give him an alibi for the entire window of time. "I met him at his house. Then we walked over to the brewery and stopped in at the main office."

"Where were you before you met him at his house?"

"At the Inkwell, working," I said. "I walked over to Grayson's."

"How long did that take?" Marquez asked.

"About five minutes."

"Did Mr. Blake ever mention Ms. Girard to you before?"

"No," I replied. "I only found out that he knew her a few minutes before we discovered her body."

"Did he bring up the subject?"

I shook my head. "The brewery's receptionist did. She mentioned that Dominique had stopped by."

"And how did Mr. Blake react to that news?"

"He was surprised to hear that Dominique was in town." I didn't add that it was clearly an unwelcome surprise.

Detective Marquez continued with her questions. "When was the last time you saw or spoke with Mr. Blake?"

"This morning. I spent the night at his house. I was walking back to the Inkwell when I saw all the police cars going up his driveway."

"Did he tell you that he was planning to go anywhere this morning?"

"No."

"Have you heard from him since then?" she asked.

"No."

"Have you tried to get in touch with him?"

"I texted him a couple of times," I said, glad that I'd had the presence of mind to do that. "He hasn't responded."

Marquez jotted something in her notebook and then studied me closely with her dark eyes. "Do you know where he is?"

"No, I really don't."

Now that I sat facing the detective, I was glad I could answer that question truthfully, and I appreciated that Grayson had made sure that would be the case.

"He didn't kill Dominique," I said. "Any time spent investigating him is time wasted. The real killer could be slipping through the cracks as we speak."

"I'm required to follow the evidence," Detective Marquez

said. "And currently, it points at Mr. Blake. My mind isn't closed to other possibilities, but things aren't looking good for him."

"But it wasn't him," I stressed. "He wouldn't kill anyone."

"Are you aware that he and the victim had a history?"

So the police knew about that already.

"Yes," I said. "But if Grayson had wanted to harm Dominique—which he didn't—he would have done it a long time ago."

"I understand your feelings on the matter," Marquez said, shutting her notebook. "I have to caution you that this is a police investigation and if you're in possession of any pertinent information, you'll need to disclose it. We have a warrant for Mr. Blake's arrest. If you know or become aware of his current whereabouts, I expect you to bring that information to me. Otherwise I'll consider you to be aiding and abetting a fugitive."

My mood hadn't been great when I arrived at the station, but now it darkened considerably. I'd always respected Detective Marquez, but at the moment I couldn't help but see her as the enemy. I knew she was just doing her job, and it was an important one, but I also knew that Grayson was innocent, and I wasn't going to stand by and let him get railroaded by the police.

"Am I free to go?" I asked.

Detective Marquez pushed back her chair. "I'll walk you out."

She escorted me to the parking lot and I climbed into my car, slamming the door a little harder than necessary. Marquez didn't notice. She'd already gone back inside the station.

I rested my head against the steering wheel, thinking. I needed to return to the Inkwell, but I also needed to help Grayson. How I was going to do that, I didn't yet know, but I focused on what little information I did have.

Dominique had stayed at the motel at the edge of town.

That seemed like as good a place to start as any, so I took a detour on my way back to the pub, driving out to the highway, where the motel was located. I parked in the lot in front of the building and remained sitting in my car. The drab, two-story motel looked in need of a good power washing, and I doubted it would attract anyone other than visitors trying to find the cheapest accommodation possible beyond a tent at a campsite.

There was no police tape in sight, confirming what I'd overheard at the station. The police were done searching Dominique's room. I wondered if that meant they'd cleared out all of her belongings. Maybe it wouldn't hurt to ask.

I climbed out of my car and crossed the parking lot. I peered through the glass window of the motel's office door before opening it. A heavyset, balding man sat behind the desk, his focus on a small TV mounted on the wall across the room. He didn't turn his gaze to me until I was right up at the counter.

"Hi," I said, giving him a cheery smile. "I understand the woman who died the other night was staying here at your motel."

The man narrowed his eyes at me. "You a reporter?"

"No," I replied quickly. "But I knew the victim—slightly—and wanted to make sure that her family would know where to find her personal effects."

The man seemed disappointed. Maybe he'd hoped I was a reporter, here to give his motel a headline.

"The cops took all that. Or at least whatever was left."

"What do you mean?"

"Someone ransacked the room before the cops arrived."

"Any idea who?" I was hoping he could identify the culprit, who was likely also the killer.

"Nope," the man said, clearly losing interest in our conversation.

"What about security cameras?"

"The system broke months ago. Haven't had a chance to get it fixed. Unless you want to rent a room, I can't help you." He turned his attention back to the TV.

Disappointment weighed heavily on my shoulders. "Thanks, anyway," I said before heading for the door.

I frowned as I stepped outside. So much for that line of investigation. All I'd learned was that the killer had likely wanted something of Dominique's. Something they hadn't found on her body. Or, the killer searched the room first and then went after Dominique when they didn't find what they wanted. Either way, I had no clue what the killer might have been searching for.

When I reached my car, I paused, noting that there were four other vehicles parked in the lot. Dominique must have had a car. Otherwise, getting to and from the motel would have been a chore. Had she driven to the brewery on the night of her death?

I thought back. When I arrived at the brewery, there was a single car parked in the lot. I was pretty sure it was gone after Grayson and I had found Dominique. The car probably belonged to Annalisa. She'd been on her way out when we'd seen her at the office.

I pictured the events unfolding in my head.

Yes, I was certain that when the police cars arrived, the parking lot was otherwise empty. So Dominique must have parked elsewhere and walked to the brewery.

That probably wasn't significant. There was a small community parking lot tucked out of sight of the village green. She could have parked there and then walked around town. I figured Grayson's theory was right—she'd returned to the brewery after dark because she was desperate to talk to him and hoped to take him by surprise so he couldn't avoid her. But who had followed her in there and killed her? And why?

Those were both million-dollar questions.

Finding the answers would be worth far more to me than any amount of money, though.

Before I could find those answers, I had to get back to the pub.

Hopefully, while I worked, I could figure out a plan of action.

Chapter 11

Even though I knew roughly what time my mom was planning to arrive in Shady Creek, I couldn't stop myself from checking out the Inkwell's windows every few minutes. I managed not to mess up any orders, but my mind was definitely on other things. It didn't help that several of the pub's customers were discussing the murder at the brewery. Some of them peppered me with questions, now that it was widely known that Grayson and I had discovered the body, and others shared theories about how Dominique might have met her end.

I eavesdropped now and then whenever I could do so inconspicuously, but I didn't learn anything new. I hoped for a different result later when I took a more in-depth look at the folder of information Grayson had given me. Aunt Gilda and I were having dinner with my mom, but I planned to go through the folder's contents before going to sleep that night, no matter how late I got back from dinner.

When the anticipated hour of my mom's arrival drew closer, my glances out the window grew more frequent. An order for six different drinks diverted my attention, forcing me to wait several minutes before I could have another look. When I'd finally delivered the drinks to the waiting customers, I peeked out the window again.

A smile spread across my face. My mom's dark blue sedan was pulling into the Inkwell's parking lot.

I spun around, wanting to get rid of the tray I was holding. To my surprise, Mel stood a few feet away. She smiled and held out a hand.

"Thanks, Mel." I passed her the tray and dashed out the door.

I couldn't contain my excitement. I ran across the lawn to the small parking lot, waving as my mom climbed out of her car. She smiled when she noticed me, and that brightened my own smile and eased some of my worries.

"I'm so glad you're here!" I gave her a hug. "How was your drive? Did you enjoy the scenery? What do you think of Shady Creek so far?"

"One question at a time please, Sadie," my mom said.

Although her voice held a typical note of sternness, her smile hadn't faded completely.

I drew in a deep breath, forcing myself to calm down. "Sorry. How was your drive?"

"Not too bad, especially once I got out of the city."

My mom had driven from my hometown of Knoxville, Tennessee.

"Let me get your bags," I offered.

She popped the trunk and I hauled out the single suitcase while my mom fetched her purse from the front passenger seat.

"Would you like something to eat or drink or do you want to get settled at Gilda's first?" I asked.

"I'd like to see your pub." Her gaze had already locked on the old gristmill.

Pride and excitement bubbled in my chest, eclipsing any of my residual nervousness. "I can't wait to give you a tour."

I held the front door open for her and then followed her into the Inkwell. I introduced her to Mel, and then took her into the kitchen to meet Booker. After locking her suitcase in my tiny office under the staircase, I then gave her a brief tour of my upstairs apartment.

My mom listened carefully to everything I told her, but I couldn't tell if she was impressed or not. It didn't really surprise me that she was holding her cards close to her chest, but it did stoke the embers of my worries.

"What do you think?" I asked once we'd returned to the main floor.

"It certainly seems more like a cozy British pub than a wild sports bar," she said.

Of course it doesn't resemble a wild sports bar, I wanted to say. I'd explained that to her over the phone many times and I'd sent her several pictures of the pub over the past year. I held my tongue, though. I didn't want the visit starting off on the wrong foot.

"I think I'd like to head over to Gilda's now so I can get ready for dinner."

We'd arranged over the phone that she, Gilda, Grayson, and I would all have dinner together at Lumière, Shady Creek's fanciest restaurant. A hum of anxiety shot through me. Somehow, I was going to have to explain Grayson's absence.

My mom and I walked across the corner of the village green, with me pulling her wheeled suitcase. I could tell she was taking in the sight of the cute bandstand and all the charming shops on the streets that bordered the green.

"That's Aunt Gilda's salon." I pointed it out. It sat next to the local bakery and a few doors away from the Village Bean.

Aunt Gilda saw us through the large front window and waved, a bright smile lighting up her face. She hurried to the door to open it for us. After hugs and greetings, I left my mom in Gilda's charge. I returned to the Inkwell but only stayed in the pub long enough to make sure everything was running smoothly. Once satisfied that all was well, I jogged upstairs so I could change for dinner.

I switched out my jeans and blue sweater for a jersey knit dress and high-heeled boots. Wimsey was curled up on the couch, but as soon as I opened the fridge, he jumped down and wound around my feet, meowing impatiently, as I prepared his dinner.

I set his dish on the floor and gave him a pat on the head as he dug into his meal.

"See you later, buddy," I said as I pulled on my coat.

I'd arranged to meet my mom and aunt at Gilda's place, since it was situated two doors down from Lumière, so I sent a quick text message to say I was on my way and then hurried out of the gristmill. Darkness had settled over Shady Creek and the old-fashioned street lamps lit up the streets. Even at night, I found the town charming. I hoped my mom did too.

She and Aunt Gilda came out the front door of the salon as I was crossing Sycamore Street, and I greeted each of them with a hug.

"Gilda mentioned that Grayson might not be able to join us this evening after all," my mom said as we walked the short distance to the restaurant.

"Unfortunately." I hoped my aunt hadn't said *why* Grayson was unavailable. "He had some . . . urgent business to take care of."

"Brewery business?" my mom asked.

"Personal business," I said, doing my best to sound unconcerned.

I was dancing around the truth, but at least I wasn't outright lying. I figured that trying to clear your name when you're suspected of murder qualified as urgent personal business.

Aunt Gilda and I exchanged a glance. Luckily, my mom seemed to accept my explanation.

"That's too bad," was all she said.

"He really wants to meet you," I assured her.

"When will he be free?"

"I don't know precisely when, but hopefully very soon."

To my relief, she didn't ask any further questions. She didn't look impressed, though.

So much for things going smoothly in terms of my mom meeting my new boyfriend. Hopefully, he really would be free—in more ways than one—in a few days' time. Introducing my mom to Grayson while he was behind bars and wearing an orange jumpsuit wouldn't exactly be ideal.

It's not going to happen that way, I told myself silently before my spirits sagged too much.

When we reached the restaurant, I realized it was a good thing we'd reserved a table. Lumière was a popular establishment at any time of the year, but with the food and drink festival currently under way, the place was packed. Several people sat in the waiting area, hoping for a table to come free. Fortunately, all I had to do was give the hostess my name and she quickly led us toward the back of the restaurant, where a table set for four awaited us. We took our seats, and I tried not to stare at the empty chair next to Aunt Gilda. If not for the previous night's events, all four places would be taken, with Grayson seated next to me.

Despite the evening getting off to a dicey start with Grayson's conspicuous absence, we enjoyed our dinner. We chatted about Shady Creek, my brothers, and my sister-in-law's pregnancy. Jennifer was married to my older brother, Michael, and their first child was due in three months. I was excited to be a first-time auntie and my mom was thrilled about having a grandchild.

"What do you want to do tomorrow morning?" I asked my mom while we enjoyed slices of delicious chocolate cheesecake for dessert. "Zoe will be handling festival duty for me."

Sunday would be the final day of the events happening at the town hall, although A Taste of Shady Creek would run through the following week in a variety of other ways. Since I didn't have anything left to do for the event, I now had more time available to spend with my mom.

"We're planning on going to the winery in the afternoon," Aunt Gilda said. "Maybe you'd like to go to the cidery in the morning?" she suggested to my mom.

"That sounds like a nice idea," my mom agreed.

With that settled, we finished our desserts.

A short while later, I paid the bill, after insisting it was my treat over my mom's and Aunt Gilda's protestations. As we headed toward the front of the restaurant, I hoped we wouldn't run into anyone I knew well. By now, news of Grayson's status as a murder suspect might have been passed along the town grapevine and I didn't want anyone bringing up that subject in front of my mom.

Fortunately, none of my friends appeared to be dining at Lumière that evening. I smiled at a couple of familiar faces, but I didn't see anyone I knew well enough to stop and talk with.

"I lost my favorite cashmere sweater this afternoon," a woman said as I passed by the table where she sat with another woman. "Actually, it was *stolen*. Right off my back porch!"

"Really?" her companion said with surprise.

I paused next to a potted plant, pretending to check for something in my purse. The theft allegation had caught my attention.

"I took it off while I was out reading in a brief spell of sunshine," the first woman said. "I went inside to grab a drink, and when I came back out it was gone." She snapped her fingers. "Just like that! And then there was that murder last night! What's going on in this town?"

Her companion murmured sympathetically, and I realized I couldn't hover any longer without appearing suspicious. Besides, my mom and Aunt Gilda were already out on the sidewalk, waiting for me.

"Everything all right?" my mom asked when I joined them outside.

"Fine," I said with a smile.

As we walked together down the street, I wondered if the theft of the cashmere sweater was in any way related to the disappearance of Dominique's Gucci scarf. I didn't think about it much longer. I said good night to my mom and aunt outside the salon, and then I carried on home. As soon as I was on my own, I couldn't think about anyone or anything other than Grayson and his terrible predicament.

Chapter 12

Once I'd changed into my pajamas and had my teeth brushed, I climbed into bed with the file of information on Dominique. Wimsey hopped up beside me and curled up at my feet. He promptly drifted off to sleep, but I intended to stay awake until I'd reviewed the contents of the folder.

First, I took a closer look at Grayson's notebook. I skimmed through all the entries, but nothing in particular stuck out. Aside from attending Samantha's funeral, it appeared as though Dominique had simply gone about ordinary college-student business in the weeks following her former friend's death. She'd gone to campus, a bank, restaurants, a grocery store, a couple of bars, and residences where her friends lived. If any of her movements had struck Grayson as suspicious, he hadn't indicated that in the notebook.

Next, I sifted through the pile of photographs. Many of them were similar to the ones I'd looked at before. They showed Dominique going about her daily life, on campus and otherwise. Several of the photographs also showed other people in Dominique's company. None of them looked familiar to me, which wasn't surprising. I didn't know any of Dominique's friends or associates beyond Phoebe Ramone, and I'd never been to Fenworth, Maine, where Dominique was living at the time.

That wasn't where Grayson had lived. When he'd worked as a private investigator, he'd done so in Syracuse. After Samantha's death, he must have gone to Fenworth to investigate. Judging by the contents of his notebook, he stayed there for a few weeks, looking into the explosion and his prime suspect. He probably would have stayed longer if he hadn't ended up in trouble with the local police.

I set the photos aside and focused on the pile of papers I'd pulled from the folder. The first few pages gave me some details about Dominique's life eight years ago. One page listed basic information about her, and I figured it was probably something Grayson had typed up and printed. It included the fact that Dominique attended Summerville College and was a media studies student. That made sense, considering that she had worked at a magazine at the time of her death.

The typewritten notes also revealed that Dominique had been a classmate of Samantha's. They were both media studies students when Samantha was killed. That wasn't how they'd met, however. Apparently, they'd been friends since middle school.

I wondered what had happened to cause a rift between them, especially one so wide as to drive Dominique to arrange for Samantha's death. Grayson said he thought it had something to do with a guy, but his notes didn't enlighten me any further in that respect.

My mind strayed away from the task at hand, and I again wondered if Grayson had shelter for the night. I hated the thought of him huddling beneath a tree in the forest, especially since I could hear rain pelting the roof over my head. I hoped he hadn't hidden in the old cellar where I'd been trapped a year ago. The mere thought made me shudder. In this weather, the cellar would be flooded. Grayson would know that, so he must be elsewhere. That didn't bring me much comfort, since I had no idea where that could be.

I told myself to focus on the notes in front of me. As much as it pained me, I couldn't do anything to help Grayson stay safe and warm that night. All I could do was try to clear his name so he could come back home as soon as possible.

With renewed determination, I turned my attention back to the papers on my lap. One was a property document of some sort. From it, I gleaned that the houseboat that had exploded was owned by someone named Jonathan Northcroft. What the document didn't tell me was Samantha's connection to Jonathan or why she was staying at his houseboat. Maybe he was another classmate?

The next document was an investigative report on the explosion. The fire was started deliberately, with the help of an accelerant. Propane tanks on board had then exploded, causing the houseboat to ignite into a fireball. I was impressed that they'd been able to figure out that an accelerant was used. It sounded like there had been very little left of the houseboat once the fire was put out.

I flipped over to the next page. The incident had happened shortly after midnight on a blustery winter night. The explosion and fire had been so devastating that the investigators had recovered very little of Samantha's remains. It was believed that everything else had been swept away by the current. No one else had been on board that night.

By the time I finished going over all the rest of the documents, my eyelids had grown heavy. Although I now knew more about Dominique and the explosion that had killed Samantha, I didn't see how any of that would help me clear Grayson's name.

Frustrated by the lack of real clues, I shoved the folder and its contents into the drawer of my bedside table and switched off my lamp.

Physically, I was tired enough to fall asleep. My mind, on the other hand, was wide awake.

I grabbed my phone, knowing I wouldn't have any messages from Grayson but needing to check, anyway. As expected, he hadn't contacted me. I knew that was for the best, but I missed him terribly.

I'm worried about you, I wrote in a text. **I hope you're okay. Miss you.**

I sent the message, even though I knew he wouldn't see it. If anyone saw it in the next day or two it would probably be the police. The text would help me to keep up the pretense of not being in on Grayson's plan to go on the run. If I could even call it a pretense. I wasn't in on the plan, but I did know more than I'd admitted to.

After setting my phone aside, I huddled down beneath my blankets and tried to sleep. It didn't take long for me to give up. My mind refused to settle down. I was so worried about Grayson. Was he even in Shady Creek still? I didn't know, and not knowing threatened to drive me crazy.

I threw back my blankets and switched on the lamp. I retrieved a notebook and pen from the living room before returning to bed. While Wimsey slept soundly near my feet, I propped myself up against my pillows and tapped the pen against my chin as I thought. The only way to get Grayson back home safely with his name cleared was to find Dominique's killer. Going through the information Grayson had collected on her eight years ago hadn't helped me at all, so maybe it was time to focus on her more recent life.

Not everyone in Shady Creek had been pleased to see her here. As far as I knew, aside from Grayson, the person most upset by Dominique's presence in town was George Keeler. I wrote his name in my notebook. Next, I added his wife's name,

Miranda Keeler. Although she hadn't been quite as angry as George when she saw Dominique at the Village Bean, she definitely wasn't a fan. Maybe she'd wanted to seek revenge on her husband's behalf. Or maybe even on her own behalf. She could have been a partner in George's restaurant. It probably wouldn't be too hard for me to find out if that was the case.

I thought back over the past couple of days and quickly came up with another name to add to my suspect list: Phoebe Ramone. She and Dominique had argued in the restroom at the Inkwell. There was no love lost between them, that was for sure.

Then there was Alicia Jollimore. Her brother, Caleb, had said something about Dominique crushing Alicia's dreams. I thought I'd heard him say that Alicia should start writing again. Had she dreamed of becoming a writer? If so, how had Dominique spoiled that dream? I needed to find out more about Alicia's connection to Dominique.

That would have to wait until morning, at the earliest.

I set my notebook aside and switched off the lamp again.

Eventually, I fell asleep, but my dreams were filled with heartache and worry.

Chapter 13

I had to gulp down two cups of coffee before I could get out the door the next morning. The fitful few hours of sleep I'd had weren't enough to leave me feeling anywhere close to well rested. At least the sky had cleared overnight, giving the sun a chance to shine. If it had been pouring rain, I might never have made it out of bed.

Even having consumed those two cups of coffee, I grabbed my travel mug on the way out the door. My first destination of the day was the Village Bean. There was a short line at the coffee shop, but I soon had my travel mug filled with a mocha latte. My mouth watered with anticipation so I took a sip as I pushed out the door. I winced as the hot beverage burned my tongue. I needed to be more patient.

A woman strode past me on the sidewalk, a cell phone held to her ear. It was only when I heard her voice that I realized it was Phoebe Ramone.

"Can you believe she had the gall to accuse me of stealing her scarf?" Phoebe said into her phone.

I followed Phoebe, walking a few steps behind her, wanting

to hear what else she was going to say. She had to be talking about Dominique and my sleuth senses were definitely tingling.

"Like I'd want anything of hers," Phoebe continued. "I mean, so it was Gucci. So what? The colors totally didn't suit her."

Her attitude made me feel slightly ill. It struck me as callous to speak that way about someone who had recently been murdered. Nevertheless, I continued to follow Phoebe and eavesdrop.

"I'm going to send my resume to Jan Rodenburg again," she said to whoever was on the other end of the call. "That job should have been mine in the first place. I intend to make it mine now."

Phoebe stepped off the curb and strode across Hillview Road. I was about to follow when a car drove by, forcing me to pause. On the other side of the street, Phoebe tucked her phone into her purse, the call obviously finished.

I turned and retraced my steps as far as the bakery, thinking over what Phoebe had said. She didn't sound the least bit sad or shaken up about Dominique's death. She'd sounded hateful and bitter. She certainly wasn't waiting to move in on Dominique's now-vacant job at *Foodie Fare* magazine. At least, I figured it was safe to assume that from what I'd heard.

I rested my travel mug on the bakery's window ledge while I dug my phone out of my purse and quickly accessed the Internet. When I did a search with Jan Rodenburg's name and *Foodie Fare*, I confirmed my suspicion. Rodenburg was the editor of the magazine where Dominique had worked.

As I tucked my phone away, I decided that Phoebe was a strong suspect. I wasn't yet sure if she was more likely than George Keeler to be the killer, but they both had solid motives to want Dominique dead. Now I needed to figure out if they—or anyone else on my suspect list—had had the opportunity to commit the terrible crime.

I took a cautious sip of my latte. It was still hot, but at least I didn't scorch my tongue this time. I savored the delicious and invigorating combination of chocolate, sugar, and caffeine as I entered Sofie's Treat, the local bakery. There were three people ahead of me in line at the counter, but it wasn't long before I had a box of half a dozen muffins tucked under my arm. I carried it to Aunt Gilda's salon, where I said good morning to Betty, Gilda's coworker, before heading upstairs to my aunt's apartment. She and my mom were seated at the kitchen table, chatting over cups of coffee. I'd texted Aunt Gilda when I first got up, letting her know that I'd bring breakfast, so they had been awaiting my arrival.

Once we'd all eaten, we piled into Aunt Gilda's car for the ride out to the local cidery, located on the outskirts of town. I'd been there a couple of times before, and I used the local cider in the newest cocktail I'd added to the Inkwell's menu, Kiss of the Cider Woman. I loved the fact that I was able to feature a locally made ingredient.

"Have you heard from Grayson this morning?" my mom asked as Aunt Gilda drove us out of the center of town. "Is there any chance I could meet him today?"

"Um." I frantically tried to figure out what to say. "I haven't heard from him yet today." That was the truth, unfortunately. "I think he's going to be tied up at least a while longer."

"Hmm," was all my mom said in response.

It wasn't a good sound. I shifted in my seat and then stared out the window.

An awkward silence descended upon us. Thankfully, Aunt Gilda jumped in to dispel it by chattering about the sights we were passing.

When we arrived at the cidery, I practically leapt out of the car. I gulped in a few breaths of crisp autumn air. Hopefully, my mom was done with questions about Grayson for the day. I didn't think I could count on that, though.

A tour was about to start, so we joined a group of half a dozen tourists and followed the guide into one of the cidery's smaller buildings. Although I'd taken the tour before, I still found it interesting, and I was glad to see that my mom seemed to be enjoying herself. I was also glad that she seemed to have forgotten about my missing boyfriend, at least for the time being.

After the tour, we strolled around the grounds, admiring the beautiful old barn that had been transformed into the cidery's main building. The maple trees in the background still held on to a few colorful leaves, but their branches were mostly bare. The site had probably been even more beautiful earlier in the month when the fall foliage was at its most impressive.

Several tourists were also admiring the place and snapping photos. I did a double take as I realized one of the people I'd assumed was a tourist was actually the travel writer Nick Perry. He took a photo of the renovated barn with his phone and then set off in the direction of the apple orchard.

I snapped a photo of my mom and Aunt Gilda out on the grounds and then we headed indoors. After my mom had sampled some cider, we wandered around the store. In addition to apple and pear cider, the store offered T-shirts and hats featuring the cidery's logo, and some snacks and other merchandise. My mom and Aunt Gilda browsed the shelves, apparently interested in what was on offer, but my attention was focused solely on the person manning the cash register.

I'd recognized the young woman with her strawberry blond hair as soon as I'd walked into the shop. She was Caleb Jollimore's sister, Alicia, and one of the people on my suspect list, thanks to the conversation I'd overheard at the Inkwell. I wanted to know how Dominique had destroyed Alicia's dreams, and there was no way I could pass up the opportunity to do a little sleuthing.

In order to give myself an excuse to talk to Alicia, I grabbed a packet of apple cider caramels to purchase. I waited while two women paid for several cases of cider, and then I approached the counter.

"Is that all for you today?" Alicia asked, as she scanned the package of caramels.

"Yes, thanks," I said before casually adding, "I think I've seen you at my pub, the Inkwell."

Alicia looked at me properly for the first time. "I go there every so often. I was there with my brother the other night."

I tapped my credit card to pay for my purchase. "Right. It's hard for me to forget that night. That poor woman who died was at the pub."

"Oh?" Alicia acted as though she hadn't known and didn't care.

I tried another angle. "You've lived in Shady Creek a long time, right?"

"My whole life."

"Do you remember the woman who died? Dominique? I'm told she visited Shady Creek a few years ago."

"No," Alicia said, her voice clipped. She tore my receipt off the register and handed it to me. "Have a nice day."

I didn't budge. "I'm sorry," I said, not ready to give up. "I thought someone mentioned to me that you knew her. I can't remember how, exactly. Maybe something to do with writing?"

To my astonishment, Alicia burst into tears. She turned and fled, disappearing into the back of the store, pausing only briefly to say something to one of her colleagues on her way by.

"Is that young lady all right?" my mom asked as she set two jars of apple cider jelly on the counter. "She looked upset and sure took off in a hurry."

"Maybe she has bad allergies," I said, not about to confess that I'd triggered Alicia's tears.

My mother would have been horrified. I was slightly so myself. I hadn't meant to upset Alicia, but I did want to get to the truth about her feelings toward Dominique. If she turned out to be the killer, I'd no longer feel so bad for making her cry.

I stuffed my receipt into my purse and moved out of the way. Another employee came rushing forward to take over the cash register. I lingered by the door as my mom paid for the jars of jelly, but Alicia didn't reappear.

When we left the cidery a few minutes later, I had a snack in hand to assuage any physical hunger pangs that might strike, but my appetite for clues remained unsatisfied.

Chapter 14

My mom and Aunt Gilda dropped me off at the Inkwell. They were going to take a drive through the surrounding countryside before visiting the Five Owls Winery, where they planned to have a late lunch. Aunt Gilda was going to cook dinner for my mom so they could have a quiet evening in. I'd spend more time with my mom the next day, and throughout the coming week. I was looking forward to it, but I wasn't entirely sure how I'd balance sleuthing with visiting with my mom. I'd have to play it by ear.

I had a busy afternoon at the Inkwell, with many locals and tourists stopping by for a drink and a bite to eat. I stamped nearly a dozen cards for the bingo game that was part of the food and drink festival. The game was designed to get more people eating at Shady Creek's various restaurants. Anyone interested in taking part could stop by the town's visitors' center and pick up a card. The cards featured twenty-five squares, with the name of a local eatery in each one, and all participating restaurants had a special stamp to use for the cards.

Customers who presented their card while paying their bill

received a stamp on the square for that particular establishment. Whenever a participant had a full line of stamps, they could take their card back to the visitors' center, where they would receive a coupon or gift certificate to use at a local business. I was pleased to see how many tourists and locals were taking part in the bingo game, and it seemed to be having the desired effect, as many of the cards I stamped had already received several stamps from other restaurants.

In the middle of the afternoon, Zoe brought the empty coolers back from the town hall and reported another good day. All the drink samples had been given away and the pile of menus and fridge magnets had dwindled down to just a few. I set what remained out on the bar for customers to take and soon every last one was gone.

In the early evening, my friend and local reporter Joey Fontana showed up with an appetite. He ordered a pint of beer, a burger with fries, and a slice of Once Upon a Lime, a delicious key lime cheesecake that I'd recently added to the menu after Booker came up with the idea. I'd taste-tested several slices before offering it to my customers. Far more than I really needed to, but better safe than sorry, I figured.

Joey sat at the bar, chatting with a man who worked at the local hardware store, but when I brought him his cheesecake after he'd polished off his burger, he was alone, the other man having left minutes before.

"I was hoping we'd get a chance to chat," Joey said as I set the plate of cheesecake on the bar in front of him.

"Me too."

Joey knew that I couldn't keep my nose out of a real-life mystery, and since he was a reporter and co-owner of the *Shady Creek Tribune*, he was always chasing down leads and clues as well. We'd traded information in the past, but I always had to offer Joey something to get something in return. I didn't share everything I knew with him, though. Sometimes there were things that I didn't want showing up in the next edition of the local newspaper.

"I'm sorry Grayson's in hot water," Joey said as he sank his fork into his cake.

"I hope you know he's innocent."

Joey took a moment to enjoy the first bite of his cake before speaking again. "I don't believe he did it for a second, but it's not looking good for him."

Even though I knew that was the case, I didn't like hearing it stated out loud.

"His name will be cleared," I said with determination.

Joey grinned. "And you'll be the one to do it, right?"

"If need be. And it does seem like it needs to be."

"Any idea where he's hiding out?" Joey asked.

I looked at him like he'd lost his mind. "You seriously think I'd say if I did?"

He laughed. "No, but I had to try." He dug his fork into the cake again. "Do the police think you know where he is?"

"I'm not sure, but I told Detective Marquez the truth when I said I don't know." My spirits threatened to do a nosedive when I spoke those words. I didn't think I could get used to not knowing.

"I'd say either they think you know or they think Grayson might try to get in touch with you," Joey said.

"That's probably safe to assume."

"It's not just an assumption. Not exactly."

Apprehension prickled down the back of my neck. "What do you mean?"

"When I was on my way here, I noticed an unmarked car parked in Grayson's driveway, facing Creekside Road. It's far enough up the driveway that it doesn't stick out like a sore thumb, but whoever's sitting in the front seat still has a view of this place."

The prickling at the back of my neck intensified.

I was under surveillance?

I probably should have expected that, but the thought sent my stomach into a twist.

"They're most likely wasting their time," I said, trying to sound unfazed by the news. "Grayson has purposely kept me in the dark so I can't get in trouble with the police."

"That doesn't surprise me," Joey said. "Still, I thought you should know."

"I appreciate it." I really did. I knew he too was trying to keep me out of trouble.

Even though I was glad to know that I was being watched, that knowledge made me nervous. I realized I'd been holding out hope that Grayson would make an appearance at some point. Now I doubted that would happen. He probably knew the police were watching the gristmill. It would be too risky for him to show up here, even in the dead of night.

Never mind, I told myself as my spirits started to sink again. I just needed to get Grayson's name cleared quickly so we could be together again. Not quite thirty-six hours had passed since I'd last seen him, but I already missed him like we'd been apart far longer. It didn't help that I had no clue where he was or whether he was okay.

"Have you got anything to share?" Joey asked after I'd mixed a few cocktails and delivered them to waiting customers.

I considered what I wanted to tell him.

"There's another food writer in town," I said. "Phoebe Ramone."

Joey nodded, unimpressed with that bit of intel. "I've already met her."

"Did you know that she and Dominique didn't get along?"

Now he appeared more interested. "How do you know that?"

I told him about the spat the women had in the Inkwell's

restroom. "And Phoebe sure doesn't seem cut up about Dominique's death," I added.

"Huh." Joey didn't say anything more, but I knew he was tucking that information away in his mind.

I moved out from behind the bar to clear and clean a couple of tables before returning to Joey.

"Dominique was staying at the motel off the highway," I said.

"I know. The cops searched her room, but someone beat them to it and tossed the place. The killer, most likely."

I nodded. "I heard that from the manager."

"Her car was found here in town," Joey continued. "Not surprising, seeing as she was at the brewery."

"But it wasn't parked in the brewery's lot," I said.

"I heard it was found on Maple Street."

That was within easy walking distance of the brewery. Had Dominique parked there early in the day and walked to multiple places before heading to the brewery? Or had she left her car on Maple Street so she could approach the brewery surreptitiously?

"One of the car's windows was smashed," Joey added.

That was interesting.

"Was anything taken?" I asked.

"Impossible to know without Dominique to ask."

Of course. I should have thought of that.

"Do you have any suspects aside from Phoebe?" Joey asked.

"I'm guessing you know about George Keeler's history with Dominique."

"It's hard not to. And I hear he wasn't too happy to see Dominique back in town."

"You heard right," I said. "I was at the Village Bean when he ran into her. It wasn't a pleasant scene."

"So the guy's got a motive," Joey said. "What about opportunity?"

"That's what I intend to find out."

"Let me know when you do?"

"Maybe," I said with a smile.

He grinned at that and drained the last of his beer. "I need to get going."

"Chasing down leads?" I guessed.

"Not tonight. I've volunteered to help out with the haunted corn maze. There's a meeting over at the community center in fifteen minutes. I'm walking so I'd better get a move on." He pulled some bills out of his wallet and left them on the bar for me. "Let's compare notes again."

I hoped by the next time I saw him I'd have more information worth sharing, and I hoped he would too. It would be even better if there was no longer any need to compare notes.

The good-sized crowd in the pub kept me busy for the next couple of hours. Business had slowed slightly when Jason claimed the bar stool that Joey had vacated earlier.

I delivered pints of beer to a middle-aged couple at the other end of the bar and then headed over Jason's way.

"Any news?" I asked him in a quiet voice.

"Not really," he said, to my disappointment. "I was going to ask you the same question."

"I've learned a few things," I said.

"We shouldn't talk about it here."

I agreed. I didn't want to risk anyone overhearing us discussing Grayson.

"Upstairs?" I suggested. When Jason nodded, I turned to Damien, who was mixing cocktails at the other end of the bar. "I'll be up in my apartment for a few minutes. Text or holler if you need me."

"Things should be fine down here," Damien assured me.

I left the main part of the pub for the back hallway, with Jason following me. We didn't speak again until we were up in my apartment with the door shut.

"Have you heard from Grayson?" I blurted out as soon as I thought it was safe to do so. "Is he okay?"

His response triggered another pang of disappointment. "I haven't heard from him. That's probably a good thing, considering that the cops are keeping an eye on me. You too."

"Joey gave me a heads-up on that." I sat on the arm of my couch, suddenly feeling Grayson's absence more keenly than ever. "You really don't know where he's staying?"

"All I know is that he had a place in mind, but he didn't tell me anything more than that. Maybe I could guess where he is, but it's probably better not to. You can't be going looking for him, anyway. You could end up leading the cops right to him."

"I know. I just wish . . ." I didn't bother finishing my sentence.

What was the point in wishing things were different? The situation was what it was. The only way to change it was to make progress with my investigation.

A thought struck me. "What if we clear Grayson's name and he doesn't realize it because he's gone so deep into hiding? How will he know when to come back?"

"He'll know," Jason assured me. "He won't go far. He's as determined to find the real killer as you are. He can't do that if he's on a beach in the Cayman Islands."

"True."

Wimsey was lying on the back of the couch. I stroked a hand over his fur, and he closed his eyes and purred. The sound soothed me.

"The police found the wrench," Jason said.

"I figured they must have. Have you heard anything else? Anything that could help us find the real killer?"

"All I know is that Grayson thought it would be good to dig into Dominique's more recent life."

"But he didn't have a chance to do that before he took off?" I asked.

"After you left, he packed a few things and then he was gone."

"Okay," I said, thinking. "I can look her up online."

"I did that earlier, but I didn't come up with much. She angered a few restaurant owners over the years with harsh reviews, but it seems like she'd mellowed since then. Her recent reviews haven't been as scathing as some of her early ones."

"So if one of those restaurant owners wanted to kill her, they probably would have done it a while ago," I said. "Unless, like George Keeler, they came face-to-face with her and that brought up all their old anger."

"As far as I can tell, George is the only one with that sort of grudge here in Shady Creek," Jason said. "I looked into his background. He's had a couple of speeding and parking tickets, but otherwise he hasn't had any trouble with the police."

"That doesn't mean he's not the killer."

"No, it doesn't," Jason agreed. "I talked to a couple of people about George. Apparently, he hangs out at the pool hall now and then. A couple of times he almost came to blows with another guy who frequents the place, but the police never had to be called in."

"So being violent wouldn't be out of character for him."

"Not by much."

"I'm going to find out more about him tomorrow." I was determined to make that the truth. "Once I know if he had the opportunity to kill Dominique, I'll know if he should stay on my suspect list or not."

"Don't do anything dangerous," Jason cautioned. "And don't give George a chance to turn his temper on you. If you need backup, text me. Day or night, okay?"

I nodded, suddenly fighting tears. "Thank you."

"We'll get Grayson's life back, Sadie."

I could only nod again.

He left, but I stayed up in my apartment for a few minutes

longer, stroking Wimsey's fur as I went back over everything Jason had said.

If Grayson wanted to stay involved in finding the real killer and wanted to dig into Dominique's more recent life, he would need access to a phone or computer. He couldn't turn on his own phone without risking the police tracking him, and he also couldn't come here or return home or to the brewery.

Where else could he go?

I could think of one possibility.

Now I just had to wait.

Chapter 15

The next hour seemed to pass at a crawl. I kept looking at the Guinness wall clock and ended up double-checking the time on my phone to make sure the clock was working properly, which it was. I tried to distract myself by chatting with the pub's patrons, and it worked—sort of—but I was still overly aware of the minutes slowly passing.

Finally, it was time to say good night to the last of the pub's customers. Teagan left on their heels, and I locked the door behind her before cleaning tables with help from Damien. Eventually, Damien left too and I was on my own. I figured I should probably wait a while longer, until the majority of the town would be fast asleep, before going ahead with my plan.

I checked my e-mail and my social media accounts, but by then I was practically twitching with impatience. I gave up on waiting any longer and hurried upstairs to my apartment, where I dug around in my closet for some appropriate clothing. I didn't wear much black, but I managed to find black leggings and a matching hoodie that I hadn't worn for at least a year.

Wimsey observed me from his comfy spot on my bed as I changed my clothes. I thought he watched with a critical gaze.

"I'm not getting up to any mischief," I assured him.

He didn't appear convinced.

"In fact, I'm probably wasting my time," I continued. "But if there's even the slightest chance that I could see Grayson . . ."

Wimsey shut his eyes, no longer interested in my explanations, if he ever was.

I zipped up my hoodie and gave him a quick kiss on the head.

"I'll be back before you know it."

I made sure all the blinds and curtains in my apartment were closed, and I turned off all the lights save for a lamp in my bedroom and another in the living room. All that was left to do was to figure out how to get away from the gristmill without the police noticing. Considering the size of the Shady Creek Police Department, I figured there was a good chance that there was only one car stationed outside to keep an eye on me. Going by the information Joey had provided, the officer watching the gristmill was stationed to the east and had a view of three sides of the building. That meant they couldn't see the pub's front door, which was on the west side of the mill. That probably didn't worry the police much, since the only obvious route to take from the door was toward Creekside Road and into the watching officer's line of sight. That meant I needed to take a less obvious route away from the gristmill.

Even before I was out the door, my heart was pounding away in my chest. I told myself I wasn't doing anything wrong. Not really. I had every right to come and go from the gristmill. The only problem was that I didn't want to lead the police to Grayson.

I slipped quietly out the pub's front door and locked it behind me. I stayed standing close to the door for almost a full minute, watching and listening. Aside from the hoot of an owl coming from the nearby forest, I didn't hear a sound. Everything was still and quiet.

It was time to take a chance. I eased away from the door and walked briskly across the lawn and past the Inkwell's parking lot, making sure to stay in line with the pub's western door the entire time. Once beyond the Inkwell's property line, I slipped into deeper darkness cast by the shadow of a maple tree and glanced back the way I'd come. Still nothing moved. I didn't think anyone would be able to spot me now, especially not from the distance of the brewery's driveway.

Nevertheless, I stuck to the deepest of shadows as I crept around the old Queen Anne house that sat next to the Inkwell. I considered it fortunate that the house was currently vacant. The owner was locked up in jail, and the place had been cleared out and put up for sale at her behest. With its charming character and its prime spot overlooking the village green, the house would likely get snatched up before long, but at this point, only a week or so after it had gone on the market, it still stood empty and unsold.

I crept through the backyard of the old house, doing my best to move quietly despite the fact that no one was home to see or hear me. I jumped with fright and nearly let out a yelp when something fluttered past my face. It was a bat, I realized. I pressed a hand over my heart and steadied my breathing.

I had a small flashlight on a key chain in my hoodie pocket, and a flashlight app on my phone, but I didn't dare to use either in case the light attracted attention from anyone in the neighboring homes. Clouds occasionally drifted across the half-moon above me, but most of the time I had enough light to keep from tripping over anything. I moved more carefully when I passed the vacant house and started crossing the yard of the next house, which I knew was occupied. No lights were on inside, and I hoped that meant all the occupants were fast asleep.

After what felt like an hour, but was probably more like ten minutes, I made it through the yard behind the Creekside Inn, owned by Cordelia's grandmother. That Queen Anne was the last house on this stretch of Creekside Road. Next to it were some trees and bushes before a T-intersection with Woodland Road, which led to a covered bridge over the creek. I intended to head in the opposite direction of the bridge.

I made my way past the trees, getting scratched by a couple of branches in the process. Then I checked to make sure Creekside Road was empty before dashing across. I followed Mulberry Street southward until I hit Briar Road, which I followed eastward. It was a roundabout way to get to my destination, but I now felt confident that I'd made it away from the gristmill without drawing any attention from the police or anyone else.

I picked up my pace and jogged down the street. Soon I arrived at Shady Creek's public library. I stood in the deep shadows cast by another maple tree while I took a moment to observe the front of the brick building. As I'd expected, all the windows were dark and there was no activity in the area. It was well after midnight now. The library would have closed hours ago, along with all the other businesses in the neighborhood.

Still, I wanted to be cautious. I skirted around to the back of the building, where I hesitated, not exactly keen to enter the yawning darkness of the alley. Maybe it wouldn't hurt to use my flashlight now. I flicked it on and gathered up my courage. Slowly, I made my way along the back of the building. The metal door that provided access to the alleyway was shut tight. I hadn't expected otherwise. I tried to open it, but it was locked. Again, not unexpected.

I retraced my steps until I was near the mouth of the alley. Leaning back against the brick exterior, I settled in to wait.

Maybe it was ridiculous of me to be out here, but the public library had a whole bank of computers with Internet access. If Grayson wanted to do some online research, this would be the perfect place to do so in secret. The doors were locked, but Grayson knew how to pick locks. I'd seen him do so in the past. Unfortunately, despite my repeated requests, he'd never passed on the skill to me.

Of course, there was a chance that Grayson had already used the library's computers the night before, when I'd yet to even consider the possibility. There was an even better chance that he had no intention of showing up here at all. But I knew Grayson. He wouldn't be able to resist working on the case any more than I could, not when he was so personally invested in it. He couldn't exactly go around questioning the townsfolk like I could, so to me this seemed like a good route for him to take.

Unfortunately, I hadn't thought things through before leaving home. I'd dressed in dark clothing, but it wasn't a particularly warm outfit. I was lucky that it wasn't raining, but the night air had a definite chill to it. I hadn't been waiting in the alley very long, and already I was starting to shiver. I pulled my hands up inside the sleeves of my hoodie and wrapped my arms around myself, but that didn't help much. Minutes passed, and my shivering intensified. There was no way I could hang out here all night on the off chance that Grayson might appear.

Reluctance to give up kept me there a few minutes longer, but then I had to give in. Maybe it was for the best. I needed to get some sleep, and standing in a dark alley by myself was giving me the creeps, not to mention the fact that the smell from the nearby dumpster wasn't exactly pleasant.

I cast a glance in the direction of the library's back door and then flicked on my tiny flashlight, the narrow beam of light leading me out of the alley. I wasn't looking forward to taking a circuitous route home, but I knew that would be the wise decision. If the police saw me arriving home in the middle of the night, they'd be even more suspicious of me. The fact that they hadn't seen me leave might make them think they needed to watch me more carefully, something I wanted to avoid.

I reached the end of the alleyway and switched off my flashlight.

At the exact moment when the light extinguished, a scream tore through the night.

Chapter 16

I ran in the direction of the scream as my heart raced with fear.

Had the killer struck again?

I came to an abrupt halt when I had a view of the village green. Five teenagers were running across the grass, heading in my general direction. One of the girls shrieked as they ran. She sounded like the same person who'd screamed. But the teens didn't seem terrified. In fact, a couple of them were laughing.

Not another murder then.

I let out a sigh of mixed relief and annoyance. The scream had nearly sent me into a panic. I'd thought someone had found another dead body.

Headlights lit up Sycamore Street. I ducked back around the corner of the nearest building so the driver of the approaching car wouldn't see me. The teenagers ran across Hillview Road and continued south, never noticing me. I hid in the deeper darkness of a recessed doorway as the car passed, heading in the same direction as the teenagers. I couldn't tell if it was an unmarked police vehicle or a civilian's car. To be safe, I stayed in my hiding place until I could no longer hear it.

I figured I might as well continue on home, but something made me glance back toward the library. A shadowy figure moved swiftly out of the alley before heading east, away from where I stood.

My heart gave a leap in my chest. Even from this distance, I was sure I recognized the silhouette.

I bit down on my lip, stopping myself just before shouting Grayson's name.

The shadowy figure disappeared around a corner. I broke into a run, pursuing him. By the time I reached the corner where I'd last seen him, he was long gone. I checked in every direction, but there was no sign of him or anyone else.

I must have been right about him using the library computers, but that didn't bring me much satisfaction now that I'd missed meeting up with him. He probably wouldn't be back again another night unless he was desperate. Returning to the same place on multiple nights would increase his chances of getting caught.

I stood there on the corner, wallowing in my disappointment until I realized once again how cold I was. There was no point in letting myself freeze. I needed to get home.

"Sadie?"

The unexpected voice gave me a start. Once again, my heart was off at a run. It slowed seconds later when I recognized Booker across the street. He crossed the empty road toward me.

"I thought it was you," he said as he stepped up onto the sidewalk. "What are you doing out here at this hour?"

"I was about to ask you the same thing," I said, not wanting to answer his question.

Booker ran a hand over his braids. I got the impression he wasn't keen to answer either.

"I needed to get out and do some thinking," he said finally.

"Is anything wrong?" I asked.

This was the second time in a matter of days that I'd suspected something was weighing heavily upon him.

"Everything's fine," he said, waving off my concern. "But it's really late, and there's a killer on the loose. I'll walk you home."

We fell into step together, heading back toward the village green. I wondered how I could explain to him that I didn't particularly want to be seen arriving home at the gristmill. When the brewery's driveway came into view, I peered in that direction. It was hard to be completely sure, but I didn't think there was a car parked there. Maybe the screaming teenager had drawn the police officer's attention. Or maybe the cops had given up watching me and my earlier sneaking hadn't been necessary.

A sudden wave of weariness crashed over me. Surveillance or not, I was going to walk directly home like a normal person.

"How's your mom liking Shady Creek?" Booker asked as we crossed the village green.

"So far so good." At least, I hoped that was the case.

"What's not to love about this place, right?"

I smiled. "Are you hoping to stick around permanently then?"

Booker had grown up in Boston and had moved to Shady Creek shortly after I did.

"That's the plan," he said with a brief smile.

Again, I got the distinct impression that there was something he wasn't saying.

As curious as I was, I told myself to mind my own business. If he wanted to talk about whatever it was, he would choose the time to do so.

When we reached the gristmill, I thanked Booker for walking with me and he waited until I was safely inside. Once upstairs, I quickly exchanged my black outfit for my fluffy robe. Wimsey cracked open one eye, but then promptly went back to sleep. I took a hot shower, letting the water run over me until I was finally warm. Then I dressed in cozy pajamas and crawled beneath the blankets on my bed. Despite my weariness, however, I wasn't quite ready to give in to sleep.

Since I couldn't confer with Grayson about what he'd found out about Dominique's more recent life, I'd have to do my own digging in that regard. I propped myself up with pillows and settled my laptop on my legs. Several Internet searches later, I shut the computer off with a growing sense of frustration. I'd learned about Dominique's employment history and the fact that she enjoyed sailing and kayaking. I'd seen plenty of pictures she'd posted online of various vacations over the years, and she'd also made a couple of recent trips to Fenworth, Maine, where she'd gone to college. None of that gave me any insight into why someone would have wanted to kill her.

I shut off the lamp on my bedside table and scooted down farther into bed, but my mind wasn't quite ready to slumber. For a brief moment, I wondered if I should try looking at the murder from another angle. Perhaps Dominique had accidentally interrupted the killer while he was doing something surreptitious and the killer then struck out on the spur of the moment.

No, I decided. The mysterious figure in the dark rain jacket had followed Dominique, I felt certain of that. So it was a planned murder. Or at least a planned encounter that went awry.

I sighed and turned over, trying to get comfortable. I really needed to make some progress with looking into my suspects.

Tomorrow, I decided with determination. Tomorrow I would find some answers to all the questions in my head.

Since the next day was Monday, the one day of the week when the Inkwell was closed, I didn't have to worry about the pub. I had plans to meet my mom, Aunt Gilda, and my best friend, Shontelle, for lunch, but until then, I was free to go in search of clues.

The problem was that I had no idea where George Keeler

lived. I could have asked Aunt Gilda, since she'd lived in Shady Creek a lot longer than I had, but I didn't want her to know that I was looking into the murder. She probably could have guessed that I was, given my history, but I didn't want to make it plain to her. She would only worry about me putting myself in danger.

Fortunately, I had other potential sources I could go to for that information, and one happened to be located at my first destination of the day.

When I reached the Village Bean, several locals and tourists had already beat me to it. Half a dozen tables were occupied and four people stood in line ahead of me. I stifled a yawn as I waited for my turn to order. After my nighttime excursion and my online sleuthing, I'd managed to grab a few hours of sleep, but not nearly as many as I would have liked.

After I'd paid for my pumpkin spice latte and my chocolate chip muffin, I leaned against the counter so I could have a private chat with Nettie Jo. Luckily, no one was in line behind me.

"Do you happen to know where George and Miranda Keeler live?" I asked in a low voice.

Nettie Jo popped the lid onto the top of my travel mug and slid it across the counter to me. "Sure. They're over on Meadowsweet Road. Three or four houses in on your left if you're heading west. The house has a blue door and rosebushes growing out front, courtesy of Miranda."

"Great. Thank you," I said, picking up my mug and the paper bag that held my muffin.

Two new customers came in the door of the coffee shop. Nettie Jo called out a greeting to them, but then turned back to me, appraising me with knowing eyes.

"Are you thinking George killed Dominique?" she asked quietly.

"I think it's a possibility."

Nettie Jo glanced at her waiting customers. "Stay safe, Sadie," she said before moving along the counter.

"Always," I said with a parting smile.

I tore a piece off my muffin and savored it as I followed Sycamore Street toward Meadowsweet Road. It didn't take long to get there. I tucked the remains of my muffin back in the bag and searched for the Keeler house as I walked slowly along the quiet residential street. The blue door and rosebushes were easy to spot, even though the flowers weren't in bloom at this time of year.

Even without those characteristics to watch out for, I would have been able to identify the Keeler house, because George was out in the front yard, raking leaves. A tall maple tree stood near the property line, its branches all but bare. From the looks of things, George hadn't kept on top of the falling leaves and now had quite a job ahead of him.

"Good morning," I called out cheerily as I stopped on the sidewalk in front of his house.

George squinted at me through the morning sunshine and grunted out what I thought was meant to be a greeting.

"You're George Keeler, right?" Uninvited, I joined him on the grass.

"Who are you?" He sounded like a grumpy bear.

I suspected that was the norm for him.

"Sadie Coleman," I replied, still keeping my tone cheerful. "I own the Inkwell."

He remained as unfriendly as ever. "What are you selling?"

"Nothing. I just remembered seeing you at the Village Bean a few days ago when that food writer was there."

George's expression, not exactly bright to begin with, darkened considerably. "So what?"

He really wasn't going to make this easy. Maybe I needed to be more direct.

"After what happened that day, I wondered if the police sus-pected you of killing her."

George's already ruddy face flushed. "I'm not sad she's dead, but I didn't kill her. It was that guy from the brewery."

"I know for a fact it wasn't him," I said, struggling to keep my voice neutral.

"Well, it wasn't me either." He got back to raking, acting like I was no longer there.

It wasn't going to be that easy to get rid of me.

"Do you have an alibi?"

He turned on me, his hands gripping the handle of the rake so tightly that his knuckles had gone white. "What?!" He prac-tically bellowed the word.

The gate at the side of the house opened and Miranda Keeler came out into the front yard, wearing dusty jeans, a long-sleeved T-shirt, and gardening gloves. "Hello," she said as she walked our way, studying me.

I could tell she was trying to place me.

"Hi, Mrs. Keeler. I'm Sadie Coleman. I own the Ink-well pub."

"Right," she said slowly.

Now I was pretty sure she was trying to figure out why I was standing on her front lawn.

"I was concerned that the police might suspect your hus-band of having something to do with the food writer's death. You know, after that scene at the Village Bean."

Miranda's eyes widened, but she quickly got her expression under control. "I thought the police already knew who did it."

"They haven't arrested anyone yet," I said truthfully. "Any-way, if Mr. Keeler has an alibi, he won't have anything to worry about." I addressed her husband again. "Where were you the night Dominique was killed?"

George slid his gaze toward his wife before aggressively rak-ing a patch of grass already free of leaves. "That's none of your business." He glared at the ground as he worked, his face still flushed and his nostrils flared. "Can't you see I'm busy?"

"George!" Miranda sounded shocked at his rudeness.

"That's all right," I said with a smile. "I have a tendency to ask too many questions. I'll leave you to your work."

I offered up one last smile, seen only by Miranda, and continued on my way along the street with a hint of satisfaction.

George Keeler might not have given me much in the way of information, but judging by his reaction to my last question, I thought it was safe to bet that he didn't have an alibi for the time of the murder.

Chapter 17

After speaking with George, I ran a couple of errands and then went home, where I remained until it was almost time to head over to Aunt Gilda's. Instead of going straight to the salon, I planned to first stop in at the Treasure Chest, the gift shop owned and operated by my best friend, Shontelle Williams. Shontelle was joining us for lunch so she could meet my mom, but I wanted to have a few moments to chat with her privately first. I hadn't yet had a chance to talk to Shontelle since Dominique's death. We'd exchanged a few text messages, but because I didn't want to leave a record of anything that might not look good for me from the perspective of the police, any reference I'd made to recent events had been vague at best.

Like the Inkwell, the Treasure Chest was closed on Mondays, at least outside of peak tourist season, but Shontelle lived in the apartment above the shop with her nine-year-old daughter, Kiandra, who was currently at school. Before leaving the gristmill, I texted Shontelle to let her know I was on my way over. I received a response as I was crossing the footbridge. She said her morning spin class at the community center had run late and she'd just stepped out of the shower. Pausing on the bridge, I tapped out another message, asking her to let me know when she was ready to meet.

I could have turned around and hung out at home for a while longer, but I decided to keep going. I strolled across the green at a leisurely pace, enjoying the fresh air. Although gray clouds scudded across the sky, the sun shone through the gaps now and again. The chilly breeze made me wish I'd worn gloves, but the scents of wood smoke and crisp air seemed so appropriate for the season.

Before the Autumn Festival, which had ended near the beginning of the month, someone had decorated the white bandstand with pumpkins and garlands of fake colorful leaves. I'd noticed the week before that a couple of the pumpkins had gone missing, and one was left smashed in the grass, but the mess had since been cleaned up and fresh pumpkins adorned the structure.

With Halloween approaching, I hoped to carve a few pumpkins and add them to the decorations I already had up at the Inkwell. That reminded me that I needed to pick up a few new battery-operated tea lights. I still had some time to kill, so I altered my path slightly so it would take me to the general store, located a few doors down from Shontelle's gift shop.

It didn't take me long to find what I was looking for in the general store. I picked out half a dozen tea lights and then made my way toward the counter.

"Hey, Sadie," a woman said from behind me.

I turned around to see Simone Rubio, owner of Primrose Books, in an aisle I'd just passed.

"Hi, Simone," I said. "How are you doing?"

"Great, thanks. But what about you? How are you holding up?" She lowered her voice. "I heard about the police wanting to arrest Grayson."

She needn't have bothered speaking so quietly. The whole town had probably heard the news by now.

"I'm looking forward to the day when his name is cleared," I said.

"As our resident Nancy Drew, I'm sure you'll make that happen."

I smiled, appreciating her confidence in me. "I've been meaning to drop by your store. The colder the weather gets, the more I want to curl up in front of the woodstove with a good mystery."

"I've definitely got lots of those in stock." She brightened. "And when you come by, you can meet Eddie."

"Who's Eddie?" I asked, wondering if she'd hired someone new to help out at the bookstore.

"My new cat." She pulled out her phone. "I adopted him from the Happy Paws Cat Shelter." She turned her phone so I could see a picture of an orange tabby with white socks.

"He's adorable," I gushed. "I'm so glad he's got a good home. Does he hang out at the store with you?"

"Yes, he's the official mascot now. He's escaped out the door a couple of times, but he came back on his own, fortunately. Mostly he likes to lie on top of the shelves or in the front window."

"I can't wait to meet him." My own phone buzzed, letting me know that Shontelle had texted me. "I've got to run, but I'll be by the shop soon."

We said our good-byes, and I paid for my tea lights before heading out onto the sidewalk. I tucked my purchase into my purse, and as I drew close to the Treasure Chest, Shontelle emerged from the shop.

She waved at me and then locked the door before dropping the keys into her purse.

She pulled me into a hug as soon as I reached her. "I've been worried about you."

"I'm sorry I haven't told you much," I said, returning the hug. "I'm wary about saying too much in my text messages in case the police ever look at them."

Shontelle stepped back and held me at arm's length, studying me carefully. "Are you in trouble?"

"I don't think so. The police might suspect that I know more than I'm telling, but what they really want to know is where Grayson is, and I truly don't know the answer to that."

Shontelle gave me another quick hug before releasing me. "I'm so sorry, hon. This must be so hard for you and for Grayson. I can't believe he's the prime suspect. I promise you, I don't doubt for a moment that he's innocent."

"Thank you," I said. "I appreciate that."

We began walking slowly in the direction of Aunt Gilda's salon and apartment.

"Does Eldon believe Grayson is guilty?" I asked.

Shontelle had been dating the officer for several months.

"I don't think he *wants* to believe it, but he also said his opinion doesn't really matter. As a police officer, he has to follow the evidence."

"Detective Marquez said pretty much the same thing. Unfortunately, the evidence has piled up against Grayson. Did you hear about the wrench?"

She hadn't, so I quickly told her about that disturbing turn of events, with the proviso that the information wasn't to be shared with anyone. I didn't know which details of the murder the police wanted to keep quiet, but I hadn't heard that tidbit being spread around town, so I figured I should keep it contained for now. I also told her about Grayson's connection to Dominique and the fact that he suspected her of killing the daughter of his mentor.

"So the real killer is trying to frame Grayson?" Shontelle said when I'd finished telling her everything. "Why? And was that their intention right from the start?"

"I'm not sure about that last question. It could be that Grayson was simply a convenient person to frame because he owns the brewery and has a connection to Dominique. Although . . .

that would mean the killer knows about that connection. Otherwise, someone had something against both Dominique and Grayson. I guess that's a possibility, but it seems unlikely."

"But you haven't ruled it out?"

"I haven't ruled out anything yet," I said with a sigh.

"You're trying to, though." It was a statement rather than a question. Knowing me as she did, that wasn't something Shontelle needed to ask.

"I've got some suspects," I confirmed. "But I've got a long way to go."

The recent events and my forced separation from Grayson suddenly weighed heavily on my shoulders. Shontelle didn't fail to notice the flagging of my spirits.

"Hey," she said, touching a hand to my back, "you'll figure this out. Then you and Grayson can be together again."

I nodded, knowing that eventual outcome was what I needed to hold on to.

"Please don't mention any of this in front of my mom," I requested. "She doesn't know about it yet, and I'm hoping to keep it that way."

"How have you explained Grayson's absence?" Shontelle asked.

"I said that he's been busy with some personal stuff."

"You know how news and gossip travel in this town, though. Don't you think she's in danger of hearing it from someone else?"

"I know that's a possibility," I said. "But for the moment at least, I don't want to bring it up."

"Fair enough."

We'd reached Aunt Gilda's salon, but Shontelle put out a hand to stop me before I texted my aunt to let her know we'd arrived.

"I saw the food writer Dominique at the grocery store the day of the murder," she said. "It was strange."

"Strange how?" I asked.

"She had a few things in a shopping basket, but then she suddenly looked as though she'd seen a ghost. She abandoned the basket on the floor and took off out of the store like she was being chased by demons."

"Do you know what made her do that?"

Shontelle shrugged. "A man had walked into the store, and she was looking his way, but he didn't even notice her."

"A local man?" I asked, already guessing that the answer was no.

"I'd never seen him before," Shontelle said, confirming my suspicion.

"Can you describe him?"

"White. Maybe six feet tall. He had blond hair and was probably in his late twenties or early thirties."

Her description confirmed another suspicion of mine.

The man Dominique had run from in the grocery store was the same man who'd scared her the night she was at the pub: travel writer Nick Perry.

Chapter 18

The four of us walked together to the Harvest Grill, a restaurant owned by Matt Yanders, one of the members of the science fiction and fantasy book club hosted by the Inkwell. Aunt Gilda had called ahead to reserve a table for us, so we didn't have to wait to be seated.

"I'll have to visit your shop before I leave," my mom said to Shontelle as we opened our menus.

My friend smiled. "I'd love that."

I'd introduced the two of them only a few minutes ago, but I could tell that my mom already liked Shontelle. That didn't surprise me. Shontelle was easy to like.

I looked up from my menu. "And you should meet Kiandra."

"My daughter," Shontelle explained. "She adores Sadie."

I smiled at that. "It's mutual."

"Why don't we all have afternoon tea one day at Shady Creek Manor?" Aunt Gilda suggested. "Would Kiandra enjoy that?"

"She loves going to the Manor," Shontelle said. "She's got a sweet tooth, and they serve some amazing desserts."

"I can attest to that." I'd eaten at Shady Creek Manor for the first time back in the spring, but I'd returned a few times since. I was particularly fond of going there for high tea. That was something Shontelle and I tried to do together once a month now.

"It sounds lovely," my mom said. "You three choose the day, since my schedule is completely open."

"Any day works for me," Aunt Gilda said. "I've booked the week off."

"Same here," I said. "So whatever day works best for you, Shontelle."

"I'll check with my mom and see when she can watch the shop for me," my friend said. "Or, maybe I can close early one day and my mom can come with us."

"That would be perfect," Aunt Gilda said, and my mom and I agreed.

We decided that Shontelle would get back to us after talking to her mom. With that out of the way, we all studied our menus more closely.

Our waiter came by a few minutes later and took our orders. He returned again briefly to deliver our drinks before disappearing again.

I was taking my first sip of my mango margarita when Matt, the restaurant's owner, arrived at our table.

"Good afternoon, ladies. How are you doing?"

"We're doing great, thank you," I said before introducing Matt to my mom.

He chatted with her about how she was enjoying Shady Creek, and then he turned his attention to me.

"I can't believe what's going on with Grayson," he said. "Anyone who knows the guy thinks it's crazy that he's wanted for murder."

My mom choked on the sip of wine she'd just taken.

"Are you okay?" Matt asked with alarm.

My mom patted her chest as her coughing subsided. "Yes, thank you. I'm fine."

She took a careful sip of her drink and then fixed her eyes on me.

I wanted to slide down underneath the table.

"I'm sure everything will turn out all right for Grayson in the end," Aunt Gilda said with forced cheeriness.

"I sure hope so," Matt said. "If you get the chance, let him know the town is behind him, Sadie."

"Thank you," I said faintly as he left our table.

I took a gulp of my margarita, but even that didn't help matters much. The cat was well and truly out of the bag. No amount of alcohol or anything else was going to undo that.

"Sadie. Elizabeth. Coleman." My mom's gaze bore into me.

I slid down in my seat, wishing again that I could disappear beneath the table. Or maybe to the center of the earth, never to be seen or heard from again.

"I can explain," I said.

"I should certainly hope so."

"It's all a misunderstanding," Aunt Gilda chimed in.

My mom raised an eyebrow, thoroughly unconvinced. "Murder is a misunderstanding?"

Shontelle sent an alarmed glance my way. "It's more the fact that the police suspect Grayson that's the misunderstanding," she said, trying to help out.

My mom's expression was only growing more forbidding.

"A woman was murdered at Grayson's brewery the night before you arrived," I said, deciding to spill the details and get it over with. "Grayson and I found the body, and Grayson knew the victim once upon a time. Since he suspected her of murdering his friend's daughter, they didn't exactly get along."

I still couldn't bring myself to mention the bloody wrench that was found in Grayson's kitchen, or the surveillance footage of the killer wearing a jacket that looked similar to my boyfriend's.

"So the police think Grayson did it," I said to wrap up, "but he didn't."

"He definitely didn't," Shontelle agreed.

I flashed her a wavering smile of thanks, grateful for the support.

"So he's in jail?" my mom asked, sounding scandalized.

"No." I sank down in my seat a little more. "He went into hiding so he couldn't be arrested. He used to be a private investigator and he wants to investigate his own case. It would be difficult for him to do that from behind bars."

I didn't mention the fact that I intended to help clear his name. That was another detail that didn't need to be shared. If I did tell my mom, she'd probably lock *me* up and throw away the key. Which was exactly why I'd never told her about my previous ventures into the realm of investigating murders. Thankfully, Aunt Gilda had agreed to keep those stories quiet as well, even though she didn't approve of my snooping because she thought it was too dangerous.

Silence settled over our table, but it was a silence fraught with tension and apprehension. My mother stared at me from across the table and I had to fight to keep from sliding down any farther. I was already in danger of falling off my seat.

"So let me get this straight," my mom said finally. "Your boyfriend is a wanted man. Wanted for murder."

"Yes," I said. "But he's innocent."

"But he *is* your boyfriend?"

I sat up in my seat, surprised by the question. "Huh?"

"Please don't 'huh' me, Sadie," my mom scolded. "Answer properly."

I glanced at Aunt Gilda and Shontelle, who both seemed as puzzled as I was by the question.

"Of course he's my boyfriend," I said. "I've been telling you that for months."

"I'm aware of that, but you've been so cagey about his whereabouts and why I haven't been able to meet him that I was beginning to wonder if you'd made the whole thing up."

I almost laughed but then realized my mom was entirely serious. "Hold on. You thought I'd *made Grayson up*? But I've sent you pictures of him!"

"I didn't doubt that the man existed. I simply questioned whether you were really in a relationship with him."

"Why would she lie about that?" Aunt Gilda asked, saving me the trouble.

"I figured perhaps Sadie was so determined to prove to me that she had a perfect life here that she wanted to present herself as having not only a successful business life but a successful personal one too."

This time I really did laugh, but it had a touch of hysteria to it. "You thought I'd invented a relationship and kept up the lie for nearly six months?"

We all fell quiet as our waiter arrived with our meals.

"Anything else you need at the moment?" he asked once all our plates were on the table.

"No, but thank you," Shontelle said.

She might have been the only one capable of normal speech right then.

Silence descended again once the waiter left us, but it didn't last more than a few seconds.

"Seriously, Mom?" I blurted out.

"You can't exactly blame me," she said as she unfolded her cloth napkin and placed it over her lap. "What was I supposed to think?"

"Not that I'd invented a boyfriend!"

"In my defense, I knew you were keeping something from me since I arrived in Shady Creek. And Gilda wasn't any help. She was being as vague and evasive as you were."

I mouthed the words "thank you" to my aunt. Then I let out a sigh as I dug my fork into my southwestern pasta salad. "I'm sorry, Mom. I should have told you everything right from the beginning."

"You should have," my mom agreed. "Why didn't you?"

"I want so desperately for you to like and accept Grayson. I really love him, Mom, and I don't want this whole situation to color your view of him. He doesn't deserve any of this."

"He really is a good man," Aunt Gilda said in support. "I can promise you that."

"And he and Sadie are great together," Shontelle added.

"Until I can meet the man myself, I'll take your word for it," my mom said.

"You will?" I asked with surprise. It wasn't always easy to get my mom on my side.

"All three of you vouch for Grayson, and I have no reason to doubt your judgment."

"Not even mine?" I asked. I often thought she doubted my judgment.

"Of course not," my mom said. "Why would you think otherwise?"

I could have brought up the fact that she hadn't—in the past, at least—approved of my decision to buy a pub and live in Shady Creek. However, I didn't see any point in rippling the waters, which were far smoother than I'd expected.

"Thanks," I said instead before taking a bite of my lunch.

"Is Grayson all right?" my mom asked. "Have you spoken to him since he went on the run?"

"I don't know how to get in touch with him," I said with what was now becoming a familiar ache in my heart. "He doesn't want me getting in trouble with the police, so he didn't even tell me he was going into hiding."

My mom gave a nod of approval as she cut into her gnocchi. "He was right not to tell you." She surprised me yet again by adding, "You must miss him terribly."

"More than I can put into words," I said.

My mom reached across the table and gave my hand a squeeze. "Everything will turn out all right in the end, Sadie."

"I hope you're right."

With my secret now out in the open, I was able to relax and enjoy the meal, although for every single second, I keenly felt Grayson's absence.

After finishing our lunch at the Harvest Grill, I wandered back to the Treasure Chest with Shontelle. My mom and Aunt Gilda were going to visit the Caldwell Cheese Company before heading over to my place, where I would cook them dinner. In the meantime, I needed another chat with my best friend.

"That went better than I expected," Shontelle said. "I really like your mom. You had me worried that she'd completely freak out if she found out about Grayson's troubles."

"I thought she *would* freak out," I admitted. "She totally surprised me there." Much to my relief.

"After meeting her, I'm sure she's going to love Grayson."

"I just need to make sure she gets that chance," I said.

"She will. With you and Grayson on the case along with the police, the real killer will be caught soon."

"You're right," I said, deciding to be optimistic. "Between all of us, someone is bound to solve the mystery."

"Do you want to come upstairs for a cup of coffee?" Shontelle asked as she unlocked the front door to the shop.

"That would be great, thanks," I said.

Shontelle led the way through to the back of the shop, where a staircase provided access to her apartment. Once upstairs, we found nine-year-old Kiandra at the kitchen table, brushing orange glaze onto pumpkin-shaped sugar cookies. Shontelle's mom, Yvette, was in the process of sliding another sheet of cookies into the oven.

"Wow!" I exclaimed. "You two have been busy. Those cookies look great."

"We're making them for a bake sale at the elementary school," Yvette said.

"But we're keeping some too," Kiandra said with a smile. She picked up a cookie and bit into it as if to emphasize her words.

"Remember to save some for the sale," Shontelle said, ruffling her daughter's cloud of curly hair.

A phone rang somewhere in the apartment.

"That sounds like mine," Yvette said. "Excuse me."

She disappeared into the living room as Shontelle set about making a pot of coffee.

"Sadie, is it scary living next door to a haunted house?" Kiandra asked as she glazed another cookie.

"A haunted house?" I echoed, puzzled. "You mean the brewery?"

I wondered if she'd heard about someone dying there and had equated that with the place being haunted.

She shook her head. "On the other side of the mill."

"The vacant house?" Shontelle asked.

This time Kiandra nodded, her eyes wide and solemn. "Except it's not really vacant. There's a ghost living there."

"Oh, honey, there's no such thing as ghosts," Shontelle said. "You don't need to worry about that."

"No, it's for real," Kiandra insisted. "My friend Cherry's older sister Leanne has a boyfriend named Chad. He was there one night with another boy. They sneaked inside the house and heard footsteps in the attic. The next night, they took Leanne and another girl there to look for the ghost, but Leanne got too scared and they ran away before they saw anything." Kiandra froze. "Oops. That was meant to be a secret. Leanne wasn't supposed to be out that late."

"Well, I don't know Leanne or her sister, so their parents won't hear about it from me," I said.

"And I'll pretend I didn't hear," Shontelle added as she took three mugs down from a cupboard.

"Phew," Kiandra said with relief.

Dots connected in my head as I recalled the teenagers who'd run across the green after one of them had screamed. "Was it last night that Leanne was at the house?"

Kiandra nodded. "Cherry told me about it this morning."

So the boys heard the footsteps two nights ago.

"I don't think I have any reason to worry," I said. "I doubt there was actually a ghost there." In fact, I suspected the footsteps were made by someone altogether human.

"But it *could* be a ghost," Kiandra said before taking another bite of the cookie she'd started eating earlier. "You should wear a necklace made of garlic."

"I think that's for warding off vampires," Shontelle said.

Kiandra shrugged as her grandmother returned to the room.

"Did I hear you talking about ghosts and vampires?" Yvette asked. "You'd think Halloween was coming or something,"

Kiandra laughed. "It is and I can't wait!"

Shontelle groaned. "I can. I'm not looking forward to the sugar high."

"I can have a sugar high right now," Kiandra said, biting into another cookie. "We all can."

"The cookies do look tempting," Shontelle admitted.

I had to agree.

Even though Shontelle and I had just finished a filling lunch, we both indulged in a cookie with our coffee. After Kiandra finished glazing the last batch of cookies, she showed me the pirate princess costume her grandma was making for her for Halloween.

After that, I didn't stay much longer. I needed to get some groceries and clean my apartment before my mom and Aunt Gilda showed up for dinner. Shontelle walked me out through her shop and locked up behind me. Once I was alone on the sidewalk, I paused to gaze across the village green at the vacant house next to the gristmill. It was a struggle to keep myself from running straight over there. If Grayson really was hiding out there, as I suspected, the last thing I wanted to do was to alert the police to that fact. Maybe they weren't watching me now, but I didn't know that for sure. I'd have to wait until I could sneak over there under the cover of darkness, and nightfall was still hours away.

With great reluctance, I turned away and walked to the grocery store, counting down the hours until I could go in search of Grayson.

Chapter 19

When I reached the grocery store, I realized I had no idea what to make for dinner. Maybe I should have come up with a plan when I'd invited my mom and aunt over for a meal, but I'd had so much going on in my life and inside my head lately that I hadn't found the time. It didn't really matter in the end. As I pushed my cart around the grocery store, I came up with a plan on the go. I'd cook some salmon fillets and serve them with asparagus and little potatoes. My mouth watered at the thought. I loved little potatoes smothered with butter.

I filled my cart with all the ingredients I needed for dinner as well as other items that I was running low on. I needed some chocolate chips, which I loved to melt on my oatmeal, so I turned down the baking aisle. A woman stood at the other end of the aisle, examining the different types of liquid extracts on offer. She glanced my way when I brought my cart to a halt next to the chocolate chips. As soon as she was facing me, I realized she was Miranda Keeler, George Keeler's wife. She recognized me at the same moment. Her eyes widened and she dropped the bottle of extract she had in her hand into her shopping basket. Then she fled from the aisle like she'd seen a terrifying ghost.

I stood staring at the spot where she'd been a moment before, trying to process what had happened. Was Miranda Keeler scared of me?

I glanced over my shoulder. I was the only person in sight, so it must have been my presence that sent her running.

Leaving my cart where it was, I hurried to the end of the aisle and peeked around the corner. Miranda was at the express checkout, hastily emptying her basket onto the counter. When she turned her head my way, I ducked out of sight.

Why would Miranda Keeler be frightened of me?

I pondered the question as I returned to my cart. The only answer I could come up with was that she knew I was looking into Dominique's death and that was what had her scared. She'd heard me ask George if he had an alibi for the time of the murder. Even if she hadn't overheard that part of the conversation, she could still know about my reputation for sticking my nose into murder investigations. She was probably afraid I'd corner her and interrogate her. Maybe I would have, although I liked to think my questioning would have been subtle enough not to be labeled an interrogation.

I stared at the goods lining the shelves without really seeing them, my thoughts still on Miranda. If she was worried about me investigating the crime, then surely that meant she had something to hide, something she didn't want me finding out.

She definitely needed to stay on my suspect list. I still didn't know if she'd had a stake in her husband's restaurant. Even if it had been his venture alone, the loss of the business likely would have affected them both, and she certainly hadn't liked seeing Dominique in Shady Creek.

Maybe she and George killed Dominique together.

I quickly discounted that idea. Only one person had followed Dominique into the brewery building. That didn't mean the husband and wife hadn't planned the murder together, but only one had carried it out.

I definitely needed to investigate the Keelers further, I decided.

If I got home and cleaned my apartment quickly, maybe I'd have a chance to do some sleuthing before I needed to start preparing dinner.

I grabbed a package of chocolate chips and plunked it into my grocery cart. At the other end of the aisle, I added a box of Earl Grey tea bags to my groceries. It was my mom's favorite tea, and I didn't have any at home. I really hoped she liked my apartment. She hadn't said much when I'd given her the brief tour, but after our talk at lunch, I felt more optimistic about her opinions. She'd surprised me by being much calmer and more accepting about Grayson's situation than I'd ever anticipated.

Another ache shot through my heart at the thought of Grayson. I didn't think that would stop happening until we were back together with his name cleared of any suspicion.

I headed for the checkout counter, noting that Miranda was no longer around. I joined the shortest line aside from the express checkout and parked my cart while the one woman in front of me unloaded her groceries onto the counter.

"Maybe we need to spread the word more about the local food bank," the cashier was saying. She appeared to be in her late forties, and the tag pinned to her shirt revealed that her name was Gloria. "It's not the first time I've seen someone taking food from the store's dumpster out back, but this woman was dressed in expensive clothing."

"Anyone can fall on hard times," the woman in front of me said. "And isn't it true that lots of perfectly good food ends up in the dumpsters of grocery stores?"

"That is true, unfortunately," Gloria agreed as she scanned groceries.

"Did you recognize the woman?" the shopper in front of me

asked. "Maybe there's a way we could tactfully let her know about the food bank, in case she's new to town and doesn't know it exists. Or maybe it's not a financial issue. Aren't there people who dumpster dive simply because they don't want good food going to waste?"

"I've heard of that," Gloria said as she scanned the last item. "But I didn't recognize her, so she could be new to the area. I'd say she was in her late twenties. She had gorgeous long, auburn hair."

"That doesn't ring a bell." The woman in front of me pulled out her credit card.

I started unloading my grocery cart as she paid for her purchases. Even though I'd heard the conversation going on in front of me, my mind was still mostly focused on Miranda and my other suspects. As soon as I'd paid for my groceries, I picked up my two bags and headed for home. I couldn't help checking the windows of the abandoned house as I approached the gristmill, but I tried to be discreet about it. I didn't see any signs of life, though that didn't surprise me. The way the light was reflecting off the glass, it was hard to see much of anything, and Grayson knew better than to stand by the windows when he was trying to stay hidden.

Before crossing the footbridge, I cast a quick glance toward the brewery's driveway. Sure enough, a car was parked there, mostly hidden by the trees and bushes. The sight of the vehicle only added to my determination to get the case solved quickly. Even if I hadn't planned to sneak around that night, I wouldn't have liked being under police surveillance. It made me uncomfortable, overly aware of every move I made.

I was able to relax once inside my apartment, thankfully. I put the groceries away, groomed Wimsey—much to his displeasure—and then got to work cleaning. By the time I had every surface sparkling, I needed to start preparing the food. My fingers itched to get hold of my laptop, but I didn't have a chance to do some online sleuthing before dinner, because my mom and Aunt Gilda arrived shortly after I got the food out of the fridge.

I did my best to push all thoughts of the murder to the back of my mind so I could enjoy the time with my family. My mom and Gilda both loved the meal I cooked, which made me happy. I wasn't the most skilled cook in the world, so I was glad I was able to put together something that tasted good.

While we ate, we chatted about my brothers, other relatives, and our lives in general. I found myself relaxing, no longer so worried about what my mom might think about everything. She seemed to like my apartment, and she was pleased to see Wimsey again. The feeling must have been mutual. When we settled in the living room to chat some more after dinner, Wimsey hopped up onto my mom's lap and purred away while she stroked his fur. Wimsey was typically more aloof, allowing people to pet him for a short while but not usually snuggling up to them. Even with me, he typically didn't curl up on my lap except on cold winter nights.

When I said good-bye to my mom and aunt for the night, a big yawn escaped me. Sleep would have to wait, however. I didn't think it was quite late enough to risk sneaking next door to the vacant house, but I had plans for the interim. I grabbed my laptop and settled on the couch again, Wimsey now sleeping on the armchair across from me.

It was time to see what I could find out about my suspects.

I started with Miranda and George Keeler, but that turned out to be a waste of time. Neither one of them seemed to have social media profiles, and aside from the one restaurant review from years ago, nobody else had written anything about them, at least not that I could find. Even unearthing the review took quite a bit of digging. I winced when I read it. Dominique sure hadn't pulled any punches. Phrases like "deep-fried cardboard would have tasted better" had me feeling sorry for George and

Miranda until I remembered that one of them might be a cold-blooded killer. I decided I should set my sympathy aside until I knew whether they were innocent or not.

I gave up on the Keelers and shifted my attention to Alicia Jollimore. I figured since she was in her early twenties she'd be more likely than the Keelers to be active on social media. That turned out to be the case. She'd posted lots of photos of her best friend's adorable Yorkipoo puppy on Instagram. I scrolled through the pictures with a smile on my face until I reminded myself that I was on a mission that had absolutely nothing to do with puppies.

After checking out Alicia's other profiles, I was almost ready to turn in my amateur sleuthing badge, if I'd actually had one. This search hadn't turned up anything useful about any of my suspects but I had one more name I wanted to check out.

I found far more information about Nick Perry than I had about Alicia and the Keelers. He'd written numerous travel articles that had been published online and he also had professional social media accounts. At first nothing I found made my sleuthing senses tingle, but then I dug up an interesting tidbit. Nick had attended the same college as Dominique and Samantha. I stumbled upon that information on one of his social media profiles, where he'd posted a photo of himself with his soccer teammates from his college days. I did some more searching and discovered that he'd been an elite athlete in his early years of college, but in his senior year, a serious knee injury had put an end to his chances of becoming a pro soccer player.

Nick's truncated athletic career wasn't what I was really interested in, however. I reeled myself in from that tangent and refocused on the fact that he'd studied at the same college as Dominique. Nick had majored in English, but he'd attended the college around the same time as Dominique. It looked like he'd graduated one year ahead of her.

I sat back on the couch, staring at the far wall as I thought things over.

The college connection was potentially interesting, but it didn't explain why Dominique was so frightened of Nick. I tried and failed to find anything online that shed any light on that issue.

Rubbing a hand over my eyes, I gave up for the night.

It was late enough now to go in search of Grayson.

Chapter 20

I wished I had Grayson's night vision binoculars on hand. With the lights in my apartment turned off, I checked out the eastern window with my regular binoculars to see if I could tell if the police were still watching the gristmill. Unfortunately, it was too dark for me to tell if anyone was parked in the brewery's driveway. I checked out all the other windows as well, in case I spotted a surveillance vehicle stationed in a different location. The streets were empty and quiet. That didn't mean the police weren't out there, but I was going to proceed on the assumption that they were parked in the brewery's driveway, watching from the east.

As with the last time I'd sneaked out at night, I dressed in dark clothing. This time I remembered to wear gloves, and I added a black winter hat to the ensemble to help keep my ears warm. I tucked my keys, mini flashlight, and phone into the pocket of my hoodie and crept out of the gristmill through the pub's main door on the western side of the building. Cautiously, I slipped past the maple trees and into the neighboring backyard. Once again, I wished Grayson had taught me how to pick locks. That would have made the next step of my plan easier. I knew the teenagers had managed to get into the vacant house, but I didn't know how they'd done so. I hoped it wasn't through the front door. I'd feel far too exposed going that route.

I started with the back door. I expected it to be locked, so I wasn't surprised to find that was the case. There were two windows I could reach from the back porch. I tried opening them, but neither would budge. I wasn't going to risk breaking a limb by trying to scale up to the second-story windows. Most likely those were locked too. While it was possible that one or more of the teens had been adventurous enough to get inside through an upper window, I thought it more likely that they'd found an easier way in.

Sticking to the darkest of shadows, I made my way around to the western side of the house, where there were two first-floor windows. Unfortunately, the porch didn't wrap around the house and I couldn't quite touch the windowsill with the tips of my fingers even when I reached as far as I could over my head. The window closest to me was shut all the way, but as I drew closer to the other window, I noticed that it was open a crack. A maple tree grew next to the house, with one sturdy looking branch reaching close to the window. Maybe the teenagers hadn't scaled the house, but it seemed likely that at least one of them had climbed the tree. It looked as though I would have to do the same.

I made sure that my keys and phone were sitting in the deepest part of my pocket and then grabbed hold of the lowest branch and hauled myself up into the tree. I paused for a moment, wondering about the wisdom of what I was about to do. I'd climbed trees all the time during my childhood, but I hadn't attempted to do so in at least fifteen years.

The thought of possibly seeing Grayson spurred me on. I climbed up to the branch that reached toward the window and then sat down on it, carefully shifting myself along inch by inch. When I was within reach of the window, I stopped and carefully leaned forward, hoping desperately that the branch would continue to support my weight.

At first, I couldn't get the window to budge. I tried and tried, but only ended up with sore fingers for my efforts. I shifted a few inches farther along the branch, bringing me closer to the window. I tried opening it again, and this time I had more leverage. After some initial resistance, the window shifted upward.

The next challenge was to get myself from the branch to the windowsill. I decided the safest way to go about that would be to grab hold of the windowsill and then haul myself up and in through the window. It would be too risky to stand up and step from the branch to the sill.

I glanced around to make sure I was still alone and unobserved. I was, as far as I could tell. Holding my breath, I reached out and grabbed the sill with one hand. I managed to get my other hand on it just as I slipped off the tree branch. My legs hit the side of the house with a thump that I feared would bring someone running. My hands and arms were already beginning to protest, so I didn't delay my next maneuver. I summoned up all the strength I could find and hauled myself up and over the windowsill.

I was glad there was no one to witness my awkward and clumsy entry into the house. I toppled over the windowsill and landed on the floor with a thud.

"Ouch." My voice sounded loud in the dark, vacant house.

I lay still for a moment, listening and wondering if Grayson was here and had heard me. I didn't hear a sound.

Rubbing my hip where it had hit the hardwood floor, I climbed to my feet. Dust tickled at my nose. Before I could stop it, a sneeze burst out of me. I really wasn't doing a very good job of being stealthy. Although, now that I was inside the house, I probably didn't need to worry about that so much. After all, I didn't want to stay hidden from Grayson.

I fished my mini flashlight out of my pocket, where it had mercifully stayed while I climbed the tree and toppled into the house. I turned it on, being careful to aim the beam of light away from the window. The last thing I wanted was to draw attention from someone outside and have the police come looking to see what was going on.

I took in my surroundings and found that I was standing in the dining room. The place had been cleared of furniture, but the low-hanging chandelier gave away the room's purpose. I shone the light at the floor. A jumble of footprints had disturbed the dust. They weren't all of the same size. The teenagers were probably responsible for at least some of them, but I hoped Grayson had walked on this floor too.

The silence in the house had an eerie quality to it. I crept forward as quietly as possible, suddenly worried that someone other than Grayson might jump out from around a corner even though I had no reason to think that anyone else might be here. If the teenagers had returned, I probably would have heard them. Even so, I couldn't quite get myself to relax.

I made a quick circuit of the main floor, shutting off my flashlight whenever I had to pass by a window. Other than a single candy bar wrapper, I didn't find anything.

When I reached the front foyer, I gripped the banister and started up the stairs to the second floor. The third step creaked beneath my feet, almost making me jump with fright. Maybe it was the fact that Halloween was right around the corner, or maybe it was simply the dark and empty house, but I was feeling thoroughly spooked.

I froze halfway up the staircase, too frightened to continue.

There's nothing to be afraid of, I chided myself. *If anyone is here besides you, it's Grayson.*

I resumed my progress, more determined than scared now. I checked every room on the second floor, but there wasn't even a candy wrapper this time. A doorway halfway down the hall stood open a few inches. Behind it, a narrow staircase led up to the attic. I paused at the base of the stairs and aimed my light up toward the top.

"Grayson?" I called out.

I hadn't raised my voice much, but it still sounded far too loud.

The silence that followed felt as though it was pressing against my eardrums.

Aiming the narrow beam of my flashlight ahead of me, I crept up the stairway. At the top, I found myself in an attic that stretched the whole width of the house. Unlike downstairs, a couple of things had been left behind. A chair with one broken leg lay on its side, covered in dust and cobwebs. A mirror leaned against one wall, its surface so grimy that it sent only a weak reflection of my flashlight's beam back at me.

Those items had most likely been there a long time. I didn't think that was the case with everything, though. At one end of the attic, an orange juice carton and an empty glass bottle stood by the wall, along with a small stack of plastic containers. There was a space on the floor where the dust had been thoroughly disturbed.

I moved closer and inspected the labels on the plastic containers. One had held doughnuts, another fresh pineapple chunks, and the third an assortment of pastries. They looked as though they'd likely come from the grocery store. The glass bottle had once held chocolate milk. Now only a few drops remained at the bottom.

I recalled what I'd overheard when buying my groceries. The cashier had seen a woman dumpster diving behind the store. Maybe Grayson had done the same thing? I hated the thought of him having to get his meals out of a dumpster, even though I knew grocery stores often threw out plenty of good food.

No matter where the bottle and other containers had come from, Grayson wasn't here.

I called his name a couple of times, in case he'd heard my arrival and hadn't realized it was me. There didn't seem to be anywhere he could have hidden, but maybe he knew more than I did.

Nobody responded when I called out and my spirits quickly sank. I'd really hoped that I'd find Grayson here, but even if this had been his hideout at some point, he wasn't here at the moment. I should have expected that. After the teenagers had sneaked into the house, Grayson would have wanted to move somewhere safer. Still, I couldn't help but feel disappointed. I missed him so much that my chest ached.

Forcing myself to accept that my quest to find Grayson had failed, I returned to the main floor. I stowed my phone in my pocket again and considered my options for getting out of the house. I didn't want to invite vandals by exiting through the back door and leaving it unlocked, but I wasn't sure how I could climb out onto the tree branch and get the window closed behind me. Somehow the gap between the branch and the windowsill seemed bigger and more dangerous than it had been when I was trying to get in the house.

The drop wasn't all that far to the ground below. I could let myself hang from the windowsill and then drop to the grass, but then the window would still be wide open.

Now that I had no chance of seeing Grayson that night, all I wanted to do was get some sleep. I shut the window and hurried into the kitchen, where another window overlooked the back porch. The frame creaked in protest as I opened the window, but I wasn't as worried about making noise now that I was on my way out. I quickly climbed out onto the porch, managing to land on my feet this time. I shut the window behind me, hoping no one with ill intent would realize that it was unlocked.

Minutes later, I was back home in my warm apartment. I crawled into bed, with Wimsey at my feet, and soon drifted off into an uneasy dream about a spooky house filled with shadows and beams of moonlight.

Chapter 21

I really needed to identify the real killer, not only to get a murderer off the streets and to clear Grayson's name, but also so I could get a decent night's sleep. My late-night sleuthing and Internet searches were starting to take a toll on me. I overslept by half an hour, despite my alarm going off as scheduled, and I only woke up at all thanks to Wimsey meowing loudly while trying to pull the blankets off me. Even after I hauled myself out of bed and took a shower, I couldn't clear the grogginess from my head.

Yawning at regular intervals, I set out for the Village Bean, hoping a good dose of caffeine and sugar would be enough to wake me up fully. I'd have a hard time solving Dominique's murder if I couldn't get my brain to function properly.

When I opened the door to the coffee shop, a blast of warm, heavenly scented air hit me in the face. The delicious smells perked me up a little bit, although I still had to stifle a yawn as I got in line. As I waited for my turn to order, I checked out the display of muffins and pastries. What I really wanted was a chocolate chip muffin to go with my mocha latte, but I decided to be at least a tiny bit healthy and instead went with blueberry.

I'd just finished paying for my order when someone tapped me on the shoulder.

"Hey, Sadie." Joey Fontana grinned at me, looking far too awake. "Here for some brain fuel?"

"Everything fuel," I said as I moved down the counter, letting him step up to the cash register.

After he'd ordered, Joey joined me at the other end of the counter.

"Not sleeping much?" Joey guessed as I covered my mouth to hide yet another yawn.

"Not as much as I'd like, anyway."

Nettie Jo's part-time helper, Ruthie, set my latte and muffin on the counter in front of me. I thanked her and turned around to survey the coffee shop, looking for an empty table. There were three or four free, but instead of claiming one, I nudged Joey with my elbow.

"Check it out. Nick Perry is here."

Joey picked up the coffee and chocolate croissant that Ruthie had set on the counter for him. "I noticed that when I came in the door. I was hoping to ask him some questions. He knew Dominique."

"They went to the same college. Is that how they knew each other?"

"Apparently," Joey said. "They had some friends in common back then."

"He knows Phoebe Ramone too," I said, remembering how cozy they'd seemed at the town hall.

Joey wasn't surprised by that information. "They dated for a while back in their college days."

"Really? Did Phoebe go to the same school?"

"No, she was at a nearby college, just outside of Fenworth, Maine."

"Interesting," I said.

"But is it relevant?" Joey asked.

"I have no idea." I knew I'd burn my tongue if I took a sip of my latte, so I contented myself with inhaling the scent wafting up from the cup. "What are you hoping to ask Nick?"

Joey shrugged. "If he can tell me about Dominique and who might have wanted to harm her."

We were definitely on the same wavelength.

"I'm going to ask him some questions myself," I said.

With my latte and muffin in hand, I threaded my way around the tables to get to Nick.

"I hope you don't mind me crashing the party," Joey said from over my shoulder.

I didn't. In fact, having a reporter with me might make my questions seem more legitimate and less flat-out nosey.

Nick had his attention fixed on his phone, which was set on the table next to a plate holding a half-eaten blueberry Danish. He also had a cup of what I assumed was coffee in front of him. When I stopped right next to his table, he glanced up.

"Nick, right?" I said, even though I didn't need confirmation. He barely had a chance to nod before I added, "I'm Sadie Coleman."

Joey stepped up next to me and set down his coffee and croissant before offering his hand to Nick. "And I'm Joey Fontana from the *Shady Creek Tribune*. Do you mind if I ask you a few questions?"

Joey and I were already pulling up chairs to sit down when Nick replied, "Sure. I guess that would be okay."

If he thought I was with the *Shady Creek Tribune* as well, I wasn't going to correct him.

"Let me guess." Nick pushed his phone aside and drew his coffee mug closer to him. "This is about Dominique, right?"

"We understand you knew her," I said as I broke a piece off my muffin. When I took a bite, a delicious blueberry exploded in my mouth.

"I did," Nick confirmed, although I thought I detected a hint of wariness in his blue eyes.

"From college, is that right?" Joey asked.

Nick took a drink of his coffee. "How did you find that out?"

"I was looking up background information on Dominique," Joey said. "Your name came up in the process."

Nick seemed to accept that explanation. Maybe it was completely true on Joey's part. I wasn't about to add that I'd uncovered the connection while investigating Nick as a murder suspect. Instead, I took a cautious sip of my latte. It was still hot, but not so much as to burn my tongue.

Joey had his phone out, ready to take notes. "What can you tell us about her?"

Nick took a moment to consider his words. "She was a determined and tenacious woman. She'll be sorely missed by everyone who knew her." He stared down into his mug of coffee with a somber expression.

"We're very sorry that you lost a friend," I said, realizing that we should have led with that.

Nick raised his gaze. "Thanks. I guess we were more like acquaintances than friends, but it's still hard to believe she's gone."

"Acquaintances?" I echoed. "I thought there was more of a history between you two than that."

His gaze sharpened. "What makes you say that?"

I could tell that Joey had turned his attention on me too.

"I own the local pub," I said. "Dominique was in there one night before she died. When you arrived, she looked frightened and took off."

I didn't bring up the similar incident that Shontelle had witnessed at the grocery store. I didn't want him to know that I was snooping into his life.

Nick took a sip of his coffee and gave me a sheepish smile. "You're right. We did have more of a history. But that's not something I want reported in the local gossip rag."

"The *Tribune* definitely isn't a gossip rag," Joey said, although he didn't sound offended. He set down his phone. "But if you want to go off the record, we can do that."

"I'm not sure how any of this is relevant." Nick stared at us. When we said nothing, he sighed and gave a curt nod. "Off the record then. Dominique and I had a brief fling."

"While you were in college?" I asked.

"A few years after that. We ran into each other in New York and decided to have coffee to catch up. One thing led to another." He drained the last of the coffee from his mug.

"That doesn't explain why she was scared of you," Joey said, taking the words right out of my mouth.

Nick leveled his gaze at Joey. "She wasn't scared of me. She had no reason to be. She probably didn't want to run into me because things didn't end well between us. We've avoided each other ever since."

"When you say things didn't end well . . . ," I prodded.

Nick looked past me for a moment, and I got the feeling he was deciding whether or not he should tell us anything more. Finally, he seemed to come to a decision.

"This is definitely off the record," he said to Joey before addressing us both. "I cheated on her. It's not something I'm proud of, but it happened. And to make matters worse, the other woman was the editor of the magazine Dominique was working for at the time. When it all came out, Dominique felt betrayed and humiliated. She hated me from then on, and I couldn't blame her for that." He frowned at the unfinished pastry on his plate and pushed it aside. "When I heard she was here in Shady Creek, I hoped I'd have a chance to apologize to her like I should have done ages ago. Now she'll never know how much I regret what I did."

I exchanged a glance with Joey. I still had more questions, but I was afraid Nick might shut us down. Bringing up the past had clearly clouded his mood. He seemed really saddened by Dominique's death.

"Do the police know all of this?" I asked.

"They know some of it," Nick said. "I spoke to them after Dominique was killed, seeing as I knew her."

"Are you a suspect?" Joey asked.

Nick pierced him with an icy glare. "Why would I be?"

Joey shrugged. "The two of you had a romantic history. The cops might think you had it in for her."

"I guess the cops are smarter than that." Nick grabbed his phone off the table. "Besides, I wasn't anywhere near the brewery when Dominique died."

"Where were you?" I asked.

"At the inn where I'm staying. I was watching the Rangers-Sabres hockey game on the TV in my room." He stood up. "I need to get going."

"Thanks for talking to us," I said, but he was already halfway to the door and he didn't look back.

"What do you think?" Joey asked me before taking a bite of his croissant.

I took a sip of my latte before replying. "I think I need to talk to Cordelia."

Joey nodded. "To see if she can confirm Nick's alibi. I'll come with you."

"But first," I said, breaking off another piece of my muffin, "I'm finishing my breakfast."

With food and caffeine now in my system, I felt ready to face the day, and to hunt down more information. Nick's word wasn't enough for me to believe his alibi, but if Cordelia could confirm it, I'd be happy to strike his name off my suspect list. Maybe then I'd feel like I was making some progress.

Joey and I cut across the green and headed straight for the Creekside Inn. The beautiful Queen Anne sat on a spacious lot along with several sugar maples. The creek ran along the back of the property, with the forest beyond it. The front windows of the stately house offered a view of the village green, and I'd often seen visitors relaxing on the wraparound porch during warmer months.

It was no wonder that the inn was a popular place for tourists to stay while in Shady Creek. The inside was just as beautiful as the exterior. Over the years, the various homeowners had maintained the charming character of the house, and Cordelia's grandmother had furnished the place with gorgeous antiques. Now that Grace King was nearing eighty years of age, Cordelia was taking on more of the responsibilities associated with running the inn. Grace intended to hand the business over to Cordelia in the near future.

Grace answered the door when I knocked, but she informed me and Joey that Cordelia wasn't at home. We stayed on the porch chatting with Grace for a few minutes. I considered asking if she could confirm Nick's alibi, but I decided to leave that as a last resort. The look I shot Joey seemed to effectively pass that message on because he didn't ask her either.

"I didn't want to worry her," I explained to Joey as we walked away from the inn a short while later. "If she couldn't confirm Nick's alibi, she might be scared that she has a murderer staying under her roof."

"I figured that was the reason you didn't bring it up," Joey said. "Won't Cordelia worry too?"

"Probably, but hopefully Nick isn't the killer. Then nobody at the inn will have reason to worry." That thought gave me pause. "Do you know where Phoebe Ramone is staying?"

"At Shady Creek Manor," Joey replied.

"Right," I said, remembering that Cordelia had mentioned that. "No expense spared then."

Joey shrugged. "She's freelance, so I guess she's footing her own bill. It does seem like a pricey place for a food writer to stay, though."

I wondered if that was significant, but pushed the thought to the side for now.

When we reached the village green again, we paused.

"Where are you off to now?" I asked.

"I'm going to interview a couple of people about the recent rash of thefts."

That brought a memory rushing back to me. "I overheard a woman saying her cashmere sweater was stolen from her back porch."

Joey nodded. "Marianna Delmer. She's one of the victims. One of her neighbors, Alita Sanchez, had a pair of leather gloves stolen out of her car while she was unloading groceries the other day. And another woman in the same neighborhood had a diamond brooch go missing while she was out running errands. She'd left a window open and I guess the thief couldn't resist the opportunity."

"The thief got in the house but didn't take anything else?" I asked. "Just one brooch?"

Joey shrugged. "That seems to be the case. But it was a family heirloom and worth quite a bit, so the owner is pretty upset about it."

I thought things over. "A sweater, gloves, and a brooch." Another memory popped into my head. "What about Dominique's Gucci scarf?"

"Someone stole it from her before she died?"

"Possibly. She was upset because her scarf went missing at the town hall. Someone might have picked it up by accident, but I think it's more likely that it was stolen."

"I didn't know about that," Joey said. "Sounds like it could be the same person at work."

"Clothes, accessories, jewelry," I said. "All of the items stolen belonged to women."

"So maybe the thief is a woman?" Joey said.

I considered that. "Or a man who can't afford to buy presents for a special woman in his life."

"Or a man who's too cheap to buy presents."

I conceded that possibility with a nod.

"Are the police involved?" I asked.

"They've been notified, but with a murder to solve . . ."

He didn't need to finish his sentence. Thefts, most of which were petty, weren't going to be a top priority for the police department as long as the murder remained unsolved.

"Let me know if you hear anything more," Joey said.

"About the murder or the thefts?"

He grinned. "Both."

Joey set off toward Sycamore Street while I continued on to Primrose Books, the town's only bookstore. I wanted to make sure that the owner, Simone, had remembered to order copies of *A Riesling to Die* by J. C. Eaton, the novel that the Inkwell's mystery book club was planning to read for their November meeting. Most likely she had remembered, as she always had in the past, but I wanted an excuse to visit the store. Even though I had a stack of books waiting to be read at home, there were a couple of new releases I wanted to get my hands on.

I smiled when I reached the bookshop. A large orange tabby cat lay in the front window, snoozing in a patch of sunshine. He had to be Eddie, the cat Simone had recently adopted from the local shelter. He looked right at home among the books displayed in the window.

The bell above the door jingled as I entered the store. Simone was in the process of shelving a box of books. She had her wavy brown hair tied up in a bun and she wore a maxi skirt with a peasant blouse, a beaded necklace, and several bangles. She tended to dress in similar outfits, no matter what the weather.

"Hi, Sadie!" Simone greeted as the door drifted shut behind me. "How's the investigation going?"

"Slowly," I said.

She gave me a sympathetic smile. "You'll get there. Looking for a fictional mystery to take your mind off the real one?"

"Probably two or three." I tipped my head in the direction of the front window. "That must be Eddie."

Simone beamed. "Isn't he adorable?" She followed me over to the cat. "That's his favorite spot, especially when it's sunny."

"Has he managed to sneak out of the store again?" I asked.

"No, thank goodness. He's mostly content to sleep and visit with people. He did sneak out on me this morning when we were at home, though. He came back a while later, but it worries me when he wanders. I'm thinking of building him a catio in my backyard so he can enjoy time outdoors without me having to worry."

"That sounds like a good compromise," I said. "I could do that for Wimsey too, although he's such a homebody that he never strays out of sight of the gristmill."

"That's lucky." Simone gave Eddie a scratch on the head. He opened his amber eyes and purred. "There's actually another reason—"

The bell above the door jingled, distracting Simone from what she was about to say.

"Cordelia!" I said when I saw that it was my friend who had entered the store. "You're just the person I wanted to see."

Chapter 22

"Is anything wrong?" Cordelia asked, hesitating a step inside the store.

"No," I rushed to assure her. "I just want to ask you something."

The phone by the cash register rang, so Simone quickly excused herself and hurried to answer it.

"I stopped by the inn a few minutes ago," I told Cordelia. "But you weren't there, obviously. I'm glad we ran into each other here."

"I had some books to return to the library," Cordelia said. "I thought I'd stop here on my way home to pick up a copy of *A Riesling to Die*."

Cordelia was one of the members of the Inkwell's mystery book club.

The bell jingled again, heralding the arrival of two more customers.

Cordelia joined me by the window. "What did you want to ask me?"

I glanced at the other customers and lowered my voice. "Is it okay if I ask you after we're done here?"

She caught on right away. "Sure," she whispered. "It's about the murder, isn't it?"

I nodded, not wanting to say anything since the other customers were walking right past us.

"I'll meet you outside in a bit," Cordelia said.

She caught sight of Eddie then and we spent a few minutes showering him with attention before we wandered over to the mystery section. Cordelia picked up a copy of *A Riesling to Die* by J. C. Eaton as well as a mystery by Linda Reilly. By the time I made my way over to the cash register, I had books in hand by Ruth Ware, Megan Miranda, Chanel Cleeton, and Debra Sennefelder.

I paid for the books and then joined Cordelia over by the window again, where she was saying good-bye to Eddie. I gave the cat a pat too, and then we wandered out of the store.

"Joey and I talked to Nick this morning," I said once we were outside.

"Is he a suspect in the murder?" Cordelia asked with wide eyes.

"He's one of *my* suspects. I don't think there are any official ones other than Grayson." That fact still irked me, and likely would until the police accepted that he wasn't the guilty party.

Cordelia gave an exaggerated shiver. "A possible killer staying in my house?"

"There might not be any reason for concern," I said quickly. "Nick says he was in his room at the inn when Dominique was killed. I was wondering if you could confirm that."

She took a moment to think, and then smiled. "That's true. Phew! I'm glad he's not a killer."

"Are you sure he was there that evening?" I pressed, not wanting to leave any room for doubt.

"He got back to the inn around six-thirty. I remember because it was right after I sat down to read by the fire in the parlor."

"So you had a view of the front door," I said, picturing the layout of the main floor of the inn.

Cordelia nodded. "He was soaking wet when he arrived. He didn't have a jacket on, just a hoodie, and it had started pouring a little while earlier."

I remembered clearly the weather that night. The driving rain, rumbling thunder, and flashes of lightning seemed a fitting backdrop for the terrible events that unfolded at the brewery.

"I asked him if he needed anything," Cordelia continued. "He said he was fine and was heading up for the night. He had some takeout from the pizza parlor with him. We said good night, and he went upstairs. That's the last I saw of him until the next morning."

"But could he have left without you seeing him?" I asked. "Dominique was killed around seven o'clock."

Cordelia shook her head. "I was reading in the parlor until nearly ten. I couldn't put the book down until I'd finished it. Have you read *Reclaimed* by Sarah Guillory? It's so good."

"I read it a year or two ago," I said. "And I totally get why you couldn't put it down until you'd finished."

"Nothing was going to stop me. Not even—" Cordelia let out a yelp and hopped to the side.

Bird poop splatted onto the grass, right where Cordelia had been standing a split second earlier. Overhead, a pigeon flapped away from us.

"Nice save," I said.

Cordelia patted her hair as she fell into step with me again. "That was a little too close for comfort."

I tried to get my thoughts back on track. "You didn't leave the parlor at all on the night of the murder?"

"Not even to use the bathroom. I was there for over three hours. I got up once to light some candles, but I didn't have to leave the room to do that."

"Could he have gone down the back staircase and out through the kitchen?" I asked.

"Not without my grandma seeing him. She was baking that evening. I can ask her if she saw him, but she didn't mention that he'd gone out when she went up to bed around nine-thirty."

"Please do ask her."

"I will," Cordelia promised. Her gaze focused on something in the distance. "Who's that waving at us?"

We'd reached the edge of the village green. My mom stood over by the bandstand, waving.

I smiled. "That's my mom. Do you have time to meet her?"

"Sure," Cordelia said. "I'd love that."

We altered our path slightly so we'd meet up with my mom.

"Were you so into your book that you wouldn't have noticed someone coming or going?" I asked as we walked. Sometimes I could get so deep into a story that I didn't know what was going on in the world around me.

"I do forget where I am sometimes when I'm reading, but I didn't that night," Cordelia said. "Whenever the front door opened, a blast of cold, damp air hit me and the fire got a bit wild. Besides, the wood floors in the foyer and the stairs to the second floor are pretty creaky."

"What about coming and going through the window of his room?" I asked, not wanting to miss any holes in Nick's alibi. "Could that have been possible?"

"No way," Cordelia said without hesitation. "He's staying in the third-floor tower room. He probably would have broken his neck if he'd tried that. Especially with how rainy it was."

"Then I guess it's safe to cross him off my suspect list," I said.

"I'm glad. I wouldn't have been able to sleep tonight if I thought he was a murderer."

"I would have worried about you too, even though I'm pretty sure Dominique's murderer isn't someone out to kill random victims. And it's nice to finally shorten my suspect list, if only by one name."

"Is Grayson doing all right?" Cordelia asked.

"I wish I knew."

We'd reached the bandstand by then so I gave my mom a quick hug.

"Hi, Mom. This is my good friend Cordelia King. She runs the Creekside Inn with her grandmother." I pointed out the Queen Anne in the distance.

"I was admiring that house earlier," my mom said. "It's so nice to meet you, Cordelia."

"You too, Mrs. Coleman," Cordelia said with a smile.

"Would you like to join us for lunch today?" my mom asked her.

Cordelia looked disappointed. "I would love to, but I've got a long list of chores to do at the inn."

"Perhaps another day before I leave town then."

Cordelia's smile made a comeback. "I'd really like that."

"I'll text you later," I promised her.

We exchanged a few more words, and then Cordelia set off for home.

"I don't suppose you have any news about Grayson," my mom said as we walked slowly in the direction of Aunt Gilda's salon.

"No," I said glumly. "But I should check in with Jason." I dug my phone out of my purse. "He's the head of security at the brewery," I explained. "He's also Grayson's best friend."

"Does he know where Grayson is?"

"No. Grayson didn't tell anyone where he was going." I thought about the empty food containers I'd found in the attic of the vacant house, but I didn't bring that up. I didn't want to have to admit to my mom that I'd basically broken into the house to look for him.

I sent a quick text message to Jason, asking how Bowie was

doing. When we reached Aunt Gilda's salon my phone chimed, signaling a new message.

Bowie's good, Jason had written. **And the brewery's reopening today.**

That was one small bit of good news. At least Grayson's business wouldn't have to suffer more losses. As long as people weren't too scared to visit the place where someone had recently been murdered. Worry gnawed at my stomach. I hoped people wouldn't feel that way. It was bad enough that Grayson was hiding from the police. If the brewery suffered financially, that would be an extra blow.

I really wanted to ask Jason if he'd had any contact with Grayson since we'd last spoken, even though I knew it was unlikely. It wasn't a good idea to ask that by text messages, though.

"Would you like to check out Grayson's brewery this morning?" I asked my mom, thinking that might give me a chance to talk to Jason in person. "It would have been nicer if Grayson could have shown you around, but I'd still like you to see the place."

"That sounds like a lovely idea," my mom said. "Why don't we ask Gilda if she'd like to come?"

We found Aunt Gilda up in her apartment, folding laundry. When we told her our plans, she encouraged us to go to the brewery without her. She'd been there a few times before and wanted to get some household chores done.

According to the weather app on my phone, the afternoon would bring rain showers and possibly more thunderstorms. At the moment, however, the sky was only partly cloudy, with the most ominous of the dark clouds still off in the distance. My mom and I decided to chance it and walk the short distance to the brewery. Hopefully, we wouldn't end up regretting it.

On our way there, I took my mom along the private branch of Grayson's driveway so she could get a look at his house. I wondered if Bowie was inside, but I didn't peek through the windows to check. If he was there, I didn't want him to get excited only to be disappointed. I didn't have a key, so I couldn't let him out for a proper greeting.

When we reached the brewery buildings, I showed my mom the way to the tasting room. I waved at Caleb, who was pushing a dolly with kegs on it toward one of the other buildings. Seeing him reminded me of his sister, Alicia. I felt bad about the fact that I'd caused her to burst into tears at the cidery the day before. I hoped she was feeling better by now. If she wasn't the killer. If she had murdered Dominique, she didn't deserve to feel good.

I still needed to figure out if Alicia was a solid suspect. As nice as it was to have crossed Nick's name off my mental suspect list, removing a second name would be even better.

My mom and I spent close to an hour at the brewery, tasting the different craft beers and wandering around the store, which offered beer for sale along with miscellaneous gifts and merchandise that catered to the tourist crowd. My mom wasn't a beer drinker, so I thought she was a good sport for tasting the different brews. I didn't drink much beer myself, but when I did, it was beer brewed by Grayson. I knew enough to recognize how good his products were. Since before we started dating, and even before we were friends, I'd been serving his beer at the Inkwell. His brews were always popular with the local crowd and the tourists.

Unfortunately, Jason wasn't available for a chat while my mom and I were at the brewery. I'd have to try to meet up with him another time. I did collect one piece of information, though. As we walked down the driveway, I checked my phone and saw that Cordelia had texted me. She'd talked to Grace, her grandmother, as promised. No one had passed through the kitchen of the Creekside Inn on the evening of the murder. That helped to confirm Nick's alibi.

After a quiet lunch at Aunt Gilda's apartment, my mom and I walked around town, visiting some local stores, including Shontelle's gift shop. While we were there, we arranged with Shontelle to meet at Shady Creek Manor for tea the next afternoon. Kiandra wouldn't be able to join us because she was heading to a friend's birthday party right after school, but Shontelle's mother, Yvette, would come along. It happened that the tea would be the same day as my own birthday, a happy coincidence.

By the time we'd visited all the shops my mom was interested in, the first drops of rain had started to fall. We retreated to my apartment above the Inkwell and spent the afternoon chatting and drinking tea. My mom didn't have a critical word to say the whole day, and it warmed my heart to think she was starting to accept that I had a good life here in Shady Creek. If only she could meet Grayson so she'd have a complete picture of my new life. That would have to wait, but it *would* happen. I was going to make sure of that.

My mom borrowed an umbrella so she could walk through the now pouring rain to Aunt Gilda's apartment as darkness was falling. She was tired and ready for a quiet evening spent reading a book or watching television. I was tired too, thanks to my recent lack of quality sleep, but I was also restless, so I headed downstairs to the pub to help out with serving customers. I hoped that Alicia Jollimore might show up at the Inkwell, but I wasn't surprised when she didn't. She came by occasionally, but she wasn't a regular customer. I'd have to seek her out the next day, perhaps at the cidery.

After closing, when all the customers had left, I helped Damien clean up the pub. Eventually, I was the last person in the building. By the time I switched off the lights and headed upstairs, it was a minute or two past midnight. I thought I was finally tired enough that I might sleep soundly, despite the unsolved mystery that still troubled me.

At the top of the stairs, I opened my apartment door and flipped on the overhead light. Wimsey stood in the middle of the living room, looking at me. As I shut and locked the door, a floorboard creaked in my bedroom. I froze.

I stared at Wimsey. He stared back at me and then suddenly looked behind him.

A shadow moved in the doorway to my bedroom.

A scream rose up in my throat.

Chapter 23

"It's me, Sadie."

Those three words killed my scream before it broke free. My fear immediately changed to relief and elation.

Grayson stepped out of my bedroom, into the light.

A smile broke out across my face, but a shot of panic wiped it away.

I pressed a hand to my chest as I remembered with relief that I'd closed all the blinds and curtains in my apartment before heading downstairs.

"Are you okay? I didn't mean to scare you." Grayson crossed the distance between us.

I threw my arms around him and kissed him. "I'm fine." I put both hands to his face. "Are *you* okay?"

He was unshaven, with his stubble almost resembling a beard. He looked tired, with dark rings beneath his eyes, but otherwise he seemed in decent shape. His T-shirt was a bit rumpled, but he'd changed clothes since I'd last seen him.

"I'm fine too," he said. "Especially now. Happy birthday."

I hadn't even realized that it was now my birthday.

Grayson pulled me close for another kiss.

"Thank you, but you shouldn't be here." Even as I said that, I didn't let go of him. "How did you get in here without the police noticing? They've been watching the gristmill." My blood ran cold. "What if they saw you?"

This time Grayson put his hands to my face. "Shh. It's okay. No one knows I'm here."

"Are you sure?" The thought of the police knocking on the door and dragging him off to jail terrified me.

"Positive. The cops have been watching this place, but I've been watching them. They must have got called out to respond to a situation elsewhere, because they drove off in a hurry about an hour ago."

"What if other officers are watching from a different spot?"

He rested his hands on my shoulders. "They aren't. I made sure of it. I guess the fact that we've got a small police department here is working in our favor at the moment."

"And no one else saw you?" I asked, wanting to be absolutely sure.

"Nobody. I cut through the forest and came in through the back door."

"You picked the lock?" I hadn't given him a key to my place, although that was something I'd thought about doing.

He pulled me closer again, wrapping his arms around me. "You don't mind, do you?"

"No. And I'd mind even less if you taught me how to do that."

His low rumble of laughter nearly made my heart burst. I was so happy to have him there with me.

"Maybe I will," he said into my ear. "One day."

I decided that conversation could wait.

"You must be hungry," I said. "Have you been eating?"

"Not much."

I surrendered my hold on him so I could open the fridge.

"Have you had any sleep?" I asked as I gathered up sandwich fixings and set them on the counter. "Did you find another place to stay after you left the house next door?"

"The house next door?" He sounded puzzled.

I shut the fridge and turned to face him. "The vacant house. You were staying there, right? Some local teens thought you were a ghost. I figured with them poking around you decided to find another hiding place."

"I was never there," Grayson said.

"Really?" I'd been so sure that I'd located his hideout, a day too late to find him there.

"I've been staying out in the woods."

I was still taken aback by the fact that it wasn't him who'd been in the attic of the house next door, but I pushed my surprise to the back burner. "In the woods? How have you stayed dry in the rain?"

"I had shelter," he assured me.

His stomach gave a loud growl. The sound reminded me of what I'd set out to do.

"Is a sandwich okay?" I asked as I pulled half a loaf of bread out of the breadbox. "Or I could cook you something."

Grayson snaked his arms around my waist from behind me. "A sandwich would be great, but I really just wanted to see you and wish you a happy birthday."

I turned around in his arms so I could see his face. I couldn't get enough of looking at him. "And I'm really, *really* glad you're here. But your stomach says you need a good meal." I tugged a lock of his dark hair, which had lost its usual luster. "And you could use a shower."

"I won't say no to either of those."

I got back to work on the sandwich. Grayson grabbed a

knife and sliced a tomato and some cheese while I buttered the bread and added slices of roast turkey. I ended up grabbing two more slices of bread and putting together a second sandwich. That one I packed in a brown paper bag for Grayson to take with him.

When his stomach gave another loud growl, I dug out the half-dozen chocolate chip cookies that remained of the dozen I'd bought from the local bakery a few days earlier. I added three of them to the plate with Grayson's sandwich and tucked the others into the paper bag.

"Don't leave without this," I said as I put the paper bag in the fridge for the time being.

Before shutting the fridge, I grabbed a can of root beer.

Grayson was at the kitchen table, already at work devouring his sandwich. I passed him the root beer and poured him a glass of ice water before sitting down across from him.

"We should compare notes," I said.

He downed half the glass of water in one go. "Before we do that, do you know how Bowie's doing?"

"He's good. I haven't seen him, but Jason says he's doing well."

"I hope he doesn't think I've abandoned him." Grayson had adopted the German shepherd from a shelter two years ago. He and the dog adored each other.

"I bet he knows you'll come back," I said. "And he'll be so excited when you do."

Grayson nodded as he ate, but his eyes had grown somber. I hoped he wasn't doubting that we'd be able to clear his name.

"What have you found out so far?" he asked before I had a chance to question him on his thoughts.

As he continued to eat, I outlined my suspects and everything I knew about them.

Grayson listened carefully as he polished off his sandwich

and the cookies. He'd downed the rest of the water and most of the root beer by the time he spoke again.

"You've been busy," he said.

"Not busy enough." I sighed. "I still haven't found the real killer."

Grayson reached across the table for my hand. "We will."

"What have you found out?" I asked, returning the pressure when he gave my hand a squeeze. "What were you looking up at the library?"

Grayson's surprise lasted only a split second and was quickly replaced by a smile. "You know about that?"

"I figured if you wanted Internet access, you'd have to go there. I was watching for you one night, but then a girl screamed and I went to see what was happening. When I got back to the library, I saw you leaving, but I couldn't catch up to you."

"I didn't realize you were there," he said with disappointment. "I was worried the scream might draw the attention of the police parked in my driveway."

"I think it did. Those were the teens who thought they heard a ghost in the house next door."

"Maybe it was a transient staying there for a night or two."

"Could be," I said. "But one of the cashiers at the grocery store saw a well-dressed woman picking food out of the dumpster. I found empty containers from the grocery store in the attic. The woman might have been the one in the vacant house."

"Maybe someone local has fallen on hard times," Grayson suggested, as one of the women at the grocery store had done.

The cashier hadn't recognized the dumpster diver, but that didn't necessarily mean that she wasn't a local woman. I shoved those thoughts aside.

There were more pressing things to worry about at the moment.

"What leads do you have?" I asked.

"I found out some of the same things as you did," Grayson said. "Like the fact that Nick Perry went to college with Dominique. And both their paths have crossed with Phoebe Ramone's, Nick's in a personal way and Dominique's in a professional capacity. Maybe I'm way off base, but I can't help but think that everything has something to do with Samantha. Dominique was her best friend until shortly before the houseboat explosion. If Dominique knew Nick Perry back then, maybe Samantha did too."

"And Phoebe dated Nick, so she could have known Samantha. Dominique sought you out, and three people who knew or might have known Samantha showed up here in Shady Creek at the same time."

"Exactly. But the only plausible connection I've come up with is that maybe Dominique didn't kill Samantha."

"But you were so sure she did. And even if she didn't, even if she knew who did, why not go to the Fenworth police? Why come looking for you?"

Grayson scrubbed a hand down his face and I was struck again by how tired he looked.

"I'm not sure," he said. "I'm not even ready to believe that Dominique didn't kill Sam. But if she didn't, maybe she didn't feel safe going to the police for some reason."

"Okay. But if that was the case, what do Nick and Phoebe have to do with it? Were they involved in Samantha's death in any way?"

"I have no reason to think so. I did some digging into Nick's past, and Phoebe's too. Aside from a few speeding tickets, it looks like Phoebe's been living life pretty much on the straight and narrow. Nick got busted for possessing marijuana several years ago, but other than that his record is clean. He's got a cousin who is serving time for murder, but I couldn't find anything to suggest that the two of them had much to do with each other."

"Could Nick's cousin have had something to do with Samantha's death?"

Grayson shook his head and leaned back in his chair. "He was already locked up at the time of the explosion."

"Nick's a dead end, anyway," I said. "He's got an alibi for the time of the murder."

"That's good to know." Grayson drained the last of the root beer from the can. "Is it okay if I take that shower now?"

I pushed back my chair. "I'll get you fresh towels."

While Grayson was in the shower, I switched on a lamp next to my bed and turned off the overhead light in the living room. If the police were watching the gristmill again, I wanted them to think I was going to bed as usual. I peeked out the eastern window, careful not to move the curtains much, but it was too dark outside to tell if anyone was watching from the brewery's driveway.

When Grayson emerged from the bathroom with damp hair, I slipped my arms around him and rested my head against his chest. If I'd missed him while he was taking a shower, how was I supposed to live without him for however long it would take to clear his name? I didn't want to think about that.

Grayson held me close as I listened to the beat of his heart. We stood like that for a long moment before he spoke.

"I should get going," he said quietly into my ear.

"No," I whispered, not letting go of him.

He made no move to release me either. "I shouldn't be here at all."

"I'm glad you are."

"So am I. But the longer I stay, the greater the risk."

I knew that was true, but I still couldn't bring myself to let him go.

"Please stay," I said. "Just a while longer."

Even as I spoke the words, I knew I shouldn't have asked that of him.

Reluctantly, I stepped back.

He took my hands and tugged me closer again.

"I'll stay," he said.

Then he kissed me in a way that made me forget about all our troubles.

Chapter 24

I sat up like a shot, my heart beating so hard I thought it might burst out of my chest.

My first thought was that the police were here to haul Grayson off to jail. It took half a second for me to realize that his side of the bed was empty. Something had woken me abruptly, but I wasn't sure what until my apartment's buzzer sounded for what had to be the second time.

I threw back the blankets and ran out into the living room.

"Grayson?" I whispered.

Even as I spoke his name, I knew he was no longer there.

I peeked into the bathroom, anyway, just to be sure.

Empty.

The buzzer rang again, grating on my nerves. I hurried across the room, stubbing my toe on the coffee table on the way.

"Oh, for the love of Frodo!" I grumbled as I hobbled over to the intercom.

"Yes?" I might have sounded grumpy, but I couldn't help it.

"Ms. Coleman, it's Detective Marquez. May I speak with you?"

My heart rate picked up again. Had Grayson been caught

sneaking away from the gristmill? Was Detective Marquez going to arrest me for aiding and abetting a murder suspect?

"Just a moment," I said into the intercom.

I dashed back into my bedroom and grabbed my robe. As I pulled it on over my pajamas, I surveyed the room for any signs that Grayson had been there. The only potential give-away I could see was the indent in the pillow next to mine. I fluffed up the pillow and straightened the blankets on one side so it looked as though I was the only person who had slept in the bed.

On my way back to the door, I ducked into the bathroom. A set of fresh, unused towels sat on the counter. All the other towels were in the washing machine outside of the bathroom. The washing cycle had already finished.

Grayson had thought of everything.

I checked the kitchen as well. I'd cleaned up Grayson's dishes the night before, and a quick peek in the fridge told me that he'd remembered to take the second sandwich with him. I didn't know what time he'd left my apartment, but I hoped he'd done so under the cover of darkness and had managed to slip away unseen.

With a heavy sense of trepidation, I hurried downstairs. I felt a hint of relief when I saw that Detective Marquez was the only person waiting outside the gristmill's back door. She had a tablet in hand, but no handcuffs that I could see. Still, I wondered if my relief was premature. Maybe there were other officers around the corner of the building, waiting for word from Marquez to come and arrest me.

The detective took in the sight of my robe and tousled hair. "Did I wake you?"

"Yes." I wasn't in the mood to provide a more polite answer.

"I'm sorry about that."

I couldn't tell if the apology was sincere or not.

"May I come in?" she asked.

I wasn't keen to let her into my apartment. Even though I was pretty sure Grayson had left no visible signs of his presence, I still worried that he and I both might have missed something that the detective's sharp eyes would pick up on.

I decided on a compromise. I stepped back to let her in the building, but when I shut the door behind her, I didn't lead the way upstairs. Instead, I opened the door to the pub.

"I'm afraid I don't even have a pot of coffee going yet," I said as I pulled out a chair at the nearest table. I sank down into it, realizing that my legs were trembling slightly. I still wasn't entirely sure why the detective was here, and that had me worried.

"That's fine," Marquez assured me. "I won't take up much of your time."

"Is this about Grayson?" I couldn't keep the fear out of my voice when I asked my next question. "Have you arrested him?"

"Mr. Blake's whereabouts are still unknown." Marquez took a seat across from me. "Unless you have new information to share?"

I shook my head.

"Can you tell me if Mr. Blake owns a rain jacket?" she asked.

I knew where this line of questioning was going. I didn't want to give the detective any information that would help her build an even stronger case against Grayson. At the same time, I knew Grayson wouldn't want me to lie to her. And I doubted I could convince her of anything other than the truth. Considering my close relationship with Grayson and the recent weather, she probably wouldn't find my answer plausible if I said I had no knowledge of any rain jacket owned by him.

"Yes," I said, the word tasting bitter in my mouth.

"And what color is it?"

I had to force the answer out of me. "Black."

"We weren't able to locate a rain jacket when we searched Mr. Blake's house."

"He probably took it with him when he went . . . wherever he went," I said. "It's been raining a lot lately."

Detective Marquez didn't give me any indication of what she thought of my answer. She set her tablet on the table. "There's something I'd like to show you." She tapped the screen a couple of times and then propped the tablet up in its holder. The surveillance footage from the brewery started to play.

"I've already seen this," I said as I watched Dominique enter the building where Grayson and I had found her. I glanced at the detective, but she didn't seem surprised by what I'd said.

"Can you identify this individual?" She pointed to the mystery person following Dominique into the building.

"No. I can't even tell if it's a man or woman. I saw the footage on a bigger screen before and I still couldn't identify them. I only know that it's not me and it's not Grayson."

"But you have no evidence to prove that it wasn't him." It was a statement, not a question.

"I have suspects," I said. "George and Miranda Keeler. Phoebe Ramone."

I would have continued, but the detective cut me off.

"Sadie, I hope you're not attempting to find evidence to help Mr. Blake."

"If I don't clear Grayson's name, who will?"

"You need to leave the investigating to the professionals."

It wasn't the first time she'd said that to me.

I so badly wanted to remind her that the professionals weren't investigating, at least not in the way they should have been. They might be searching for evidence to strengthen the case against Grayson, but I doubted they were actively looking into other possible suspects.

With great effort, I kept quiet. I wasn't in the mood to argue with the detective.

"Was there anything else?" I asked.

Detective Marquez regarded me with her dark eyes for a

long moment before speaking again. "I wanted to ask you about the house next door."

I crossed my arms over my stomach as a chill ran through me. I hoped I wasn't being backed into a corner of some sort. If the police had seen me sneak into the vacant house and wanted to arrest me for trespassing, wouldn't they have done that already? I wasn't entirely sure of the answer to that question.

"What about it?" I asked, doing my best to sound unconcerned.

"Have you noticed any activity over there recently?"

"I heard a scream a couple of nights ago," I said. "When I went to have a look, I saw some teenagers running away from the house. Or at least from that general direction." I didn't mention where I'd been when that had occurred. "I figured it was simply pre-Halloween silliness. Was it something more serious?"

"No, we don't believe there was anything more to that incident. However, it seems someone has been camping out in the attic."

"And you think it was Grayson?"

"We certainly consider that a possibility. Whoever was staying there has moved on, it seems." Detective Marquez got up from the table. "I won't keep you any longer. I apologize again for waking you."

I didn't relax until I had the door locked behind her. Dancing around the subject of Grayson had left me drained. And hungry. Upstairs, I quickly showered and dressed before eating a bowl of oatmeal for breakfast. My plan was to drive out to the cidery and attempt to speak to Alicia again. I hoped I'd have more luck this time. If I made her cry again, I might get banned from the cidery, something I didn't want to happen.

The cidery wouldn't open for a while yet, and I had to stick close to the pub until midmorning anyhow. I was expecting a delivery from the Spirit Hill Brewery and needed to be on hand when it arrived. In the meantime, I parked myself in my small office and took care of some of the administrative matters that had been building up while I was enjoying time off with my mom.

When I headed outside to meet the delivery man bringing kegs of beer to the pub, I saw an opportunity to gather more information. Caleb Jollimore was the deliveryman that morning. Since the gristmill was separated from the road by the creek, he had to wheel the kegs across the footbridge and around the back of the building using a dolly. When he arrived with the first load, I held the door open for him.

"Your sister works at the cidery, right?" I asked after we'd exchanged greetings. "I was thinking of heading out there this morning. Maybe I'll see her there."

"She's not working today," Caleb said as I followed him to the storage room, where he unloaded the kegs. "It's her day off."

So much for my morning sleuthing plan. Caleb headed back to the truck to pick up another load of kegs. While he was gone, I tried to figure out a way I could ask him about Alicia's whereabouts without sounding like I was prying. Since I hardly knew Alicia, and didn't know Caleb much better, I didn't see a way to go about that without coming off as a nosey Parker.

Maybe I needed to approach things from a different angle.

"How are things running at the brewery with Grayson absent?" I asked when Caleb returned with more kegs.

"Smoothly, as far as I can tell." He brought the dolly to a stop. "I'm sorry about the mess Grayson is in. That woman keeps causing trouble, even after her death."

"What kind of trouble did she cause while she was alive?" I asked, pretending to have no clue.

Caleb got to work unloading the kegs. "She was a dream crusher."

"Really? Whose dreams did she crush?" I worried that Caleb

might clam up on me, but I followed him as he wheeled his empty dolly toward the door, and he kept the conversation going.

"George Keeler's, for one. His restaurant went bust after that woman tore it apart in a review. And my sister's."

I continued following Caleb out the door and around the building.

"What kind of dream of your sister's did Dominique ruin?"

Caleb parked the dolly by the back of his delivery truck. "Alicia wanted to be a writer. When Dominique was in town a few years back, Alicia asked her to read some of her work."

"And she declined?" I guessed.

"I wish she had." Caleb loaded another keg onto the dolly. "She read what Alicia had written, and then she told my sister she had no talent and had no chance of a career as a writer."

I winced as I followed him back into the building. "That was harsh."

"That's an understatement. Being a writer was all Alicia ever wanted. Now she's working a dead-end job and won't dare to dream about achieving anything better. And she *did* have talent as a writer. I might not be a professional, but I know she could have made a career out of it, if only that witch hadn't shattered her hopes and confidence."

"Poor Alicia."

No wonder she was upset by Dominique's reappearance in town, even several years after her first encounter with the food writer. I felt even worse about making her cry the other day. Then I reminded myself that I still didn't know if she was innocent. Everything Caleb had told me strengthened her motive for murder. Alicia was still clearly distraught about her previous encounter with Dominique, so it wasn't much of a stretch to imagine her wanting to exact revenge on the woman who'd crushed her dreams.

I wanted to ask Caleb if he knew if his sister had an alibi for the time of the murder, but I couldn't come up with a way to ask that without revealing that I suspected her. I doubted Caleb would take kindly to me considering his sister as a possible killer. When he left the Inkwell a few minutes later, I still hadn't figured out a tactful way to ask the alibi question.

Frustration simmered inside me as Caleb drove away. I had more information, but I still needed to talk to Alicia, and I didn't know where to find her. At least I knew not to waste my time by driving out to the cidery.

Not knowing what to do with myself for the rest of the morning now that I'd scrapped my original plan, I wandered over to Aunt Gilda's salon. Her friend and coworker, Betty, was accepting payment from a client as I arrived.

"Happy birthday, Sadie!" she said to me as she handed over some change to the other woman. "Your aunt and mom are up-stairs."

I smiled at her. "Thanks, Betty."

"Do you have any special plans for today?" she asked as I crossed the salon.

"Tea at Shady Creek Manor."

"That sounds lovely. Have a good time."

I thanked her again and headed into the back, where a stair-case led up to the apartment. After climbing two steps, I paused and turned around. When I poked my head back into the salon, I saw that Betty's client had left. She was now alone in the salon, sweeping up hair clippings.

"Hey, Betty," I said. "Do you happen to know Alicia Jol-limore?"

Betty paused in her sweeping. "Slightly. Gilda cuts her hair every so often. Such a sad story."

"What's a sad story?" I asked, intrigued. I had a feeling she wasn't talking about Alicia's broken dreams.

"Alicia's parents both died in a car accident when she was in her early teens."

"That's terrible," I said with a wave of sympathy for the young woman and her brother.

"Tragic," Betty said with a nod. She started sweeping again. "Her older brother, Caleb, was about nineteen or twenty when their parents died. He took over raising Alicia."

A lump of guilt settled in my stomach. Here I was suspecting the poor girl of murder when she'd already been through so much. Of course, she did have a motive to kill Dominique, and her tragic past didn't eliminate the possibility that she was a murderer.

Nevertheless, I decided I needed to be gentle in my questioning, if I ever saw her face-to-face again in the course of my investigation. If she was innocent, I didn't want to upset her any more than I already had.

"Do you know where I might find her?" I asked Betty. "There's something I need to talk to her about."

Betty swept the clippings into a dustpan. "She works at the cidery."

"It's her day off, apparently," I said. "I wasn't sure where else to find her."

"She and her brother still live in the family home. It's on the corner of Yew Street and Ashcroft Road. A two-story white house with blue trim."

"I'll stop by there sometime. Thanks, Betty."

As much as I wanted to head straight to the Jollimore house to see if Alicia was home, I figured I'd better visit my mom and aunt first. If Betty mentioned to them that I'd stopped by but had left without seeing them, they might ask me where I'd gone. I didn't want to give them any reason to suspect that I was searching for a killer. Aunt Gilda probably knew I wouldn't be able to leave the case alone, but I didn't need to confirm any suspicions she might have. I preferred to avoid any lectures about minding my own business, and I didn't want either my mom or my aunt to worry.

I heard laughter when I reached the top of the steps. I tapped on the door and let myself in. My mom and Aunt Gilda were seated at the kitchen table, cups of tea in front of them.

As soon as they saw me, they both jumped up and hurried over to hug me and wish me a happy birthday. I soaked up the love and good wishes, so happy that my mom was in town to spend my birthday with me. In fact, I was so happy in that moment that I almost forgot that I was itching to keep investigating Dominique's murder.

Chapter 25

"Come and open your presents," my mom said as she led the way into Gilda's living room.

"You didn't have to get me any presents," I protested.

My mom and aunt both waved off that statement.

Aunt Gilda pressed one of the wrapped presents into my hands. I sat down on the couch and tore off the paper. My aunt had bought me a gray jersey dress that I'd admired through the window of a local shop recently. It was exactly the type of dress I liked to wear while working at the pub—comfy and casual without being *too* casual. My mom had bought me a set of silver earrings with a matching bracelet. I loved the presents and hugged both my mom and aunt.

I stayed a while longer, enjoying a cup of coffee and a chat, before I set off to the Inkwell with my gifts in hand. I'd meet up again with my aunt and mom to drive over to the manor for tea later, but in the meantime, I planned to chase down more information.

I dropped off my gifts at my apartment and spent a minute or two cuddling with Wimsey before leaving the gristmill again. The Jollimore house wasn't far, so I traveled there on foot, hoping I'd find Alicia at home. Finding the house Betty had described was easy. The white, two-story home with blue trim looked well maintained, and the grass was neatly trimmed. A man down the street was out mowing his lawn, but otherwise the street was quiet. I climbed the steps to the front porch and knocked on the door. My hopes sank with every second that passed without a response. I noticed a doorbell and rang that. I heard the bell chime inside the house, but I still received no response.

Maybe I'd have to come back another day. The loss of time irked me, though. The longer it took me to solve Dominique's murder, the longer Grayson had to remain in hiding.

I was about to leave but decided to check around back first. I didn't want to get accused of trespassing, so instead of going through the gate into the backyard, I walked around the end of the street to the back alley. When I reached the white picket fence that bordered Alicia and Caleb's backyard, I was glad I hadn't given up.

Alicia was kneeling at the edge of a flower bed, planting bulbs. Since I didn't want her running off in tears again, I didn't hail her until I was in the midst of opening the gate.

"Alicia?" I said as I stepped into the yard. "It's Sadie Coleman from the Inkwell."

Alicia looked surprised when she saw me, but she didn't burst into tears or run off, so I figured that was a good start.

She got to her feet and brushed dirt from the knees of her jeans as I approached her.

"What are you doing here?" she asked, watching me with wariness in her eyes.

"I've come to apologize," I said quickly. "I didn't mean to upset you the other day at the cidery."

Alicia glanced down at the flower beds she'd planted. "I appreciate the apology, but I probably overreacted at the time. You took me by surprise."

"I should have been more sensitive," I said, relieved that she seemed receptive to my apology. "I know now that your history with Dominique is one that you understandably wouldn't want to talk about."

She met my gaze with a hint of surprise. "Someone told you about that?"

"Your brother mentioned how she crushed your dream of becoming a writer."

Alicia's cheeks flushed. "I wish he hadn't told you that."

"I'm sorry."

She shook her head. "Never mind. I'm just embarrassed about it. I should be over it by now."

"I don't know about that," I said. "What Dominique did was cruel. If being a writer was what you had envisioned for your future, it's understandable that her words would have hit you hard."

Alicia shrugged, aiming for casual dismissal, but I detected a shimmer of tears in her eyes before she quickly blinked them away.

"Silly dreams of a teenager, I guess," she said.

"You don't know that."

"Dominique seemed to think so, and she was a professional."

"One known for being unnecessarily unkind, at least back then. And besides, that's only one opinion. Writers get rejected all the time, but that doesn't mean they don't ever achieve their dreams. What kind of writer were you hoping to be?"

"I wanted to write fantasy novels for teens."

"There you go," I said, hoping I could prove my point. "Dominique was a food writer. She probably didn't know anything about writing fantasy novels."

"Maybe not." Alicia didn't sound convinced.

I decided to get to the real reason for my visit. "I know you saw Dominique at the pub last week. Did you run into her any other time before she died?"

"No. If I'd seen her walking along the street, I would have crossed to the other side. I didn't want anything to do with her."

"Then I guess you wouldn't have any idea about who might have killed her."

"Of course not. I hear the police think it was my brother's boss, Grayson Blake. I don't really know Mr. Blake, but Caleb believes he's innocent and that's good enough for me. He's your boyfriend, right?"

I nodded. "I'm trying to clear his name."

"I wasn't anywhere near the brewery that night. I was out for pizza with friends. Caleb was working that evening, but he left before Dominique was found and didn't know anything had happened until the next morning. He was so shocked."

Was he? I wondered. *How upset was he on his sister's behalf? Was he angry enough at Dominique to lash out and kill her?*

I stifled a groan. I wanted to eliminate people from my suspect list, not add more names.

I refocused my thoughts. "The Inkwell hosts a writers' group. You should think about joining."

"I don't know about that," Alicia said. "I haven't written anything in years."

"Maybe it's time to change that."

She didn't say no outright, but she didn't seem ready to say yes either.

"It's an open invitation," I told her. "I'll leave you to your gardening."

As I walked away from the Jollimore house, I considered my next move. I needed to stop by the bank but decided I'd visit the local pizza parlor afterward. I was hoping somebody there could confirm Alicia's alibi for the night of Dominique's murder. Now that I'd talked with Alicia, I really hoped she wasn't the killer. She seemed like a nice young woman, and it was such a shame that the harsh words of one person had completely derailed her quest to follow her dreams. I really hoped she'd try writing again, whether or not she joined the Inkwell's group.

It didn't take me long to get finished at the bank, and from there I headed straight for Spice and Slice. My stomach was rumbling with hunger, but I didn't want to eat a large lunch. I needed to save room for all the delicious treats I knew I'd be eating at Shady Creek Manor later on. One slice of pizza wouldn't hurt, though. That would be enough to tide me over until tea time. Besides, I figured I might have a better chance of getting information out of the pizza parlor employees if I was a paying customer.

It was nearly noon when I arrived at the restaurant. The place was fairly busy, but there were several stools free at the counter. I claimed one and picked up a menu. Instead of reading it, I glanced around. I recognized one of the waitresses who was busy serving customers. Her name was Amy, and she'd served me and my friends several times in the past when we'd eaten at Spice and Slice.

After carrying a stack of empty plates into the kitchen, Amy stopped by the counter to take my order. I requested a slice of Veggie Heaven pizza and a glass of sweet tea.

"Do you know Alicia Jollimore?" I asked Amy as she jotted down my order.

"I know who she is, but that's about it. I think Jenny's friends with her."

"Friends with who?" Jenny appeared by Amy's side. She was a few years younger than Amy and had her dark hair tied back in a long, sleek ponytail.

"Alicia Jollimore," Amy said. To me she added, "I'll have your drink for you in a moment."

"You know Alicia?" Jenny asked.

"Not well, but I was talking to her earlier. She said she was here on the night of the murder."

Jenny nodded, her eyes wide. "I was working that night. Alicia was here with a bunch of friends. We didn't have a clue that anything bad had happened. I didn't even hear any sirens. Of course, the thunder was pretty loud. We were lucky we didn't lose power like some parts of town did." She flicked her ponytail over her shoulder. "What were you talking about that night?"

"Alicia had an unpleasant history with the woman who died," I said. "I was thinking that it was good she had an alibi. You know, so the police won't suspect her of having anything to do with it."

Jenny's eyes widened again. "Oh my gosh! You're right! That really is a good thing. I know what happened with Alicia and the food writer. It's terrible that she was murdered, but she wasn't a nice person."

Someone called Jenny's name from the kitchen.

"Oops!" she said. "Gotta go!"

She dashed into the kitchen and out of sight.

Amy appeared seconds later with my drink and my slice of pizza.

As I ate my lunch, I struck Alicia's name off my mental list of suspects.

Unfortunately, I added her brother's name in her place. I didn't want Caleb to be a killer, but I couldn't discount the possibility.

I thought back to the security footage from the night of the murder. Caleb had left the brewery building where Dominique was killed moments before she appeared on the video, heading inside. Maybe he'd spotted her and followed her back to the building.

He was wearing coveralls when he walked off screen, but he could have grabbed a dark jacket from his car before going after Dominique.

Maybe Jason had security footage of the parking lot. That might help me figure out if Caleb had driven away or simply retrieved a jacket from his vehicle.

I made a mental note to talk to Jason soon, and then I considered my other suspects as I enjoyed my delicious pizza. It seemed too coincidental that Dominique, Nick, and Phoebe ended up here in Shady Creek at the same time when they'd possibly all known each other back in their college days. I definitely needed to keep investigating Phoebe.

Then there was George Keeler and his wife, Miranda. George was hiding something, and I needed to find out what.

So much work left to do.

I pulled out my phone and found Dominique's Instagram account. Most of her photos were of food and restaurants. Not surprising, considering her profession. Occasionally, a photo showed Dominique with friends, but I didn't recognize any of the other people.

As I sipped at my drink, I found Phoebe's account and scrolled through her photos. She had plenty of pictures of food and restaurants too, but she'd also posted a lot of selfies and pictures of people at parties. Again, I didn't recognize anyone other than Phoebe.

I tucked my phone away and finished the last sip of my drink. Phoebe was staying at Shady Creek Manor, the same place I'd be having tea that afternoon. My hope was that I could squeeze in some sleuthing while enjoying time with my friends and family. Maybe some birthday luck would turn up a juicy clue or two.

I left the pizza parlor feeling upbeat and optimistic. If I could cross more names off my suspect list—without adding new ones—maybe Grayson would be back to living his normal life by Halloween.

Chapter 26

Shady Creek Manor sat on an expansive property at the edge of town. The stone mansion, once a private residence, had been converted into a hotel by the current owners, Gemma and Brad Honeywell. I admired the view from the backseat of Aunt Gilda's car as we drove up the long driveway. It was a beautiful day, and the hotel grounds looked amazing, as they always did. The grass was a lush shade of green and although the flowers in the gardens weren't currently in bloom, everything was neat and tidy and well looked after.

Even though I'd had a frightening experience at the manor during the May Day masquerade a few months ago, I knew I'd enjoy the afternoon tea. The first time I'd returned after the masquerade, I'd felt uneasy for a while, but I'd eventually relaxed. Now I liked to think that I'd put the bad experience from the masquerade behind me.

Gilda parked in the lot next to the hotel and, as I climbed out of the car, I spotted Shontelle's red sedan three spots away from ours. My mom, Aunt Gilda, and I hurried around to the main entrance, then climbed the wide stone steps to the double doors.

We found Shontelle and her mom, Yvette, waiting for us in the lobby.

"I hope we didn't keep you waiting long," I said after I'd introduced my mom to Yvette.

"We got here just a minute or two before you," Shontelle assured me.

Aunt Gilda had reserved a table for us, in case the place was busy, and Gemma Honeywell took us straight to the dining room. Soon we were enjoying cups of tea along with finger sandwiches, scones, chocolate-dipped strawberries, cakes, tarts, and macarons.

I desperately wanted to share the fact that I'd seen Grayson, but I knew I needed to keep that to myself. I trusted everyone at the table, but I couldn't be absolutely sure that I wouldn't be overheard, and I didn't want to put my friends or family in an awkward position if the police happened to ask them if they had any knowledge of Grayson's recent movements or whereabouts.

As much as it disappointed me to keep that news to myself, my spirits were still buoyed by the late-night visit, and I spent the meal chatting happily and enjoying the company of those around me. My mom and Yvette seemed to hit it off, and that brought me even more happiness. I wanted my mom to fit well into my life here in Shady Creek, even if she would only be a visitor now and then.

By the time there were only a few treats remaining on the tiered plates, I was no longer quite as relaxed as when we sat down. My mind had drifted from the tea and conversation and was now focused on finding a way to do some investigating while at the manor. I considered waiting until we'd all finished eating before slipping away under the pretense of needing to use the washroom, but I was afraid that someone else might decide to do the same, leaving me no chance to go anywhere other than the restroom.

While everyone chatted about the food and drink festival, I

excused myself and made my way out of the dining room. To my relief, the lobby was empty, with nobody stationed behind the reception desk. I paused on the marble floor, listening for approaching footsteps or nearby voices. All I could hear was the low murmur of conversation coming from the dining room.

With my pulse fluttering, I dashed behind the desk and nudged the computer mouse, bringing the screen alive. I quickly located the hotel's management software. Fortunately, it was easy to get into, not requiring a password, and it took me only a matter of seconds to locate Phoebe Ramone's room number: 204.

I closed the program and hurried out from behind the desk, making a beeline for the main staircase. When I reached the top of the steps, I peered down the second-floor hallway, first to the left, then to the right. The place was deserted.

As I crept along the hall toward room 204, I wished yet again that Grayson had taught me how to pick locks. Although, I wasn't sure if any of his techniques would work with the hotel room doors, which used electronic key cards. I hesitated near the elevator alcove and considered retracing my path to the lobby. Maybe I could find a master key card behind the reception desk.

I was still considering that plan when a housekeeper dressed in a gray and white uniform pushed a cart off the elevator. I smiled at her and resumed walking down the hall, trying to look as though I belonged there. When I glanced over my shoulder, I noticed the housekeeping cart parked outside room 207.

Reaching Phoebe's door, I realized I didn't know whether she was in her room or not. I thought I heard a rustle of movement on the other side of the door, but it was so faint that I wondered if I'd imagined it. I knocked, hoping for no response, not sure what I would say if Phoebe opened the door. Fortunately, it stayed firmly shut and I didn't hear any further sounds coming from inside the room.

Trying to appear casual, I sauntered down the hall, smiling

when I saw the housekeeping cart still parked out in the hall. The maid wasn't in sight, which I considered a good thing. The door to room 207 stood open. Quietly, I crept closer.

I couldn't believe my luck. The housekeeper's master key sat unattended next to a pile of clean hand towels. I took a quick peek into room 207. The maid was in the process of remaking the bed and didn't notice me.

My heart was beating so fast that I thought I might pass out, but I didn't have time for such dramatics. I grabbed the key card, sprinted down the hall to room 204, and slid the card into the lock. I heard a click and when I turned the handle the door opened. I peeked into the room and found it empty.

Knowing I could get caught at any second, I kicked off my shoes and used one of them to prop the door open. Then I dashed down the hall, replaced the card, and darted back to Phoebe's room. I grabbed my shoes, slipped inside the room, and shut the door, all without anyone noticing me.

After replacing my shoes on my feet, I leaned against the door and breathed out a sigh of relief. Sleuthing could be stressful at times.

I pushed off from the door and surveyed the room. I didn't want to get caught snooping, so I needed to get my search over with quickly. Dropping to my knees, I peered under the queen bed. There was nothing there aside from a few dust bunnies that had been missed by housekeeping. I checked the bedside tables next, but the drawers were empty and the only things on top of the small tables were a lamp, a sleep mask, and a romance novel.

Next, I checked the small desk over by the window. The drawers on the left side held some hotel stationery and a pen, but nothing else. A closed laptop sat on the surface of the desk. It powered up when I opened it, but then it prompted me to input a password.

I definitely wasn't a hacker and I didn't know what I expected to find on Phoebe's laptop, anyway, so I decided it was pointless to waste my time with it. I shut the laptop and checked the drawers on the desk's right side. In the top one I found another laptop. This one was dark blue and covered with an assortment of stickers. Why Phoebe needed two laptops, I didn't know. She was a freelance writer; otherwise I might have assumed that one was her personal computer while the other was provided by her employer.

I set the blue laptop on the desk and opened it, but as with the other computer, it wouldn't give me access without a password. Trying not to get too frustrated, I put the laptop back in the drawer and set my sights on the closet.

I didn't know what it was I was looking for, but I hoped I'd know when I found it. *If* I found it.

I'd overheard Phoebe say that Dominique had accused her of stealing Dominique's Gucci scarf. Phoebe had basically denied the accusation in the same breath, but I wasn't entirely sure if I should believe her. Maybe she stole the scarf as a way of lashing out at her rival, and then her behavior escalated to murder.

A bit of a stretch, maybe, but at this point I was willing to consider almost anything. I wasn't limiting my search to the scarf, though. There was a good chance that all of the petty thefts in town were linked and had nothing to do with the murder, so I was looking for anything that might strengthen Phoebe's motive to kill Dominique or link her to the murder in some way.

I paused in front of the closet as a tickling sensation ran up the back of my neck. I listened carefully, but heard nothing.

Reminding myself to hurry, I opened the closet door.

A hand clapped over my mouth before I could scream.

"It's okay," Grayson whispered before dropping his hand.

"Sweet Sherlock!" I exclaimed in a loud whisper. "You nearly gave me a heart attack!" I pressed my hand over my heart, which was galloping like a runaway horse. "What are you doing here?"

Grayson stepped out into the room and pulled me to him, wrapping his arms around me.

"Sorry for scaring you," he said quietly into my ear. "I'm guessing I'm here for the same reason you are."

"Trying to find out if Phoebe killed Dominique."

He kissed me briefly before speaking again. "I thought you were Phoebe or one of the housekeepers. I figured I was done for when you opened the closet door."

I stepped back out of his embrace, finding his touch too distracting. "You shouldn't be here. What if someone sees you? Most of the town knows you're wanted by the police."

"I was careful. I used the secret passageway to get up here to the second floor."

We'd discovered the secret passageway back in the spring while looking into another murder. After my last experience using that passageway, I was glad I'd been able to use the main staircase this time. I didn't want to encourage any unpleasant memories to resurface.

"Still," I insisted, worried for Grayson, "it's dangerous for you to be here."

"You're probably right about that," he conceded. "But I'm here now. We might as well finish what we started. Have you found anything?"

"Nothing. You?"

"No, and I've been over most of the room. I was about to check Phoebe's suitcase when you knocked on the door. At least, I'm assuming that was you."

"I thought I heard a noise in the room." I shook off that thought, refocusing. "Let's take a look at the suitcase."

Grayson grabbed it from the closet and set it on the bed. He unzipped it and flipped open the top. All of Phoebe's clothing had been removed from the case. We checked all the pockets but didn't find anything other than a couple of hair elastics, an old airplane boarding pass, and a rumpled fashion magazine.

"You checked the drawers, right?" I said, my gaze settling on the bureau.

"Maybe you should check them too," Grayson suggested. "You might notice something I missed."

Since Grayson didn't know about the stolen Gucci scarf, that was a possibility. I quickly rifled through the drawers, careful to put things back as close to how I found them as possible.

"Nothing," I said as I finished.

Grayson zipped up the suitcase and set it back in the closet. He was about to say something when we heard movement out in the hallway. Our gazes met and my heart rate picked up.

Someone slid a key card into the lock.

Grayson grabbed my hand and we dashed into the closet. He pulled the door shut behind us just as we heard the main door open.

My pulse pounded in my ears. It sounded so loud I worried that whoever was on the other side of the door might hear it. Grayson wrapped his arms around me from behind and gave me a gentle, reassuring squeeze. Then we stood as still as possible, listening.

I hoped that it was a housekeeper who'd entered the room, one who would tidy up, replace the towels, and then leave without coming near the closet. That hope was soon dashed.

A cell phone rang somewhere in the room and I heard Phoebe's voice as soon as the ringing stopped.

"Hey," she said to whoever was on the other end of the line. "I was about to text you."

Behind me, Grayson tensed, sensing the precariousness of our situation just as I had. Even if we avoided detection, who knew how long we'd have to hide here in the closet?

I tried not to worry about that, instead listening to Phoebe's end of the phone call.

"Yep," she said, the word followed by a sound that made me think she'd dropped down onto the bed. "Everything's going as planned."

She paused and then laughed. "You'll see. I'll get what I came here for and I'll still make it to New York in time for the meeting."

There was another, longer pause before she spoke again. "Uh-huh. But I've got to get ready now. I'll text you later."

I hardly dared to breathe as Phoebe's footsteps approached the closet.

Grayson's arms tightened around me.

I closed my eyes as my heart pounded.

I was certain we were about to get caught.

Chapter 27

The footsteps passed by the closet. I remained tense, worried that Phoebe might still discover us in our hiding spot. A few seconds later, I heard the sound of running water.

Grayson released his hold on me and carefully opened the closet door enough to show a sliver of light. He peeked out into the room and then whispered into my ear, "Quickly."

My heart raced wildly as we stepped into the open. The bathroom door was closed all but a crack, and it sounded like Phoebe had the shower running. Grayson eased the closet door shut and then we made a furtive dash across the carpeted floor and out of the room.

Luckily, there was no one out in the hallway. Grayson shut the door to Phoebe's room and grabbed my hand. We hurried down the hall to the elevator alcove, where there was also a door leading to a back staircase.

"Maybe I should take the back stairs or the secret passage-way and you should go down the front way," Grayson said, slowing his pace.

His fingers were still linked with mine, so I tugged him

through the door to the back stairway. "I want to make sure you get out of the hotel safely."

I peered over the railing, relieved to find that the stairwell was empty. We hurried downward.

When we reached the bottom of the stairs, I paused. "How did you get into Phoebe's room?"

Grayson removed a master key card from the pocket of his jeans. "I got this from the reception desk. Maybe I should drop it somewhere so it looks like a staff member lost it. I probably shouldn't take the risk of putting it back."

I took the key card from him. "I'll try to return it."

"I got it from the drawer to the left of the computer."

I quietly opened the door and took a quick look out into the corridor. The coast was clear, so I led the way.

From previous sleuthing escapades at the manor, I knew the way to one of the back doors, and we reached it without any problems. Before I had a chance to open the door and peek outside, Grayson tugged me close and kissed me. The heat of the kiss almost made me forget about the danger of him being seen on the premises.

"Happy birthday again," he said as he tucked my hair behind my ear. "I wish I could give you your present, but it's at my house."

I leaned into him and rested my head on his shoulder. "That's all right. Knowing you're okay is the only present I need."

I didn't want him to go, but I knew that every second spent in the hotel raised the risk of him getting seen and reported to the police. I opened the door and took a quick look outside. There was no one in sight.

Grayson kissed me one last time and then jogged across the back lawn to the forest. I waited until he was safely among the trees and out of sight before letting the door fall shut.

My phone buzzed and I fished it out of my pocket.

Where are you? the text from Shontelle read. **Are you okay?**

I wasn't surprised that my absence had raised questions. I'd been gone far too long for a simple trip to the restroom.

I crept along the hall and around the corner, drawing to a stop as soon as I could see the lobby.

Apparently, my luck had run out. Gemma was stationed behind the reception desk. I ducked out of sight behind a large potted fern and tapped out a message to Shontelle.

I'm fine. Can you please get Gemma away from the reception desk for a minute? I'll explain everything later.

I sent the message and waited for a response, hoping Shontelle would check her phone.

She replied almost immediately.

On it.

I tucked my phone away and tapped the key card against my leg as an outlet for my nervous energy. After all the stress of this sleuthing adventure, I could almost eat another platter of cakes and sandwiches.

"Hey, Gemma." Shontelle's voice came from the far side of the lobby. "I've always admired this painting. Do you know who it's by?"

I peeked around the fern. Gemma moved out from behind the desk and crossed the lobby.

Every second counted, so I silently scurried behind the desk. Gemma was still within sight, partway down the wide hallway that led to the dining room, but she had her back to me.

I caught Shontelle's eye and she winked at me before going back to speaking with Gemma about the painting displayed on the wall.

I pulled open the drawer to the left of the computer, dropped the key card inside, and dashed out from behind the desk. I tried to look calm and casual as I crossed the lobby. Shontelle and Gemma turned my way just as my mom, Aunt Gilda, and Yvette came out of the dining room.

"There you are, Sadie," my mom said with a hint of exasperation. "We were beginning to think you'd left without us."

"Of course I didn't," I said with a smile, hoping I didn't look guilty in any way.

"Are you feeling all right?" Aunt Gilda asked with concern. "You really were gone a long time."

"I'm sorry about that. I ran into someone I know and lost track of time."

That was true enough.

Thankfully, my mom and aunt accepted that explanation and didn't even ask me who it was that I'd run into. They were too busy talking with Gemma and Yvette about how much they enjoyed the tea.

Shontelle took my arm and whispered in my ear as we headed for the door. "You owe me an explanation." She wasn't mad, but she was definitely curious. No doubt she'd guessed that I'd done some snooping.

"You'll get one," I assured her. It was the least she deserved for helping me return the key card without getting caught.

The front door of the hotel opened as we approached it. My steps faltered when Nick strode into the lobby, dressed in dark jeans and a gray button-up shirt. Mild surprise registered in his eyes as his gaze met mine, but he walked straight past us and jogged up the main staircase, leaving the scent of cologne in his wake.

I knew Nick wasn't staying at the manor, so I couldn't help but wonder why he was there. Maybe he was paying a visit to Phoebe. I couldn't follow him without making Gemma, my mom, and my aunt suspicious, so I walked out onto the front steps and into the autumn sunshine.

When we reached the parking lot, Shontelle asked me to

THROUGH THE LIQUOR GLASS 213

wait a moment while she fetched my birthday present from her car. She opened the trunk and retrieved a plastic-wrapped gift basket.

She presented it to me with a smile. "Happy birthday, Sadie."

"Thank you so much!"

The basket was filled with an assortment of local products, including cheese and the maple butter popcorn I often bought at the farmers' market.

"Everything looks delicious," I said.

I very much wanted to sample the contents, but I figured I should leave the basket wrapped at least until I got home, especially since I'd just eaten plenty of sweets.

I set the basket safely in the backseat of Gilda's car and gave Shontelle a hug.

"Thank you again." Before releasing her, I added in a whisper, "Can we meet up tonight?"

"Text me a time," she whispered back.

The five of us spent a few more minutes chatting before we got into our respective vehicles to leave the manor.

Happiness thrummed through me as we drove back to the center of town. I'd enjoyed the tea, I loved my presents, and I treasured the time spent with Grayson, despite the rather stressful circumstances. Considering the fact that he was wanted for murder, I didn't think I could have had a better birthday.

Even so, my greatest wish was to be able to see Grayson whenever I wanted, and not in secret. My next step toward making that a reality was to talk to Jason about Caleb's potential as a suspect. Aunt Gilda was cooking dinner for my mom and me that evening, but I thought I could fit in a quick meeting with Jason, as long as he was available.

I sent him a text message while still in the car and heard back from him as I was walking across the footbridge to the Inkwell.

He was at the brewery and could meet with me anytime in the next hour. I popped upstairs to my apartment to check on Wimsey, and then walked over to the brewery.

It was good to see the business operating as usual, even though Grayson wasn't there. Despite a murder taking place on the premises, tourists were still flocking to the Spirit Hill Brewery. The parking lot was nearly full when I arrived, and I saw one of Grayson's employees leading a tour group into the tasting room.

I ducked into the main office to see if Jason was there, and Annalisa told me to go on back. When I passed by Grayson's office on my way to Jason's, I felt my boyfriend's absence keenly. I'd seen him an hour earlier, but he should have been here at his brewery, doing what he loved, not hiding out in the forest somewhere.

Jason's door stood open and he sat facing a bank of monitors that gave him several different views of the property. When I tapped on the door frame, he swiveled his chair around and got to his feet.

"How are you doing, Sadie?"

"Pretty well." I shut the door to give us some privacy. I also lowered my voice. "I've seen Grayson."

"He's okay?"

I nodded. "But I don't think he's any closer to solving this thing than I am."

"I'm no closer either. I've been tied up here at the brewery. You wouldn't believe how many people have tried to sneak a look at the murder scene." He beckoned me closer to the bank of monitors. "You said you wanted to see the surveillance footage again?"

I explained to him why I wanted to see it.

As I did so, a crease appeared across Jason's forehead. "Caleb's a good guy."

"And I'm hoping he's got nothing to do with it," I said. "But I don't want to overlook anything."

"You're right. We can't afford to do that." He nudged a second swivel chair toward me and sat back down in his own.

I took a seat and wheeled my chair closer to his while he pulled up the footage on the largest monitor. We watched the same sequence of events that we'd seen at Grayson's house shortly before he went into hiding. Jason replayed the footage several times, but watching it over and over, and even pausing it in places, didn't help. It was impossible to tell if Caleb was the person who'd followed Dominique into the brewery building that night.

Jason also accessed the surveillance footage of the parking lot for the same night. Shortly before Dominique sneaked into the building where she later died, Caleb climbed into his car and drove toward the driveway. His vehicle disappeared off the screen. After that, aside from a shadowy flicker at the edge of the screen—which may or may not have been someone scurrying by on foot—there was no movement in the parking lot until Grayson and I walked across it in the moments before we found Dominique's body. Then Annalisa left in her car and, a few minutes later, the emergency vehicles arrived.

I sat back in my chair, disappointed. "We're no further ahead."

"There's something else you need to see." Jason opened a drawer in his desk and took out a white letter-size envelope. He handed it to me. "It arrived in this morning's mail."

The envelope was addressed to Grayson. I checked the return address. It had been sent by D. Girard.

I looked up at Jason with surprise. "Dominique Girard?"

"Take a look inside."

The envelope had already been slit open. Under the circumstances, I didn't think Grayson would mind that Jason had opened his mail.

Inside was a single slip of paper. I tugged it out and unfolded it. Three words were typed on the otherwise blank sheet.

Three words that sent my head spinning.

Please help Sam.

Chapter 28

"Samantha Shields?" I asked, still staring at the sheet of paper in my hands. "It's got to be, right?"

"Makes sense," Jason said.

"But does it?" I set the paper and envelope on the desk. "Samantha died years ago."

"Did she, though?"

I tried to recall what I'd read about the explosion in the investigative report. "The only remains they found were blood and some hair."

"They always figured everything else was swept away with the current, along with a lot of the other wreckage from the explosion," Jason said. "But maybe Samantha wasn't on the houseboat when it exploded. Maybe the blood and hair were planted, so the authorities would think she was on board at the time."

I considered all of that. "So Dominique didn't want to talk to Grayson about Samantha's murder," I said. "She wanted to talk to him about *helping* Samantha, because she's still alive."

"And apparently in some trouble," Jason added.

That seemed to be the case, according to the brief note.

"Dominique must have mailed the note as a backup plan, in case something happened to her," I said. "Grayson needs to know about this. It could be linked to Dominique's murder. Maybe this is the key to clearing Grayson's name."

"You said you've seen Grayson. Where?"

"At my place last night, and then again today at Shady Creek Manor. Phoebe Ramone is staying there. We ended up snooping through her room at the same time."

One corner of Jason's mouth twitched up in a smile, but it didn't last long. "Did he tell you where he's been staying?"

"Only that he's been out in the woods somewhere."

"Then you'll have to wait until your next chance meeting with him."

I didn't like the sound of that. "Don't you have any idea where he might be?"

"If he doesn't want to be found, you won't find him," Jason said. "Besides, you don't want to risk leading the cops to him, do you?"

I definitely didn't. "Maybe our paths will cross again soon." I hoped that was the case, but I knew I couldn't count on it. "In the meantime, I'll try to figure out what this note means. Mind if I keep it in case I run into Grayson?"

"Go ahead."

I checked my phone and realized that I needed to get moving if I didn't want to be late for dinner at Aunt Gilda's place. I slipped the note and envelope into my pocket.

"Sadie, don't put yourself in any danger," Jason cautioned. "Grayson wouldn't want that."

"I don't plan to."

I didn't miss the skepticism on his face.

"Remember to call me if you need anything," he said. "Even if all you need is a bodyguard."

"I'll call," I promised.

That seemed to appease him. He walked me out of the office and I hurried home, my mind whirling like a tornado.

I wore my new dress and jewelry to dinner with my mom and aunt. I enjoyed the meal and the company, but I found it hard to sit still. I wanted to follow the new line of investigation, and it took all of my self-control to keep my mind on the conversation and to keep myself from pulling out my phone to make notes and do some online research. Most likely, I wouldn't be able to do any investigating of substance until the next day. Morning felt like a long way off.

My mom and Aunt Gilda told me they were thinking of taking an overnight trip so my mom could see more of Vermont. They invited me along, but I declined, though I didn't tell them exactly why. Hopefully, by the time they returned from their short trip, Grayson would no longer be wanted for murder. We still had a lot of work to do to clear him of suspicion, but knowing that didn't dampen my spirits.

After dinner, I texted Shontelle to see if she was free to meet up. She responded as I walked home from Aunt Gilda's place. Her mom was willing to stay with Kiandra for an hour, so Shontelle would meet me at the Inkwell for a drink and a chat. I had a few minutes before she would arrive, so I checked on Wimsey up in my apartment. Although I was sorely tempted to get on the Internet, I didn't want to neglect my business, so I popped into the Inkwell's kitchen to see how Teagan was doing.

"Happy birthday, Sadie!" Teagan said as soon as I set foot in the kitchen. "I'm glad you stopped by. Booker and I made something for you." She opened the commercial refrigerator.

I couldn't see what she removed from the fridge until she turned around and set it on the island. My eyes widened as she lifted the dome off a platter that held a round cake covered in chocolate frosting and decorated with colorful flowers.

"It's gorgeous!" I exclaimed. "And it looks delicious."

"Booker baked it this morning and then I came in a few minutes early to help him decorate it."

I hugged her. "You guys are the best. Thank you."

Teagan sliced me a piece as I pulled a stool up to the island and perched on it.

"Chocolate cake with chocolate-hazelnut Swiss meringue buttercream," Teagan said as she pushed the slice of cake toward me.

"It looks and sounds heavenly." I dug my fork into the cake and took a bite, savoring it. "And it tastes even better. Seriously, Teagan, this is amazing and the decorations are incredible."

She smiled as she got back to work. It was almost time for the kitchen to close for the night, but she had a couple of food orders to fill first.

"Speaking of Booker," she said as she prepared two platters of nachos. "Do you know what's up with him?"

I was about to take another bite of cake, but I set my fork down. "What do you mean?"

"He hasn't been as upbeat as usual, and this morning he was really down. He didn't want to talk about it, though."

"I've noticed he hasn't been himself," I said. "But I don't know the reason. I'll talk to him tomorrow."

The brief chat about Booker had me worried. I hoped nothing serious was wrong, but it really wasn't like him to be glum and it sounded as though his mood had only worsened.

I decided to leave the rest of my cake for a moment. I spent a few minutes helping out with serving drinks so Damien and Zoe could each take a short break to enjoy a piece of cake in the kitchen. When Shontelle arrived, I poured her the glass of wine she requested and then fetched my piece of cake as well as a slice for her. Then we headed upstairs to my apartment, where we'd have more privacy.

As we enjoyed the cake, I told her about my trip to Phoebe's room at the manor and how I'd run into Grayson there. I hoped telling her those details wouldn't get her into any trouble or put her in an awkward position, but I was finding it harder and harder to keep things to myself. Sharing the story with my best friend helped ease some of the pressure that had been building in my chest since my talk with Jason.

I also showed her the note Dominique had sent Grayson. While I was sharing that information with Shontelle, dots connected in my head.

"The squatter next door!" I exclaimed.

"Have you eaten too much sugar?" Shontelle asked, eyeing my empty plate. "You're not making sense."

"It's not the sugar," I assured her. "Someone was sleeping in the attic of the empty house next door. I thought it was Grayson, but then when I spoke to him, he said he'd never stayed there."

"So you're thinking maybe it was Samantha?"

"Exactly. Once Dominique died, Samantha couldn't have stayed at the motel room, not if she wanted to stay hidden."

"You don't even know for sure if she's really alive."

"She's got to be." I tapped the note, which was sitting on my kitchen table. "How else could this make sense? And besides," I said, remembering something else, "there was a woman dumpster diving behind the grocery store the other day. One of the cashiers saw her but didn't recognize her. She was the right age to be Samantha."

"Maybe you can take a picture of Samantha to the cashier," Shontelle suggested.

"Good idea." I reconsidered. "Although, if Samantha has been pretending to be dead for all these years, she must have a good reason."

"So maybe you shouldn't be cluing anyone in to the fact that she might be alive."

"Exactly." I grabbed my phone and searched online until I found a photo of Samantha included in an article written about the houseboat explosion. I showed the picture to Shontelle. "She's got dark blond hair in this photo. The cashier said the dumpster diver had auburn hair, but Samantha could have dyed it."

"She probably would have tried to change her appearance if she was hiding under a new identity."

"Good point." I saved a copy of the photo to my phone before setting the device aside. "I need to track her down. She might be the only person who really knows why Dominique was killed."

"Do you think she's still staying next door?"

"Not since some teenagers decided to sneak into the house."

"The ones Kiandra mentioned," Shontelle said with a nod. "She'd probably think it was too dangerous to stay there after that. So how will you find her?"

I smiled, my hopes rising. "I have an idea."

Chapter 29

I made another midnight excursion to the house next door. This time I didn't have to climb a tree to get in, much to my relief. The main floor window I'd exited through on my previous visit was still unlocked. I crept up to the attic and whispered Samantha's name as I shone my flashlight around the dusty space.

The food and drink containers had disappeared, likely taken by the police, but there was nothing to suggest that anyone had taken shelter in the attic since my last visit. Samantha—or whoever had been camping out in the attic—hadn't returned. That was what I'd expected, but I'd wanted to make sure before I tried searching for her elsewhere.

I returned home and tried to get some sleep. I tossed and turned for an hour or so, my mind refusing to shut off, but eventually I grew tired enough that my thoughts blurred and I drifted off. I woke before my alarm went off the next morning. My thoughts immediately focused on Samantha again, as if there'd been no interruption. I jumped out of bed with an unusual amount of energy, startling Wimsey, who hadn't yet stirred from his spot on the extra pillow.

It was time to track down some answers.

Except, it was too early to do what I really wanted to do, and my office was calling to me. Even though I'd taken the week off from work, as the pub's owner, I wasn't entirely free. There were certain administrative tasks that I needed to look after.

I stifled a groan and carried a cup of coffee with me downstairs to my office. I loved running the Inkwell, but that morning I was itching to do other things.

Fortunately, I buckled down and got through the necessary work in under two hours. Minutes after wrapping up, I was out the door. I zipped up my jacket as a chilly wind whistled past me. The sky was a mass of roiling dark clouds. It seemed we weren't done with the rain and storms yet.

I walked briskly across town, partly to keep warm and partly because I was eager to get to my destination. The real estate agent who'd helped me purchase the Inkwell worked at an office located on Ashcroft Road, a couple of streets south of the village green. When I got to the office, I was relieved to find that it was open. Bridget Yu, the agent I'd worked with, was seated at her desk. She glanced up from her computer and smiled when she saw me.

"Sadie, what a nice surprise. How are you doing?" Her smile vanished. "I'm so sorry! How thoughtless of me! I heard about Grayson. You must not be doing great."

"No need to apologize," I assured her. "The situation with Grayson is tough, but I know his name will be cleared."

Her smile reappeared. "Keeping a positive attitude is the right way to go," she said. "Grayson isn't a killer, and I'm sure the truth will come out."

"You know Grayson?" I hadn't realized that.

"I helped him negotiate the purchase of the brewery. That was years ago now, of course. He's done such a great job with the business, and he's been a great addition to Shady Creek."

And to my life, I thought.

"Anyway," Bridget said, "what can I help you with this morning?"

"I was wondering if there are any properties for sale in Shady Creek that are currently unoccupied. Aside from the house next to the Inkwell."

"Are you looking to invest in more property?"

"No," I said, wondering what to tell her. "I'm conducting inquiries for a friend." In a way that was true. I was trying to help Grayson, just not with purchasing real estate.

To my relief, Bridget accepted that explanation. "Are we talking commercial or residential?"

"Residential, at least to start with," I said.

Bridget led me over to a wall where property listings were on display. "At the moment, we've got three other homes that are currently vacant." She tapped one of the listings, and then another. "These two are right in town." She moved farther along the wall and tapped another listing. "And this one's a little farther out, on an acreage."

I checked the information next to each photo. I tried to memorize the addresses, but I knew I'd forget at least two of them by the time I was out the door.

"Maybe I'll just note down the addresses for the moment," I said.

"I can get you hard copies of the listings," Bridget offered. "Is your friend in town?"

"Not at the moment." I thought of Grayson out in the woods somewhere and felt a familiar ache in my chest.

"Then maybe you should send your friend the listing numbers and then he or she can look them up online."

"That's a great idea," I said, even though it wouldn't help me. "Thank you."

"But I'll get you the hard copies too. I've got some right here." She opened a drawer in her desk and rifled through a stack of papers. She pulled out three and handed them over. "If you plug the listing number or the address into the website, the properties will pop up."

"That's perfect, Bridget. Thank you so much."

"You know, you're the second person to ask me about unoccupied properties in the past week."

That caught my attention. "Really? Who was the other person?"

Bridget smiled, misinterpreting the reason behind my question. "No need for your friend to worry, I'm sure. The market isn't so hot right now that a little competition will do any harm."

"Oh, I was just wondering if it was someone new to town or local."

"New to town."

"I think I might know who you mean," I said. "Was it a woman in her late twenties with auburn hair?"

"That's her," Bridget confirmed.

"I can't remember her name," I said, pretending to think. "Samantha, maybe?"

Bridget shook her head. "No, I'm pretty sure she said her name was Delilah."

I didn't let that tidbit of information put me off. More likely than not, Samantha wouldn't give out her real name.

"I don't suppose I'd be able to have a quick peek inside these houses, would I?" I asked, hopeful. "That way I'd have more information to share with my friend."

Bridget checked the calendar on her computer. "There aren't any open houses scheduled for today." She glanced at her watch. "I have an appointment later this morning, but I could take you around for a quick peek at a couple of the homes."

"That would be fantastic," I enthused.

"You're free to go right now?" she checked.

"Absolutely."

She grabbed her keys and purse. "Then let's go. I'll drive."

The first house was so close to the real estate office that we could have walked there in five minutes. In Bridget's car, the trip took even less time. She pulled up to the curb and parked in front of a cute, two-story white house with a black door and a FOR SALE sign on the front lawn.

As I climbed out of the car, a flock of butterflies danced about in my stomach. When I left the Inkwell earlier that morning, my hope was that I would come out of the real estate office with a list of properties to check to see if Samantha was using one of them as a hideout. The fact that the mystery woman had very possibly been to the real estate office herself confirmed for me that I was likely on the right track. Finding Samantha was a real possibility, and that ratcheted up my hope and excitement.

Even though I didn't actually have a friend looking to buy a home in Shady Creek, I took a moment to admire the house from the sidewalk. The front porch looked perfect for sitting in a rocking chair and sipping sweet tea on a hot day. Today was not such a day, however, and the porch was bare of any furniture. The lawn was trim and tidy, though, and the house looked well cared for.

Bridget walked briskly past me, already digging a key out of her purse. I hurried to follow her up to the porch. I was so glad I'd thought to ask her to show me the homes. It wasn't likely that I'd find an unlocked window, as I had at the other house. Of course, if Samantha was hiding out in one of the vacant homes, she must have found a way in, but this strategy was less likely to get me in trouble than if I'd attended each home on my own and tried to gain access without permission.

"This is a sweet house," Bridget said as she unlocked the door. "Very charming. Four bedrooms. A full bath upstairs and a powder room on the main floor."

As she led the way into the home, she continued telling me about the various features. I only half listened as I wandered from room to room, looking for any sign that someone had been using the house as temporary living quarters.

It didn't take long to go through the whole property. Each room was empty, with no sign of the mystery woman or anyone else. I asked to get a peek at the attic and the unfinished basement, and Bridget obliged, but I had no luck in those parts of the house either.

If Samantha really was alive and in Shady Creek, she wasn't here.

After locking up behind us, Bridget drove me to the next house. The green and beige bungalow wasn't as charming as the last place, but that hardly mattered under the circumstances. It took even less time to walk through this house. Again, there was no sign of anyone squatting on the property.

I made sure to hide my disappointment.

"I'm afraid I've got to get back to the office now," Bridget said as we walked toward her car. "I've got that appointment."

"Of course," I said. "Thank you so much for showing me these two places."

"You're very welcome. Do you want to ride back to the office with me?"

"That's all right, thanks. I'll walk from here."

Bridget smiled as she opened the driver's door. "It was good to see you again, Sadie. I'm looking forward to meeting your friend one day soon."

I smiled and thanked her again before setting off down the street. I felt bad for giving her the impression that she might get future business out of my friend, but I didn't dwell on that. As I walked back toward the village green, I flipped to the last printout Bridget had given me. The third vacant property was too far to walk to, but it wouldn't take me long to get there in my car.

I slowed down when I realized I was passing Simone's house. The bookstore owner was in the side yard, raking up leaves. She wore jeans and a T-shirt today, instead of her usual maxi skirt.

"Morning, Simone!" I called out.

She smiled and stopped raking. "Hey, Sadie."

I approached the picket fence that stood between us. "Not at the store today?"

"Tina's opening for me so I can get some work done around here."

Tina was her part-time employee.

"Looks like Eddie has come to help you," I said as the orange tabby appeared from around the back corner of the house. I realized a split second later that he had something in his mouth.

"Oh no!" Simone leaned her rake against the fence. "Not again, Eddie!"

"What's wrong?" I was worried the cat had caught and killed some sort of creature, but it looked more like he was dragging a piece of clothing along.

"Eddie's got a bad habit," Simone said as she crouched down. "Here, kitty. Come here, Eddie." She glanced up at me. "He sneaks out and then he goes around stealing things from the neighbors."

Eddie paused about twenty feet away from us, eyeing me warily.

"What kind of things?" I asked, trying to figure out what Eddie had in his mouth.

"All sorts," Simone said with a hint of despair. "I've got a whole bag of things I need to return to the owners, but I don't know what belongs to whom. He's brought home sunglasses, clothing, even jewelry. My neighbors are going to hate me when they find out."

"Seriously?" I said, putting two and two together. "*Eddie* is the thief that's been plaguing Shady Creek?"

Simone's cheeks turned pink. "Does everybody know about the missing items?"

"It's getting around."

"That's it." She got up from her crouch. "I'm going to have to make the rounds of the neighborhood. I'll take the contraband with me and knock on every door until everything's been returned."

Eddie seemed to decide that I wasn't there to steal his newest find. He padded over to Simone and rubbed against her legs, purring. Then he dropped his loot at her feet.

Simone picked it up and my jaw nearly dropped.

Eddie had brought home Dominique's missing Gucci scarf.

Chapter 30

"Um, Simone?" I said, still shocked. "That belonged to the murder victim."

Simone let out a squeak and dropped the scarf. It drifted to the ground, pooling at her feet. Eddie sniffed at it and then looked up at his human, as if wondering why she didn't like his gift.

"Oh, Eddie." Simone scooped the cat up into her arms. "What have you done?"

"I doubt he stole it from the victim," I said. "It disappeared from inside the town hall last week, when Dominique was still alive."

"So where the heck did Eddie find it?"

"Good question." I wished the tabby could answer. "If we knew, we might know who stole the scarf in the first place." *And that might tell us who killed Dominique*, I thought.

Simone hugged Eddie as she eyed the scarf on the ground as if it were dangerous. "What should we do with it?"

"We should probably turn it over to the police." I let myself in through the gate. I grabbed a twig from the ground and used it to lift up the scarf. I wasn't sure if I should be touching it.

The scarf had certainly seen better days. It smelled like it had come from a garbage heap, and looked like it too. It was covered in grime and had a dark red wet splotch on it. For a second, I worried it might be blood, even though the scarf had disappeared before Dominique was killed, but then I tentatively brought the silk closer to my face and sniffed it.

Ketchup, not blood.

Instead of dropping the scarf back on the ground, I draped it over the fence.

"So Eddie usually steals things from your neighbors' yards and houses? Do you know how far he strays?"

"I don't think he goes too far. He's never gone for very long." Simone sighed. "I really need to build him a catio. Maybe then he'll stop trying to sneak out as much."

I studied the scarf, thinking.

"Do you think I should call the police?" Simone asked.

"That would probably be a good idea."

Simone's face had gone pale. She set her cat on the ground. "Do you think I'll get in trouble for what Eddie's done?"

"I doubt it, especially if you do your best to return everything he stole, but I think the police would want to know about the scarf."

I pulled out my phone and scrolled through my contacts until I found Detective Marquez's direct number. I passed the device over to Simone.

"That's the number for the detective in charge of the murder case."

Simone fished her phone out of her pocket and typed in the number. "Thanks. I'll make the call."

"Do you mind if I cut through your yard to the alley?" I asked.

"Go ahead."

I left Simone to call the detective and made my way to the back alley. I was hoping to find a clue as to where Eddie had found the scarf. That didn't take me long. It also didn't take much in the way of investigative skills.

Three houses down from Simone's, I found a garbage can that had been knocked over—probably by raccoons—its contents spilled out on the ground. The unpleasant smell made me want to give the small trash heap a wide berth, but I held my breath and moved closer. Sure enough, among the debris were a couple of takeout condiment packets, both of which were open and oozing ketchup.

I backed away from the garbage until I could breathe in clean air. From that safe distance, I turned my attention from the mess on the ground to the house the trash can belonged to. I recognized it from my last trip along Simone's street. It was George and Miranda Keeler's house.

My heart rate ticked up. Since seeing the note Dominique had sent Grayson, I'd figured that the most likely murder suspects on my list were the ones from out of town who'd known Samantha back before her supposed death. Now I wasn't sure that I should be so hasty to discount my local suspects.

I hurried down the alley, back to Simone's yard. The police needed to know what I'd discovered.

Simone was finishing up a phone call when I let myself into the yard. Eddie was lounging in a patch of sun on the paved walkway that led from the back gate to the porch. Perhaps he was done with stealing from the neighbors for the day.

"Did you get in touch with the police?" I asked Simone as she returned her phone to her pocket.

"The detective didn't answer, so I looked up the general non-emergency number and called that. I guess the police aren't too busy at the moment, because they said they'd send an officer over in the next half hour or so."

I told Simone what I'd found out in the alley. Then, since I wanted to stick around until the officer showed up, I offered to help rake leaves. Simone readily accepted and fetched me another rake. We almost had the whole backyard cleared of fallen leaves when a police cruiser parked on the street out front.

I was hoping that Shontelle's boyfriend, Officer Eldon Howes, might be the one to respond to Simone's call, but that wasn't the case. Officer Pamela Rogers climbed out of the cruiser and approached us where we waited by the gate at the side of the house. We showed her the scarf and I explained that it belonged to Dominique and how it had disappeared during the food festival at the town hall. I let Simone explain about Eddie's thieving habit. Officer Rogers raised an eyebrow at that part, but she didn't comment beyond offering to assist Simone with returning the cat's finds to their rightful owners.

I led Rogers down the alley to the spilled garbage and pointed out the ketchup. She stared at the scene for a moment, studying it, and then we both raised our gazes to the Keeler house. A flicker of movement at one of the windows drew my attention. I caught a glimpse of Miranda Keeler before she darted out of sight.

"Looks like Mrs. Keeler is home," I said. "Should we see what she has to say about the scarf?"

"*I'll* take care of that," Officer Rogers said, with a firm emphasis on the first word. "Thank you for the information, Sadie. I'll be in touch if I have any questions for you."

I was being dismissed. I really wanted to know how Miranda would react to Rogers's questions about the scarf, but the officer was waiting for me to leave, so I didn't really have a choice but to do just that.

I thanked her for showing up, and then walked off down the alley. When I glanced over my shoulder, Rogers had disappeared from sight, likely into the Keelers' yard. I let out a huff of frustration over being left out of the upcoming conversation with Miranda, but then I did my best to get over my disappointment. I needed to stay focused on finding Samantha Shields, if she really was still alive and in Shady Creek. Since my visit to the real estate office, I was more convinced than ever that the theory was a good one.

When I got back to the Inkwell, I was tempted to hop in my car right away and drive out to the last of the vacant properties, but my concern for Booker stopped me. I'd been worried about him for a while now, and that worry had only intensified since I'd last talked to Teagan. It was around the time when he usually arrived at the Inkwell to start his prep work in the kitchen, so I decided to check in on him.

At first, I thought he wasn't there yet. The pub was too quiet. That didn't necessarily mean anything lately, though. With Booker not himself, I couldn't count on his singing to alert me to his arrival.

Sure enough, when I pushed through the kitchen door, I found him there, quietly chopping up vegetables.

The near silence felt so wrong.

"Hey, Sadie," Booker greeted, glancing up briefly.

"Thank you for the birthday cake. It was delicious."

He smiled, but it didn't last long. "I'm glad you liked it. Did you have a good birthday, despite Grayson's problems?"

"I did. It was nice to celebrate with my mom."

"What is she up to today?"

I thought he was making an attempt to sound cheerful, but he wasn't quite succeeding.

"She and Gilda have gone on a mini road trip until tomorrow," I said.

"You didn't want to go with them?"

"I had some things to do around here, so I thought I'd stay home."

"Things to do like solving a murder?" He cracked a smile, but it was so fleeting I almost missed it.

"That, and other things. Are you okay, Booker?"

"Sure." He tried to sound casual, but he still wasn't fooling me.

I pulled a stool up to the island and perched on it. "You don't sing anymore, you barely smile anymore, and you just don't seem like yourself."

Booker set down his knife with a sigh. "It's that obvious?"

"Teagan and I have both been worried. You don't have to tell me what's going on if you don't want to, but I'm also here to listen if you do."

"Thanks, Sadie." He washed his hands as a kettle on the gas range began to whistle. "Tea?"

"Yes, please," I said. I knew the offer meant he was willing to talk.

Booker preferred to have important conversations over a cup of tea, served in the teacups he'd inherited from his grandmother. He took a moment to prepare the hot drinks and set two cups and saucers on the island. He pulled up another stool and sat next to me.

I waited, blowing on my tea, letting him decide when he wanted to talk. It didn't take him long.

"I proposed to Hannah two nights ago."

I didn't know what I'd expected him to say, but it wasn't that. Hannah was his girlfriend of several years, and he'd moved to Shady Creek because of her. She'd grown up here and had wanted to move home. I'd never heard Booker mention that marriage was on the horizon, though.

Judging by his mood and the melancholy look in his eyes, I could guess what had happened.

"She didn't say yes?" My heart was already breaking for him.

"Nope." The word came out on a heavy sigh. "I'd been building up to it for weeks. I bought a ring in Rutland and knew exactly what I was going to say. I cooked her dinner and then popped the question. She ended up in tears. She said she hated to hurt me, but she didn't see that kind of a future with me. It turns out she's been thinking of moving to New York City. Her high school sweetheart lives there now. They reconnected online recently and she wants to give him another chance."

The crack in my heart deepened. I leaned over to give him a hug. "Booker, I'm so sorry."

He put an arm around me and gave me a squeeze in return. "Thanks. Me too."

"She never gave you any hint before about the high school sweetheart?"

He stared into his tea, completely dejected. "If she did, I missed it. It hit me out of the blue like a ton of bricks."

"Oh no." I couldn't think of any words that were adequate for the circumstances. Maybe there weren't any. I looped my arm around his. "Do you need to take any time off from work? I could talk to Teagan and see if she can put in some extra hours."

"No, but thanks. I'd rather work. It helps to distract me. Speaking of which"—he drank down his tea and stood up—"I'd better get back to it."

I drank my tea as well and set the cup on the saucer. "I'll let you get on with things, but if you ever need to vent, or if you need someone to lean on, just let me know."

Booker started gathering up the teacups and saucers, but then he set them down and pulled me into a bear hug. His hugs always made me feel tiny, but I hoped I was able to provide some comfort when I hugged him in return.

"Thanks, Sadie," he said as he released me. "I'm lucky to call you a friend."

"I feel the same."

This time his smile lasted a little longer. "And don't worry," he said as he carried our teacups and saucers over to the sink. "You won't be short a chef. Shady Creek is my home now, and I'm not planning on going anywhere."

The thought of him leaving hadn't even occurred to me yet, although now I realized that it should have. He'd moved here for Hannah, after all. I was relieved to know he had far more to keep him here now.

"I'm very glad to hear that."

I left him to his work, hoping one day soon he'd feel good enough to start singing again.

When I emerged from the kitchen, it was almost time to open the Inkwell. Mel showed up ready to take care of everything, but I decided to stick around for a little while. Zoe wouldn't be coming into work until later, and I thought I should wait and see how busy it was going to get before leaving Mel on her own.

That turned out to be a good thing. Several tourists arrived, hungry and thirsty, right after we opened the pub. A smattering of locals followed on their heels. I helped out with serving meals and mixing drinks until everyone was looked after.

Before leaving on my quest to find Samantha, I decided to check the Inkwell's e-mail account. It turned out that I needed to make a phone call to one of my suppliers. The person I needed to talk to had stepped out for a few minutes, so I was told they'd phone me back shortly.

While I waited, I scrolled through my Instagram feed. My mind soon wandered back to Dominique's murder. I found her account again and went through it, picture by picture. I didn't know what I was looking for, especially since I'd already checked out her feed. But then something in my mind clicked. I stopped and scrolled back until I was looking at a selfie Dominique had taken, presumably in her apartment. In the background, a laptop sat on a coffee table. The laptop was covered in stickers, ones I'd seen before.

In Phoebe Ramone's hotel room.

Chapter 31

Phoebe had Dominique's laptop.

I didn't think I was leaping to conclusions by assuming that was the case.

I checked more photos on Dominique's Instagram feed and confirmed what I'd already suspected—the selfie was taken at her apartment. The picture was dated less than a month ago. Considering the animosity between the two food writers, I thought it highly unlikely that Phoebe, with her laptop in tow, had been hanging out at Dominique's place when the selfie was taken.

Phoebe must have stolen the laptop here in Shady Creek. Was she the one who ransacked Dominique's motel room? Quite possibly. Her motive might have had something to do with the fact that she wanted Dominique's job, but her motive wasn't what concerned me right then. I was far more interested in what might be on Dominique's computer. Maybe it held information about Samantha and the reason why Dominique was killed.

I needed to get a look at the laptop, but even if I could get my hands on it, the computer was password protected. I didn't know if that had prevented Phoebe from accessing the laptop's contents, but it had stopped me while I was snooping at the manor, and it would again if I didn't have a different strategy.

I scrapped my original plan for the afternoon. Checking out the vacant house would have to wait. I didn't know how long Phoebe would stay in town. The main part of the food and drink festival was already over. For all I knew, she could have already left Shady Creek, taking Dominique's laptop with her. I desperately hoped that wasn't the case.

Since I had no idea how to bypass the password requirement, I would need help to execute my latest plan. Joey was good with computers and might know how to do that sort of thing, but I didn't want to ask him. He would want to know what I was up to and why, and I wasn't ready to share that information with him.

There was one other person I could think of who might be able to help. I grabbed my phone and sent a quick text message to Jason.

Can we talk?

I paced up and down the hall outside my office, waiting for a reply. After a few minutes of that, I couldn't take it any longer. I needed a better way to distract myself.

Returning to the pub, I mixed cocktails for thirsty customers, checking my phone between orders. Half an hour later, I finally had a response.

Meet me at the brewery in an hour.

I'll be there, I wrote back.

That left me with more time to kill, so I hung around the pub, serving customers until three quarters of an hour had passed. I power walked over to the brewery, arriving several minutes early. I decided to check Jason's office, anyway. Maybe he was already there, waiting for me to show up.

Before I reached the building that housed the offices, Jason called my name from across the parking lot. With his long strides, it didn't take him long to reach me.

"What's going on?" he asked.

I glanced at a group of tourists passing us on their way to the tasting room.

"Maybe we should talk in your office," I suggested.

Jason led the way inside. Once we were in his office with the door closed, I showed him Dominique's selfie on Instagram and pointed out the laptop.

"I saw a laptop with those exact stickers in Phoebe's room at Shady Creek Manor," I said.

"So you think Phoebe stole it?"

"Most likely."

Jason rubbed his jaw. "And let me guess—you want to see what's on the laptop."

"It might hold a valuable clue as to why Dominique was murdered and who killed her."

"Maybe Phoebe's the killer," Jason said. "And you're wanting to sneak into her hotel room. What if you get caught?"

"I'll have to make sure that doesn't happen." I didn't mention that Phoebe had nearly caught Grayson and me in her room the last time.

Even though I kept that bit to myself, Jason didn't seem too impressed with my plan.

"Phoebe could leave town at any time, if she hasn't gone already," I said. "I can't let such a potentially valuable source of information slip through my fingers."

Jason crossed his arms over his broad chest. "I don't think you're here for my approval, so what is it you want from me?"

"I tried to access the laptop when I was in Phoebe's hotel room, but it was password protected. I don't know how to get around that. Do you?"

"You know Grayson will kill me if anything happens to you, right?"

"I'll be careful," I promised. "I know you want his name cleared too. What if this is the only way to get the information we need?"

He held my gaze as the seconds ticked by. Finally, he relented and released a heavy sigh. "Give me a minute."

He dropped into a chair in front of an open laptop. I let my gaze wander over the various monitors as I waited. After tapping away at the laptop for a minute or two, Jason removed a flash drive from one of the USB ports and swiveled his chair to face me.

He handed me the flash drive. "Plug this into the laptop. There's a program on it that will run automatically. It'll get you past the password requirement."

I closed my hand around the flash drive. "Thank you, Jason."

"The best way to thank me will be by not getting caught."

"I won't."

Skepticism nudged his eyebrows upward. "I'd come with you, but we've got two busloads of tourists about to arrive and I'm the only one here to cover security."

"I'll be fine," I assured him, already on my way to the door.

"Do me a favor, Sadie," he said before I had a chance to leave. "Text me once you're out of there to let me know you're okay."

"Of course."

I gave him a quick smile and vamoosed, not wanting him to have second thoughts about giving me the flash drive. Back at the Inkwell, I hopped in my car and drove straight to Shady Creek Manor. The first raindrops of the day pattered against my windshield as I followed the long driveway to the hotel. I dashed from the parking lot to the manor's front doors, managing not to get too wet.

When I entered the lobby, I realized I had a problem. Gemma was behind the reception desk. If I marched right up to the second floor, she might get suspicious. I couldn't tell her I was there to visit Phoebe because I didn't want the food writer to be in her room at the same time as me, and I certainly didn't want Gemma reporting to Phoebe that I'd come looking for her.

As Gemma greeted me cheerily, I came up with a quick plan.

"I felt like eating lunch out today," I said. "And the food here is so good."

"I'm glad you like it," Gemma said.

The phone on the reception desk rang and she answered it as I made my way to the dining room.

I cast my gaze over the room and quickly noted that Phoebe wasn't present. Unfortunately, I didn't know if that meant she was in her room upstairs, elsewhere in town, or she'd checked out. Now that I'd told Gemma I was there to eat, I decided I'd better keep up the pretense. Besides, my stomach was rumbling and I could use some sustenance before sneaking around the manor. It wouldn't be good if my grumbling stomach gave me away while I was hiding from someone.

I ordered a clubhouse sandwich and a cup of coffee. It didn't take long for the meal to arrive. As I ate, I watched the rain falling outside the floor-to-ceiling windows. It was pouring down from the sky now and I thought I heard a rumble of thunder off in the distance.

When I finished my sandwich, I worried that carrying out my plan would be more difficult than I'd expected. I was hoping that Phoebe would show up in the dining room before I was done eating, but that hadn't happened. If she was up in her room, I might have to put off trying to access the laptop for another day, and another day might be too late.

I figured I might as well find out for sure if she was up there.

After paying for my lunch, I returned to the lobby. At least luck was with me in one respect. Gemma was no longer behind the desk and I was alone in the lobby. I knew I might not have another chance to borrow a key card, so I slipped behind the desk and checked the drawer to the left of the computer, the one where I'd left the key Grayson had used.

To my relief, there was still a key card there. I grabbed it and slipped it into my pocket as I hurried out from behind the desk. I continued on up the stairs, hoping my luck wouldn't run out. When I reached Phoebe's room, I knocked on the door and held my breath.

Nobody answered.

I knocked again, just to be sure, but the door remained shut tight and I didn't hear any noises coming from inside the room.

Hoping that Phoebe wasn't sound asleep or in the shower, I slipped the key card into the slot and opened the door. I peeked into the room. It was empty.

With a quick glance down the hall to make sure I was unobserved, I slipped into the room and shut the door behind me. A silver laptop sat on the desk, just like the last time I was in the room.

I didn't know how much time I had, so I didn't waste another second. I retrieved Dominique's laptop from the desk drawer and pushed Phoebe's aside so I could set Dominique's in its place. I sank into the chair as I opened Dominique's computer. It turned on automatically, and I slipped the flash drive Jason had given me into one of the USB ports. The computer hummed as the program worked its magic.

My heart cantered along as I waited. Even if Phoebe wasn't the murderer, I could end up in serious trouble if I was caught in her room, snooping through Dominique's computer. At the very least, I'd get banned from ever setting foot in the manor again. I didn't want to think about the other possible consequences.

Fortunately, I didn't have much time to think about getting caught. Jason's program worked like a charm and I soon found myself looking at the computer's desktop. I opened the file explorer. Dominique had file folders named "work," "taxes," "poetry," "photos," "inspiration," and "miscellaneous." There were also two others named with what I thought were acronyms: "SWMB" and "PMF."

I clicked on the "work" folder first and found several subfolders. I quickly scanned through their contents. There were dozens, maybe hundreds, of files named for what I thought were restaurants. Those were probably her reviews. There were also a couple of contracts and some tax-related documents. None of those interested me.

Next, I tried the folder named "SWMB." I had to open a few files to figure out their purpose. I gathered that Dominique had helped two friends, with the initials SW and MB, plan their wedding.

I moved on, opening the folder named "PMF." The file names didn't give me any clues as to what they contained. When I tried to open the files, I ran into a problem. They were all password protected. If the software Jason had given me was capable of bypassing the passwords for the files as well as the computer, I didn't know how to make it do that. I tried all three files in the folder but ran into the same problem with each one.

Frustration sent tension creeping through my muscles, but hope also glimmered on the horizon. Maybe I was really onto something. None of the other files I'd looked at were protected by passwords. There had to be a reason why Dominique had added an extra layer of security to these files.

I opened the web browser and connected to the manor's Wi-Fi. Maybe Dominique's browsing history would hold a clue or two. There hadn't been any browser activity since the day before Dominique's death. I checked out the most recent sites she'd visited, ignoring the various social media platforms.

The first link I clicked took me to an article about a teenager in Fenworth, Maine, who died from consuming tainted drugs at a party. The article went on to talk about the increasing drug activity in the town in recent years and how it was believed that organized crime was behind it. The article was from a Fenworth newspaper and was dated six weeks earlier.

Clicking a second link took me to another article, this one about a Professor Michael Feldbloom at Summerville College. He taught biochemistry and had received a prestigious award for his research shortly before the article was written. Maybe Dominique knew the professor from when she attended the college, although she was enrolled in media studies, not science.

The next link brought up yet another article. I skimmed through it quickly. Like the first one I'd read, this one was about the drug trade in Fenworth, although it didn't talk about any specific deaths. Mostly it focused on the emergence of a new designer drug that was thought to have originated locally.

I was about to try another link from Dominique's browsing history when I heard a noise out in the hall. I froze.

Was that a woman's voice?

A second later, I knew I'd heard right. The woman was talking out in the hall, drawing ever closer.

I powered off the computer and yanked out the flash drive. I quickly but quietly returned Dominique's laptop to the desk drawer and shifted Phoebe's computer back to the middle of the desk. The voice was getting closer.

Now that I could hear more clearly, I recognized it as Phoebe's voice. Judging by the fact that I could hear only her side of the conversation, I figured she was talking on her phone.

My pulse roared like thunder in my ears as I frantically tried to decide what to do. If I hid in the closet like the last time, I could end up trapped in there for ages. Grayson and I were lucky before when Phoebe took a shower, but I didn't think I'd have the same kind of luck twice in a row.

There was only one other option I could see right in that moment.

As the door's lock clicked, I scrambled out the window.

Chapter 32

I arrived back at the Inkwell thoroughly soaked and shivering. Before getting out of my car, I sent a quick text message to Jason, letting him know I was home safe and sound. I didn't tell him anything else. The details of my adventure would have to wait to be shared until I saw him in person or talked to him on the phone.

The rain had let up by the time I hurried from my car to the back door of the gristmill. It was merely sprinkling now, but I hadn't been so lucky when I climbed out Phoebe's window.

Scratch that. I'd been lucky in certain respects.

If Phoebe's room had been on the third floor, or on a different part of the second floor, I wouldn't have been able to escape out the window. The one I'd climbed out of gave me access to the roof over a patio. I'd managed to get the window closed and duck out of sight before Phoebe had a chance to see me. Then I'd carefully shifted my way across the wet shingles to the corner of the roof, where I'd then climbed down some latticework, only having to drop about three feet to the ground. The entire time, I'd expected someone to notice me and start shouting, but that never happened.

So, really, getting soaked from the rain was a minor problem. Everything else had gone as well as it could have considering that Phoebe had interrupted my snooping. I'd even managed to slip into the lobby unnoticed and return the key card before leaving the manor.

Although my time with Dominique's computer had been cut short, I thought I'd managed to gather some valuable clues. I wasn't sure yet how all the pieces of information fit together, but I had a feeling they *did* fit together. I just needed to find more puzzle pieces to fill in the gaps. Then, hopefully, everything would make more sense.

Up in my apartment, I hopped in the shower to warm up and then dressed in dry, comfy clothes. I was craving a mocha from the Village Bean, but the rain had picked up again and I had no desire to go back outside now that I was warm and dry. I decided to settle for a cup of home-brewed coffee instead. I also filled a bowl with maple butter popcorn from the gift basket Shontelle had given me. My sleuthing at the manor had left me craving a snack.

I settled at my kitchen table with my laptop, ready to do some research. I focused on Professor Feldbloom. Dominique's interest in the man could have been unrelated to her murder or to Samantha Shields, but I suspected that wasn't the case. As I munched on popcorn, I skimmed through the professional profiles I found online, but they didn't tell me much other than the fact that the professor had left Summerville College almost seven years ago and had started teaching at another school.

When I dug deeper, things got more interesting.

It turned out that Professor Feldbloom had sued Summerville College after moving to his new job. That piqued my curiosity, so I continued my research. By the time I finished my cup of coffee, I knew that the professor had faced drug conspiracy charges seven years ago. The charges had ultimately been dropped, but the professor then sued Summerville College for suspending him after his arrest. The matter had been settled out of court, with the details of the settlement kept private, but Professor Feldbloom had never worked for that college again.

I sat back in my chair and drummed my fingers against the tabletop. Dominique was a food writer, but she had a broader journalism background. Had she been investigating the professor, or was she reading up on him for another reason?

I hoped I would soon know the answer to that question.

During my research, I'd come across a couple of small photos of Michael Feldbloom. Now, I located a larger one. When the man's face filled my screen, something about him briefly struck me as familiar. I studied the photo for several minutes, but I couldn't put my finger on what it was that was tugging at my memories. It irked me that I couldn't figure it out, but the harder I tried, the more I doubted the significance of that fleeting feeling.

I stood up and stretched. The rain had stopped while I had my attention glued to my computer, and I was craving some exercise. It wouldn't be long before it started to grow dark outside, especially with the heavy clouds still hiding the sun, but I had time to go for a bike ride. And if I rode my bike to the last of the vacant homes Bridget had told me about, I could look for signs of Samantha.

That sounded like a good plan to me.

Wimsey, however, wasn't particularly impressed. I told him what I was going to do as I pulled on my jacket. He was curled up at one end of the couch, looking as cozy as could be. He cracked open his eyes when I talked to him, but then he went right back to snoozing.

"I'll solve this thing and get Grayson's name cleared," I told my cat. "You'll see."

He gave no indication that he heard me.

No matter. I felt I was getting close to my goal and that was all I needed to spur me on.

I grabbed the printout Bridget had given me with the address of the third house. I stuffed the paper into my jacket pocket and then grabbed my bike helmet. As soon as I'd fetched my bicycle from the shed, I pedaled off along Creekside Road.

The last of the vacant houses was located on the outskirts of town. I had a general idea of where to find it, but I didn't realize until I got there that the old house was situated next door to the farm with the corn maze. Volunteers had been busy decorating the perimeter of the maze. There were bales of straw, a rather frightening scarecrow, and hand-painted signs that I couldn't read from this distance.

I turned into the driveway of the vacant property and cycled up to the old farmhouse. The place had seen better days. The white exterior was turning gray and the paint around the windows was peeling. A couple of the basement windows were cracked, and the steps to the front porch sagged in a worrying way, but with a little TLC from a new owner, it had the potential to look as cute and charming as it likely had in the past.

I leaned my bike against the porch railing, removed my helmet, and hung it from the handlebars. Then I took a few steps back so I could study the upper windows. They stared back at me like blank eyes. A shiver scurried its way up my spine. There was something lonely and eerie about the house, maybe because it had an air of abandonment about it. The weather probably wasn't helping either. The gray clouds were growing darker and thunder rumbled over the mountains as a damp wind blew across the neighboring fields, whipping my hair into my face.

I glanced back toward the road when I heard the sound of a car slowing down.

"Sadie, is that you?" Joey called out from the driver's seat.

He pulled the car into the driveway as I walked over to greet him.

"What are you doing out here?" he asked through the open window.

"Having a look at this house. It's for sale."

"You're looking to buy another property?" He sounded skeptical.

"No," I admitted. I didn't offer any further explanation.

Joey grinned. "You're up to something."

"Maybe." I gave him an enigmatic smile.

"And you're not going to tell me what that something is," he surmised.

"Not right now."

"In that case, do you have a few minutes to give me a hand? I've got some things I need to unload for the haunted maze."

"Sure." I figured that was the least I could do when I was keeping secrets from him.

"Hop in."

I climbed into the passenger seat and he drove onto the neighboring field. We bumped across the uneven ground until we were close to the maze. Then Joey parked and we climbed out.

A louder rumble of thunder rolled its way over the mountains. We both looked up at the ominous clouds overhead.

"I was hoping to get a bunch of stuff set up this afternoon," Joey said. "Looks like I might not have much time before it rains again."

"Then we'd better get busy."

Joey opened the trunk of his car and I helped him carry props and decorations over to the edge of the maze. He had several pieces of plywood that had been cut and painted to make the parts for coffins, which would be assembled on-site. He also had some rustic lanterns, fake skulls and skeletons, and pieces of large wooden gates that would be assembled at the entrance to the maze. The backseat of his car was loaded up with jack-o'-lanterns, all carved with scary faces.

"Looks like you've been busy," I said as I carried one of the jack-o'-lanterns over to the cornstalks.

Joey grabbed two others from the car. "This wasn't all me. A group of volunteers got together last night to carve pumpkins and work on some of the other decorations."

"You all did a great job."

We set the last of the jack-o'-lanterns on the ground.

Lightning flashed over the mountains. A clap of thunder, louder this time, followed several seconds later. Daylight was fading so fast it was as if it were an hour later than the actual time. The angry black clouds above us looked as though they could open up at any second.

"You know, I'm not sure you'll make it home without getting caught in the storm," Joey said. "If you don't mind hanging around for a few minutes, I can put your bike in the trunk and give you a ride home."

As much as I enjoyed riding my bike, I had no desire to do so in the middle of a bad thunderstorm.

"I'll take you up on that offer, thanks," I said. "I don't mind waiting. I want to go take a look at the house, anyway."

"Maybe one day you'll tell me why?"

"One day," I said with a smile.

I left Joey by the maze, where he started putting together the coffins with the help of a drill. As I carefully climbed the steps to the front porch of the old farmhouse, a few fat raindrops splattered down from the sky. I tried the front door, but it was locked, as I expected. Next, I peered through each of the front windows on the main floor. The house had been emptied of all furniture and looked as forlorn on the inside as it did on the outside.

Careful to avoid the rotting boards, I left the porch and circled around to the back of the house, where I found another, larger porch. This one was in even worse shape than the front one. I picked my way around the perimeter, where the boards appeared sturdiest, keeping a grip on the railing the whole time. Not that the railing would have saved me if anything went wrong. It was as wobbly as a drunken sailor.

The back door was locked tight, but one of the windows was broken, leaving a hole large enough to slip my hand through. Careful not to cut myself on the jagged glass, I reached in and turned the lock. The door creaked as I stepped into the empty kitchen.

I glanced out the window as another flash of lightning lit up the field behind the house. I thought I saw a figure dressed in dark clothing next to a maple tree, but when I blinked, there was nothing there. It was probably just a shadow. There were plenty of those, and they were growing darker as the light of the day faded away.

With thunder rumbling outside, I made my way deeper into the house. There wasn't much to see on the main floor. I didn't find so much as a discarded candy wrapper. At least the inside staircase appeared to be in good shape, in stark contrast to the outside steps and porches.

I grabbed the banister and started up the stairs.

A floorboard creaked overhead.

I froze, holding my breath as I strained to hear any further sounds. Another floorboard creaked, and a rustling sound followed.

Still holding on to the banister, I resumed my progress up the stairs, going slowly.

"Samantha?" I called softly. "I'm a friend of Grayson Blake's."

I paused halfway up the stairs, but heard no further noises. I continued on to the second floor.

I thought the sounds I'd heard had come from the front room to my left. The door to that room was closed all but a crack.

My pulse pounded in my ears as I stepped closer.

What if it's not Samantha? I wondered. *Maybe I should have brought Joey with me.*

It was too late now, though.

Mustering all the courage I could find, I stepped toward the door and pushed it open.

Someone burst out of the room and crashed into me. I stumbled back and fell to the ground. By the time I looked up, the person was disappearing down the staircase. I caught a glimpse of long, auburn hair, but that was it.

I scrambled to my feet and raced down the stairs.

This time I got a better glimpse of the woman as she jumped over the last three stairs and ran toward the back of the house.

I rushed down the stairs and along the hall.

Ahead of me, the woman yanked open the back door and flew out into the darkness.

"Wait!" I called.

I ran out the door after her, remembering too late about the condition of the porch. A board sagged beneath my foot. I lost my balance and had to do a funny hop and a skip to keep myself from falling.

"Samantha!" I yelled as I hit the ground at the base of the steps, safe and sound.

She ran across the back field. I tore after her.

A dark figure darted out from behind a maple tree and grabbed Samantha.

She screamed.

"Hey!" I yelled.

Samantha broke free of the other person and sprinted away. The darkness swallowed her up.

I was close enough now to see that the other figure wore a black hoodie. They lunged at me, and I felt fingers graze my arm. I veered off to the left and ran into the neighboring field.

Footsteps pounded on the ground behind me.

I didn't know why I was being chased. I only knew I didn't want my pursuer catching me.

"Joey!" I yelled into the wind and rain.

I was nearing the maze, but I was at the back of it, still a long way from where I'd left Joey. I'd lost sight of Samantha. I didn't know if she'd disappeared into the maze or the stand of trees nearby.

I heard a muttered curse behind me. I chanced a glance over my shoulder. My pursuer had tripped and fallen, but they were already scrabbling back to their feet.

"Joey!" I yelled again.

The maze's exit loomed ahead of me like a gaping hole in the darkness.

I plunged in among the cornstalks.

Right away, I regretted the move. The first turn I took led me to a dead end.

I spun around, planning to leave the maze and skirt around it, but a rustling of cornstalks told me that my adversary was too close on my tail.

I couldn't go back without getting caught, so I squeezed my way among the cornstalks. I tried not to make too much noise, but the cornstalks whispered and rattled, anyway. I hoped the wind, rain, and thunder would help to mask the sound of my flight.

Somewhere behind me, I could hear someone else moving through the maze.

I emerged from the cornstalks onto a pathway. I ran forward, took a right, and then spun around again when I reached another dead end. I ran back and turned left, then left again. I raced onward, wondering if I'd ever find a way out.

I charged around another corner and crashed into something solid.

Someone grabbed my arms.

I screamed.

Chapter 33

"Sadie!" Joey yelled through the driving rain. "What's wrong?"

I nearly cried with relief. "Someone's chasing me!"

A flash of lightning lit up the maze around us. A dark figure came barreling around the corner. They skidded to a stop when they saw me with Joey.

As darkness descended upon us again, the figure turned and ran in the opposite direction.

"We need to get out of here," I said to Joey, speaking loudly to be heard over the driving rain and the vicious wind.

I was scared my pursuer might regroup and come after both of us.

Joey took my hand. "I know the way out."

We ran together, Joey leading the way. It didn't take long to reach the entrance to the maze. We leapt over the jack-o'-lanterns we'd left on the ground and practically threw ourselves into Joey's car.

"My bike!" I exclaimed as Joey started the engine. Even as I said the words, I realized that leaving my bike behind was the least of my worries.

"I already put it in the trunk," Joey said as we bounced across the field and out onto the road.

I yanked on my seat belt and almost melted into the seat, weak with relief.

"Who was that chasing you?" Joey asked.

"I don't know." My voice sounded croaky and my throat felt sore from screaming.

The windshield wipers worked furiously as rain pelted the car. The headlights cut through the darkness, illuminating the downpour in its yellow-white beams.

Joey kept his eyes on the road. "Do you know *why* they were chasing you?"

"Not really," I said. "But I think I need to call Detective Marquez."

"I'll say."

I shook my head. "Not so much because of what happened to me. I think someone else is in danger."

Joey glanced my way before fixing his gaze back on the dark road before us. "Sadie, you've really got me worried here. I think we should go straight to the police station."

"I won't argue with you," I said.

I was really worried about the woman who'd run from the farmhouse, and I was more certain than ever that she was Samantha Shields. When I caught a glimpse of her face, I recognized her from the photo I'd found online.

She had a good chance to get away while our pursuer chased after me, but where would she go now? By scaring her off, I might have lost my one chance to talk with her, to find out what the heck was going on. Now she'd be warier than ever, and for good reason. I didn't think the person who'd chased me had followed me to the farmhouse. I was pretty sure they were there to hunt down Samantha.

This investigation was too out of control. Despite the fact

that Detective Marquez wanted to arrest Grayson, I needed her help. Samantha needed her help.

When Joey parked at the police station, we ran through the rain, then shook off our jackets when we got inside.

"I'll wait here and give you a ride home later," Joey said, sinking into an uncomfortable-looking chair.

It was a testament to how serious he thought the situation was that he wasn't trying to get in on my conversation with Detective Marquez. I owed him a free drink after this. Or maybe two or three.

It turned out that Detective Marquez wasn't available, so I ended up talking to Shontelle's boyfriend, Officer Eldon Howes. I started out by telling him what had happened at the vacant farmhouse, and then I went on to share my theory about Samantha Shields being alive and in danger. At that point, he started recording our conversation. I backtracked and told him about the note that Dominique had sent to Grayson, the one that had sent me along a new line of investigation.

I wanted to tell him about Dominique's Internet browsing history and the fact that Phoebe had her computer, but I didn't know how to do that without getting myself in a lot of trouble. I hoped that what I had shared with him would be enough.

I must not have told the story in the clearest of fashions. Eldon asked me to repeat several things and then went over everything again from start to finish. He took a lot of notes, even though he had an audio recording of our conversation.

When we finally finished going over everything, Eldon scrubbed a hand down his face. "Sadie, I have to tell you, it sounds a bit far-fetched that Samantha Shields could still be alive."

"I know, but can you at least consider the possibility?" I asked. "Whether she's Samantha or not, the auburn-haired woman is in danger, I'm sure of it."

"There's certainly something suspicious going on. And, yes, I'll consider the possibility that Ms. Shields is alive."

"How will you find her?"

He snapped his notebook shut. "That might take some work. It sounds like she doesn't want to be found."

"But the person who chased me could still be out there looking for her." I had to suppress a shiver at the thought.

Eldon pushed back his chair and got to his feet. "I'll head out that way and have a look around, but she's most likely taken shelter somewhere. With the storm and the darkness, I won't be able to do much searching tonight. I'll take a preliminary look, and then I'll go back in the morning when it's light."

That was probably the most that I could ask for. "Thank you."

At least he'd listened to me and hadn't written off my story as completely crazy.

"The weather is pretty bad out there," Eldon said as he walked me back toward the reception area. "Do you need a ride home?"

"That's okay, thanks. Joey Fontana is going to drive me."

Joey jumped to his feet when I returned to the reception area. We dashed from the police station to the shelter of his car and got back on the road. Thunder was booming right overhead now, and lightning lit up the road with its frequent flashes.

"Are you going to be okay here on your own?" Joey asked when he pulled up in front of the Inkwell.

"I'll be fine," I assured him. "Whoever was chasing me out there probably doesn't know where I live or even who I am."

"I hope you're right about that."

I hoped so too.

"You'll fill me in as soon as you can, right?" he asked. "I've got a feeling there's a good story behind everything that's happened."

"As soon as I know it won't endanger anyone's life, I'll tell you everything," I promised.

"In the meantime, call me if you need anything, at any time," he said.

I thanked him and kissed him on the cheek before climbing

out of the car. I put my bike in the shed and got inside as quickly as I could. Even so, I had to wipe rivulets of rain from my face.

After changing into dry clothes for the second time that day, I headed downstairs. The Inkwell was still open, and would be for a while yet, but there weren't many patrons inside.

"The storm has kept most people away tonight," Damien said when I commented on the slow pace of business.

"Understandable," I said. "It's terrible out there."

Since there wasn't much to do, I offered Damien the chance to head home early. He'd received several text messages from one of his daughters, who was anxious about the storm, so he accepted, and I took over for him. The pub emptied out nearly an hour before it normally closed, and I decided to shut things down early. The storm was still raging outside, the lights flickering now and then, and I didn't think any more customers would show up that evening.

I spent a restless night in bed, tossing and turning, grabbing only snippets of sound sleep here and there. Rain lashed at the windows, and the thunder would roll off into the distance only to wake me up with a loud clap a while later. I thought of Grayson and Samantha out there in the wild night and hoped they were both safe.

When morning finally arrived, I had to force myself out of bed. Yawning and feeling sluggish, I fed Wimsey before showering and getting dressed.

Ever since I'd left the police station, something had been niggling at the back of my mind, but every time I tried to grasp the thought, it slipped away.

While I ate my breakfast of toast with strawberry jam, I booted up my laptop and went over everything I'd found about Professor Michael Feldbloom the day before. When I looked at his photo again, I was struck once more with a sense of familiarity.

I let out a growl of frustration. Wimsey glanced up at me from the couch, where he was giving himself a bath.

"Sorry, buddy," I said. "My mind's not cooperating with me and it's driving me nuts."

Wimsey blinked his blue eyes at me and went back to his grooming routine.

If I could figure out why the professor looked familiar, I'd have more to go on. I was sure of it.

I retraced my online steps even farther back, pulling up information about Phoebe, as well as about Nick, Dominique, and Samantha from when they'd attended Summerville College. My eyes were watering from staring at the screen by the time a photo gave me pause. I enlarged it and took a closer look.

I called up another photo. Then I switched back and forth between the two pictures.

I thought back to the stormy night when Dominique had died.

Something I'd heard at the pizza parlor came back to me.

I sat back in my chair, a sense of triumph mingling with a heavy weight of fear in my chest.

I knew who'd killed Dominique.

Chapter 34

I hurried along Creekside Road with the hood of my jacket pulled up to protect me from the rain. At least the thunder and lightning had finally stopped, but even a storm wouldn't have kept me home that morning. I needed to talk to Cordelia. My theory was caught on a snag of a detail and I wanted to know if she could help me disentangle it.

As soon as I turned up the path to the Queen Anne that housed the Creekside Inn, I spotted Cordelia sweeping the front porch.

When I called out her name, she turned and waved.

"That was quite a storm last night, wasn't it?" she said when I reached the porch steps. "It blew a whole lot of leaves and even some branches up here."

When I reached the shelter of the porch, I pushed the hood of my jacket off my head. "Cordelia, there's something I need to ask you."

"You look so serious," she said with concern. "Is anything wrong?"

"Maybe."

"Why don't we talk inside?" she suggested as a gust of cold, damp wind sent her crinkly red hair dancing about her head.

I followed her into the front parlor. We seemed to be alone, but I still lowered my voice when I asked my questions.

As I'd hoped, her answers ironed out the wrinkles in my theory.

A guest came down the stairs, wanting to check out, so I left Cordelia to her work and stepped out onto the front porch to make a phone call.

The guest left and drove off while I was still talking. As I hung up a few minutes later, a car pulled up to the curb. Phoebe Ramone climbed out of the driver's seat and strode toward the inn, wearing high-heeled boots, tight jeans, and a leather jacket. Despite the rain and the heavy clouds overhead, she had sunglasses perched on the top of her head.

Nervous energy zinged through me, but I tried my best to appear calm.

"Good morning, Ms. Ramone," I greeted as she drew closer. "How are you enjoying your time in Shady Creek?"

She looked at me without recognition but still responded to my question. "It's been . . . interesting, I guess you could say." She climbed the steps to the porch and then stopped. "Do you work here?"

"No, I'm a friend of the owner's granddaughter."

As I said that, Cordelia opened the front door. "Sadie . . ." She noticed Phoebe. "Oh, hello."

Phoebe removed her sunglasses from her head. "I'm here to see Nick Perry."

"He's upstairs packing," Cordelia said, darting a nervous glance my way. "He's checking out this morning."

Phoebe tucked her sunglasses into the pocket of her leather jacket. "I know. We're both leaving today but we're having breakfast together first."

"Why don't you come inside to wait?" Cordelia held the front door open.

Phoebe took her up on the offer.

"Cordelia," I whispered as Phoebe disappeared into the house.

A phone rang inside the door.

Cordelia glanced in that direction with worried eyes. "Sorry, Sadie. Give me a minute? I should get that."

Indecision kept me standing out on the porch, alone now. I forced myself into action.

I hurried out into the rain and peered down the street. There were no cars in sight.

My stomach swirling with worry, I returned to the inn and let myself in through the front door. Somehow, I needed to keep Phoebe and Nick from leaving until Detective Marquez arrived.

Inside, I found Cordelia and Nick in the spacious foyer, with Cordelia sitting behind the reception desk. She shot a panicked glance my way before going back to tapping keys on the computer.

Phoebe sat on an antique chesterfield in the parlor to my left, focused on her phone.

Maybe I could strike up a conversation with her to delay her departure from the inn.

I'd taken three steps into the parlor when the lock on the front door clicked behind me and Cordelia let out a gasp.

I spun around.

Nick stood blocking the way to the door, holding a gun.

It was pointed right at me.

Chapter 35

"Sadie?" Cordelia's voice wavered with fear.

I stared at the gun.

"Get in there with the others," Nick ordered Cordelia, gesturing toward the parlor with his weapon.

She hesitated for a split second before scurrying over to me and gripping my arm. Out of the corner of my eye, I noticed Phoebe getting to her feet.

"What are you doing, Nick?" Phoebe asked, a hint of scorn in her voice. "Do you seriously think you'll get away with killing all of us?"

"Why not?" he said without a shred of concern. "If there aren't any witnesses . . ."

Cordelia's grip on my arm tightened. I wanted to offer her words of comfort, but they died in my throat.

"What's this about?" I asked instead, pretending I didn't know that he was a murderer.

"Please." The look he gave me was pure disdain. "You think I don't know what you've been up to? Nosing around, asking questions. If I'd caught you in that maze yesterday, I could have been out of town already."

"Really?" Phoebe stepped up beside me. She appeared completely cool and unfazed by the gun Nick had pointed at us.

I wondered if she was truly that calm or if she was a really good actress.

I nudged Cordelia a little off to the side. More than anything, I didn't want her getting hurt.

"Because if you'd left town last night," Phoebe continued, "the police would have been on your tail in no time."

"The police know nothing," Nick said with another good dose of disdain.

"Not true." I drew in a sharp breath when he glared at me with his icy blue eyes. "I've already told them that you killed Dominique. They're on their way here to arrest you as we speak."

"You're lying." He practically spat the words at me.

"She sounds pretty convincing to me," Phoebe said. "You'd better run if you want a chance to get away. If the police catch you, you're going down. I've been gathering evidence against you for days."

"Then I'll have to get rid of the evidence as well as you." Nick advanced toward Phoebe and me.

We moved backward until a coffee table blocked our path, forcing us to stop.

Nick smirked at Phoebe. "Aren't you going to wish me bon voyage?"

She returned his smug grin. "How about sweet dreams?"

Confusion barely had a chance to register on Nick's face before Cordelia smashed an antique bronze lamp base against the back of his head.

His eyes rolled back and he crumpled to the ground.

Phoebe kicked the gun aside and I pulled Cordelia into a fierce hug.

I almost laughed with relief as I squeezed her. "Cordelia, you saved our lives!"

I released her and stepped back.

She stared down at Nick's unmoving form, her face pale and her eyes wide.

Then she smiled. "I really did, didn't I?"

Chapter 36

"How did you know Nick was the killer?" Cordelia asked me as we stood outside the police station.

Along with Phoebe, we'd given statements to the police, detailing what had happened at the Creekside Inn. This was the first chance we'd had to talk with each other since Detective Marquez had arrived on the scene and taken custody of Nick, who was barely conscious at the time.

"I knew Dominique had been reading up on a professor named Michael Feldbloom before her death. I kept thinking the professor looked familiar, and it finally clicked that he reminded me of Nick. Once I realized that, I was able to find out that Professor Feldbloom is Nick's uncle."

"But what did the professor have to do with anything?"

"I haven't confirmed this, but I think Dominique was investigating the professor's ties to organized crime and the development of designer drugs. And somehow that's got to be related to the reason why Samantha Shields faked her death." I gave her a quick summary of what I knew about Samantha, her connection to Grayson, and the houseboat explosion. "I'm guessing Samantha was investigating the professor originally and he figured out that she was onto him, putting her life in danger. Then, for some reason, Dominique and Samantha picked up the investigation all these years later and the professor caught wind of it again."

"So he sent his nephew to silence her?" Cordelia guessed.

"That's my theory. His job as a travel writer gave him the perfect excuse to come to Shady Creek while Dominique was covering the food and drink festival. At some point, Nick must have realized that Samantha was still alive. He wanted to eliminate her too, but in the end, he never got the chance."

"Thank goodness." Cordelia shivered, and I didn't know if it was because of the chilly wind or what we'd been through that morning.

The door to the police station opened and Phoebe emerged from the building. She smiled when she saw us and came over our way.

"The hero of the day," she said to Cordelia, making my friend's already rosy cheeks turn a brighter shade of pink. "I'll be mentioning both of you in my article."

"You're going to write about what happened?" Cordelia asked. "I thought you were a food writer."

"I am, but I'm thinking it's time for a change. As soon as I began to suspect why Dominique had been killed, I started doing some digging. I think I've got a knack for investigative journalism."

"So you don't want Dominique's job anymore?" I asked.

Surprise registered on her face, but then she laughed. "You really do know everybody's business, huh?"

"Not exactly."

Cordelia came to my defense. "Sadie's great at solving mysteries, but she's not a snoop."

"Well, maybe I am," I admitted.

Phoebe shrugged. "Doesn't bother me. Sometimes I'm a snoop too."

"Like when you took Dominique's computer?"

I'd surprised her again.

"How'd you find out about that?"

I realized that I'd backed myself into a corner of a topic I didn't want to discuss. "I'd rather not say."

That got another laugh out of her. "You don't want to give away all your secrets. I can respect that."

"You searched Dominique's motel room after she died, right?" I said, hoping to fill in some gaps. "And that's when you took her laptop."

Phoebe's smile was in danger of turning into a smirk. "So you don't know everything after all. That must have been Nick. He was probably worried Dominique had evidence that could set the police on the trail of his uncle. The cops told me Nick stole Dominique's phone off her body when he killed her. For the same reason, no doubt."

I hadn't even realized that Dominique's phone was missing. Of course, there was no way for me to know what was or wasn't in her pockets when she died. Maybe the information on Dominique's phone was what gave Nick the idea to frame Grayson. Or maybe he'd been keeping tabs on her in the days leading up to her death and knew she had some sort of connection to Grayson. Either way, with Grayson's house so close to the scene of the crime, it wouldn't have been hard for Nick to break in and plant the wrench while retreating from the brewery. That made my boyfriend a convenient scapegoat.

"So how did you get the laptop?" Cordelia pressed, saving me the trouble.

"I took it from her car," Phoebe said. "I saw her park on a residential street. It must have been shortly before she was killed. Don't tell the cops that bit, okay?"

I still had more questions. "But why did you take the computer? Did you already know she was investigating Nick's uncle?"

"I had no clue about that until I finally managed to access the files on the computer. When I took the laptop, I was just trying to make Dominique's work life difficult. Petty of me, perhaps, but nobody's perfect, right?"

"Why did you dislike her so much?" I asked, remembering the heated argument she'd had with Dominique in the Inkwell's restroom.

"Our personalities clashed from the time we first met."

"Back in your college days?" I guessed.

"No. I dated Nick back then, and they knew each other slightly, but I didn't meet Dominique until we interned for the same magazine. We always seemed to end up competing for the same things. The same guy when we were interning and later the same job. Plus, she posted some nasty things about me online years ago. A mutual friend told me Dominique was going through an angry phase at the time, after her parents died in quick succession, but I don't think that excused the awful things she said."

Maybe that angry phase explained Dominique's scathing reviews from early in her career.

"Did Nick and Dominique really have a fling a while back?" I suspected that Nick had fed me a pack of lies when I'd spoken to him at the coffee shop with Joey.

"If Nick had his way, they probably would have, but Dominique knew all along that he was related to that shady professor. She rejected Nick's advances years ago, and he always hated her for it. The guy had some anger issues."

Maybe his hatred for Dominique was what drove Nick to crush her with the giant cask after killing her with the wrench. It seemed like such a spiteful and cruel touch.

"Anyway," Phoebe continued, "I'm getting the heck out of this town." She slipped sunglasses over her eyes, even though the sun was nowhere to be seen. "Ciao, ladies."

She strode off down the street.

"I'm not sure I like her all that much," Cordelia said as we watched Phoebe disappear around a corner.

"I'm not sure either." I zipped my jacket up, hoping to cut

out some of the damp wind. "But I do know I'm glad the killer wasn't someone local, like George Keeler or Alicia Jollimore."

"Me too," Cordelia said. "You had Miranda Keeler worried for a while, though. My grandma's known her for years and was talking to her yesterday. Miranda feels really bad about stealing Dominique's scarf."

"So she admitted to that? I guess she was kind of cornered once the police knew the scarf had been in her garbage can."

"I don't know anything about that," Cordelia said, "but Miranda told my grandma that she knows you have a reputation for figuring out mysteries. She was so scared you'd realize she stole the scarf."

That explained why she was so skittish when she saw me at the grocery store.

"She was also worried that you suspected George."

"Which I did."

"She overheard you asking him where he was at the time of the murder."

"And he didn't want to answer."

"Because he didn't want Miranda overhearing, apparently. But she knew he was hiding something and got the truth out of him. Turns out, he was doing some odd jobs for a guy Miranda doesn't like or trust. George had promised her he'd stay away from the guy."

"At least he wasn't hiding the fact that he was a murderer."

"Thank goodness." Cordelia hunched her shoulders against the wind. "I can't believe I had a killer staying in my house! I really thought he was up in his room that whole evening."

I'd believed that too until I'd made the connection between Nick and Professor Feldbloom. When I questioned Cordelia earlier, she told me that the inn had lost power on the night of the murder, so Nick couldn't have watched the hockey game on TV like he'd claimed. Then Cordelia confirmed that a guest room on the second floor had been empty that night. Its occupants had checked out that morning. I figured Nick crept down to the second floor, climbed out the window of the empty guest room, and had gone in search of Dominique. When he returned after the murder, he must have either climbed back up to the second-floor window or sneaked in the kitchen door and up the back staircase after Cordelia's grandmother had left the kitchen.

Cordelia wrapped her arms around herself. "I'm so glad he's locked up now."

"So am I. Should we start walking back home?" I suggested.

"Please." She shivered again. "I need some hot chocolate to warm me up."

Before we could get more than a few steps away from the front door of the station, a police cruiser pulled up to the curb. Eldon was at the wheel, and someone sat in the backseat. When he opened the back door, an auburn-haired woman climbed out, her gaze skittering warily around her.

"Samantha?" I said with a mixture of surprise and relief.

I was impressed that Eldon had found her and convinced her to come with him to the station. Most of all, though, I was glad to see that she was safe.

Her gaze darted my way and for a second I thought she might bolt.

Eldon put a reassuring hand on her arm. "It's all right."

I took a step toward her. "I'm Sadie, Grayson Blake's girl-friend."

Some of the tension eased out of her muscles. "Is Grayson here?"

"No," I replied with regret.

"Let's go inside." Eldon led her to the door.

Samantha glanced back at me before disappearing into the building.

I stood still, staring at the door as it drifted shut.

"Are you okay, Sadie?" Cordelia asked.

"I wish Grayson were here," I said, missing him so much that it was almost physically painful. "He doesn't need to hide anymore, but I have no way of telling him that."

"I already know."

The familiar voice sent my heart into a wild leap.

I spun around to find Grayson crossing the street toward me.

"Grayson?" I ran to him and threw my arms around him.

He hugged me tight and then kissed me. "You're okay?"

"I'm fine," I assured him. "What about you? How did you know it was safe to come out of hiding? Do you know about Nick? About Samantha?"

He laughed at my barrage of questions. "Jason filled me in."

For the first time, I realized Jason had walked up behind Grayson.

"Hold on." I narrowed my eyes at Jason. "You knew where to find Grayson?"

"I guessed," he replied. "There's an old cabin we came across once when we were hiking."

"You could have shared your guess with me."

"He didn't want you to know," Jason reminded me.

"For good reason," Grayson added.

I was too happy and relieved to be mad.

"So you know about Samantha?" I asked.

"It's hard to wrap my mind around it," Grayson said. "Are you sure she's really alive?"

Cordelia spoke up. "She's inside the police station."

"Hopefully, she can help the police make sense of things," I said. "There are still a lot of holes in the story."

Grayson pulled me close and kissed me again. "Thank you for working so hard to clear my name. I really missed you."

"I missed you too. So much."

I would have liked another kiss, but Detective Marquez chose that moment to step outside.

"Mr. Blake," she said, holding the station door open, "I'd appreciate a word."

"Of course, Detective." Grayson squeezed my hand before letting go and walking away.

I didn't want to let him out of my sight.

"Cordelia," I said, my gaze on Grayson, "do you mind if I—"

"Go on." She gave me a nudge toward the door.

"I'll walk her home," Jason assured me.

I turned back to give Cordelia a quick hug. Then I hurried to follow Grayson into the police station.

Chapter 37

"That was the best pumpkin pie I've ever tasted," my mom declared as she set her fork on her empty plate.

"Thank you, Mrs. Coleman," Grayson said with a smile. "I'm glad you enjoyed it."

"Please, call me Suzanne," my mom said.

I caught Grayson's eye as he collected everyone's empty plates, and we shared a smile. This dinner couldn't have gone better. My mom didn't just like Grayson, she adored him. I could tell. And I was over the moon.

"Would anyone like coffee?" Grayson asked.

My mom and Aunt Gilda both answered in the affirmative. I gathered up a few dishes and followed Grayson into his kitchen, where he set about putting a pot of coffee on to brew while I set the dishes in the sink.

After he switched on the machine, he pulled me into his arms.

I traced the contours of his face with my finger, still so relieved to have him back.

"What's wrong?" he asked quietly.

I realized that my expression had turned serious. "Nothing. I'm just glad I can see you on a daily basis again."

He took hold of a lock of my hair and let it slide through his fingers. "So am I. Next time I go into hiding, I'm taking you with me," he joked.

I looped my arms around his neck. "How about there is no next time?"

"Even better." He gave me a too-short kiss. "Although, I wouldn't mind another getaway with you, as long as we're not on the run."

"Nantucket *was* amazing." I released him with a sigh, remembering that my mom and aunt were expecting us to reappear soon.

I got busy putting the dirty plates in the dishwasher while Grayson got some mugs down from a cupboard.

"Have you heard from Samantha?" I asked as I loaded the last plate.

"I talked to her this morning. She's visiting an aunt in Syracuse. Now that she doesn't have to pretend to be someone else, she's looking at getting into investigative journalism, like she originally planned."

"I hope that works out for her."

Samantha had spent the years since her supposed death working as a waitress in Texas. Dominique had helped her establish a new identity and had stayed in touch with her over the years. Dominique had also helped Samantha fake her death. We'd learned that, among many other things, in the days following Nick's arrest. Grayson had spent a lot of time talking with Samantha, and I'd been present for some of the conversations.

I'd guessed right about the reason why Samantha had felt the need to disappear. When an existing drug problem on the campus of Summerville College got significantly worse and a new designer drug appeared on the scene, Samantha had decided to investigate. She came to suspect that Professor Michael Feldbloom was using campus labs to produce the designer drug, and that he had ties to organized crime, but before she could get enough proof, one of the professor's unsavory associates started following her everywhere. Then someone had tried to run her down with a truck.

With both her parents dead, she turned to her best friend, Dominique, for help. She'd heard that Grayson was planning to switch careers, and she hadn't seen him for more than a year at that point, so she decided to leave him out of it. She thought her death would get written off as an accident. She certainly never wanted Dominique to come under suspicion for her murder. They'd pretended to have a falling-out in the hope that the professor and his associates wouldn't suspect Dominique knew anything about Samantha's investigation.

The houseboat was owned by a friend of Samantha's. She knew that his family was wealthy and that the houseboat was insured, so she figured destroying it wouldn't hurt the family too much.

A few months before Dominique—and Samantha—arrived in Shady Creek, a Summerville teen had died after taking tainted drugs. That was the kid I'd read about while I was on Dominique's laptop. Samantha had babysat the boy when she was a college student. When she heard about his death, and the circumstances surrounding it, she decided she couldn't keep hiding. She told Dominique that she wanted to finish what she'd started and gather the evidence needed to put Professor Feldbloom in jail. Together, they'd worked to do just that. But again, somehow, Feldbloom got wind of what was happening and sent Nick to get rid of Dominique. At that point, Samantha and Dominique were already on their way to Shady Creek to find Grayson. They were hoping to enlist his help to keep them safe until they had enough evidence to take to the police. It was only after Nick had killed Dominique that he realized Samantha was alive, after catching a glimpse of her in town.

Now, Nick and his uncle were both behind bars.

And I had Grayson back.

"Coffee's almost ready," he said as I shut the dishwasher.

"But not quite?" I asked, hopeful.

Grayson grinned and wrapped his arms around me, knowing what I was really asking. "We can definitely squeeze in a kiss."

I'd completely lost track of time when the coffeemaker beeped. I broke away from Grayson reluctantly.

"I guess we should get back out there."

"Before they come looking for us." Grayson filled four mugs with coffee.

"Just remember . . ."

"Don't mention your run-in with the murderer," he finished for me.

"Exactly." I didn't want the evening ruined by my mom freaking out.

One corner of his mouth twitched upward. "Anything else I shouldn't talk about?"

"I don't think so."

His grin was full-fledged now. "So I can mention your tattoo?"

My eyes widened. "No way! My mom would ground me for life if she found out about it."

Grayson laughed. "I'm pretty sure she can't ground you when you're in your thirties."

"I'm pretty sure she'd still try."

"Sadie? Grayson?" my mom called from the dining room. "Do you need help in there?"

"We're fine!" I called back.

I shared a smile with Grayson.

Actually, we were better than fine.

With my heart full, I carried the coffee out of the kitchen.

Recipes

MAPLE BUTTER POPCORN

¼ cup popcorn kernels
3 tablespoons salted butter, at room temperature
3 tablespoons pure maple syrup

Pop the popcorn.

Brown the butter by heating it in a saucepan over medium low heat, stirring constantly. When the butter turns golden brown with brown flecks in it, immediately remove it from the heat and pour it into a heatproof bowl to halt the cooking process. Stir in the maple syrup. Drizzle over the popcorn and toss until evenly coated.

Serves 3 to 4 (if you're willing to share!).

KISS OF THE CIDER WOMAN

2 ounces dry apple cider
4 ounces cranberry juice
1½ ounces ginger ale

If using chilled ingredients, combine the cider and cranberry juice in a glass. Add the ginger ale and stir. If the ingredients aren't chilled, shake the cider and cranberry juice in an ice-filled cocktail shaker and strain into a glass. Add the ginger ale.

Makes one cocktail.

ACKNOWLEDGMENTS

So many wonderful people have been involved in bringing this book to publication. I'm sincerely grateful to my agent, Jessica Faust, for helping me bring this series to life and to my editor, Elizabeth May, for helping me to shape and polish this manuscript. Carina Chao came up with the title for this book and Jody Holford kindly read an early version of the manuscript. The entire Kensington team has been fabulous and I'd like to extend a special thank you to Alan Ayers and Louis Malcangi for creating such gorgeous covers for the books in this series. I'm also grateful to Larissa Ackerman and the rest of the publicity department for all their hard work. Last but not least, thank you to my review crew, my wonderful friends in the writing community, and to all the readers who have come along on Sadie's adventures in Shady Creek.

Keep reading for a special excerpt!

CLARET AND PRESENT DANGER
A Literary Pub Mystery

In this thrilling mystery by USA Today *bestselling author Sarah Fox, deadly happenings stick around like red wine stains on white tunics when the Renaissance faire visits Shady Creek, Vermont.*

The Trueheart Renaissance Faire and Circus has rolled into town, attracting locals who can't wait to spend a few summer days lost in a whimsical world of all-knowing fortune-tellers and daring acrobats. Well-read pub owner Sadie Coleman is swept up in the magic herself when she serves drinks to the faire's resident wizard, the shamelessly brazen illusionist Ozzie Stone, and scores two tickets to his dazzling performance.

Sadie has no complaints about indulging in a free show with her new beau, craft brewery owner Grayson Blake. But while Ozzie is an instant crowd-pleaser, the real surprise comes when he collapses in the middle of his set. It's not part of the act—Ozzie is dead, seemingly poisoned by someone who wasn't clowning around about writing the roguish showman's final chapter.

The terrifying situation intensifies when the police eye one of Sadie's employees, last seen caught in a suspicious fistfight at the fairgrounds. With so much at stake, Sadie must strain through a suspect list longer than her cocktail menu to find the real knave of a killer. But when another performer is murdered, it becomes clear that bringing the mixed-up murderer to justice will be about as dangerous as walking the high wire after happy hour . . .

Look for *Claret and Present Danger* on sale now!

Chapter 1

The sword blades glinted in the sunlight. The crowd watched with anticipation as the weapons clanged together again and again. The duelers managed to make it look like their fight wasn't choreographed, and now and then they hurled Renaissance insults at each other. Both men wore a combination of leather and plate armor but still managed to lunge and dodge with relative agility. I wasn't sure how they could stand the heat in their costumes. Summer was in full swing in Shady Creek, Vermont, and the sun was beating down from a gorgeous blue sky.

The taller of the two fighters parried a blow and then moved in for the kill. His opponent gasped as the sword blade slid between his arm and side, appearing from my vantage point as though it had pierced his abdomen. The wounded man staggered before dramatically falling to the ground.

The other man raised his sword in victory.

"Huzzah!" the crowd cheered, and I joined in.

"He killed him!" nine-year-old Kiandra Williams exclaimed as the crowd slowly dispersed, everyone moving on to check out other parts of the Trueheart Renaissance Faire and Circus.

"It was just pretend," my best friend, Shontelle, reminded her daughter.

"I know," Kiandra said. "I like the sound the swords make when they hit each other." She bounced up onto the balls of her feet. "Can we go watch the acrobats now?"

I checked the time on my phone. "It would probably be a good idea to go find seats."

The three of us made our way toward the red-and-white-striped tent that stood near the far end of the park, which had been transformed into a Renaissance village for the duration of the two-week event. This was my first time attending a Renaissance faire, and although I'd been at the park for less than an hour, I was already thoroughly impressed.

There were various stalls and huts where people in period costume demonstrated skills such as glassblowing, metalworking, basket weaving, leatherworking, and candle making. Many of the goods the craftsmen and craftswomen had made were available for sale, and I was considering doing some early Christmas shopping before the faire was over.

Musicians had gathered on a small stage and were playing a variety of instruments, including lutes, violins, and others that I couldn't name. Food vendors sold snacks from huts, and a tavern had been set up in one of the larger structures, where adult fairgoers could sit down for a meal and enjoy a tankard of ale. Here and there, costumed actors interacted with each other and with the spectators. Kiandra, like many other children at the faire, had already had her face painted. She now sported a unicorn on one cheek and a butterfly on the other.

At the entrance to the tent, we handed over our tickets to a woman in a tight-fitting bodice and full skirt, with a crown of flowers in her dark hair. Bleachers provided the unassigned seating in the tent. We'd arrived early, so we had our choice of spots. We decided on the third row back in the middle section.

"Sit next to me, Sadie," Kiandra requested as she plopped herself down on the bench.

I did as asked, and Shontelle sat on Kiandra's other side.

"We've got a good view from here," I said.

Kiandra's gaze traveled up and up. Her eyes widened. "Look how high that is!"

I followed the finger she was pointing up toward the ceiling of the tent. Way up high was a tightrope, as well as two trapezes. I wouldn't have the nerve to climb the ladder to get up that high, let alone swing out on a trapeze or balance along a wire.

I also noticed some silks hanging from the metal framework up near the tent's ceiling. I'd never watched a live performance with aerial silks, but I had seen one on TV and thought we could be in for a spectacular show.

When I'd first heard that the Renaissance faire was coming to my adopted home of Shady Creek, Vermont, the fact that it included circus elements had surprised me. Apparently, the faire had previously been more traditional but had recently added new attractions. Most people I knew were excited to take in both aspects of the faire, and so was I, starting with the acrobats' show that was about to start.

The bleachers quickly filled with spectators, and soon the lights dimmed. As the tent grew darker, I caught sight of a thin girl with wavy blond hair slipping into the tent while the ticket lady had her back turned. The girl appeared to be about eight or nine years old and didn't look familiar, but I didn't have a chance to notice anything more about her. She disappeared behind the bleachers, and music began to play, signaling the start of the show.

For the next hour, we were wowed by the high-flying feats of half a dozen acrobats. They walked the high wire, swung on the trapezes, flew through the air, and performed with the aerial silks. Kiandra was riveted the entire time.

"I want to do that," she whispered as a young woman let go of one trapeze and soared through the air before another acrobat on the second trapeze caught her.

"I don't think so," Shontelle said with alarm.

"Please!" Kiandra turned her beseeching eyes on her mother. Shontelle put a finger to her lips. "We'll talk about it later."

She shot me a look of dismay over Kiandra's head. I didn't blame her for her concern. The thought of Kiandra flying through the air way up high terrified me, and she wasn't even my daughter.

At one point, I caught another glimpse of the blond-haired girl who'd sneaked into the tent. She watched the show from between two sets of bleachers, her eyes as wide as Kiandra's. When the show finished, I looked for her again, but she was nowhere to be seen.

As we headed out of the tent, Kiandra bounced up and down between me and Shontelle, chattering nonstop about the amazing feats of the acrobats. She eventually wound down and asked for a snack. Shontelle and I were hungry too, so we wandered away from the tent, in search of something to eat. Along the way, we paused to study a poster affixed to the wall of one of the thatched huts. The poster advertised the most talked-about and anticipated attraction of the entire faire. Illusionist Ozzie Stone would be performing in the main tent each night.

I'd heard of Ozzie Stone before the faire had arrived in Shady Creek. He'd appeared on a televised nationwide talent show a year or so ago, and his star had been on the rise ever since. I'd hoped to catch one of his shows, but when I'd inquired at the gate that morning, I'd been informed that the tickets for all his performances were already sold out. That had disappointed me, but I was still determined to enjoy the faire as much as possible.

We moved on from the poster and spotted a hut with a sign that read ROSIE'S FARE. Another sign indicated that the vendor sold burgers, fries, cheese melts, and milkshakes. Before we reached Rosie's Fare, we paused to watch a juggler performing for passersby. He looked to be in his midtwenties and had curly brown hair. At the moment he had four beanbags in the air. He wrapped up the juggling act by catching all the beanbags. The crowd applauded, and he bowed.

"Now for some magic," he told everyone who was watching. He had three upside-down cups on a roughly hewn wooden table. He picked up one of the cups and placed a ball beneath it.

As he opened his mouth to speak to the crowd again, another man strutted over to his side, a self-assured smile on his face. I knew who he was right away—illusionist Ozzie Stone. He wore a white shirt beneath a blue velvet cape with a black silk lining, just like in the photo on his poster. He had piercing blue eyes, and his jet-black hair was a little on the long side. Despite the beautiful summer weather we'd been having in Vermont, I suspected his deep tan had been sprayed on.

There was a collective intake of breath from the crowd. I clearly wasn't the only one to recognize the illusionist.

"Lords and ladies," Ozzie said to the crowd, "if it's magic you desire, it's magic you shall get." He whipped a blue mug out from beneath his cape and snapped his fingers. "Water, please, Tobias."

The juggler frowned but handed over a small pitcher of water that had been sitting on the table.

"Observe," Ozzie commanded, "as I instantly turn this water into a block of ice."

A hush fell over the crowd as he poured the water into the blue mug. As soon as the pitcher was empty, he turned the mug upside down. No water flowed out, but a small block of ice fell into Ozzie's waiting hand.

The crowd cheered, me included.

"That's so cool!" Kiandra exclaimed with delight.

It seemed Ozzie had captivated her almost as much as the acrobats had.

Out of the corner of my eye, I noticed the curly-haired juggler slink away, looking disgruntled. I couldn't blame him.

Ozzie really had stolen his thunder, and he wasn't finished yet. For his next trick, Ozzie produced a small piece of paper and had a woman from the audience sign her name on it. He rolled up the paper and held it up for all of us to see. Then, with a flick of his hand, he made it disappear.

He fished a lemon out of his pocket, showed it to us, and then cut around the middle of it with a knife. When he pulled the two pieces of the lemon apart, a rolled-up paper protruded from one half. Ozzie removed the paper, unrolled it, and had the woman from the audience confirm that it was the same paper she'd signed. We all burst into applause as Ozzie bowed.

While the illusionist posed for selfies with fairgoers, we headed over to Rosie's Fare and purchased our snack, which turned out to be more of an early lunch. Shontelle bought some fries and a cheese melt to share with Kiandra, and I bought a cheese melt for myself. All three of us ordered chocolate milkshakes. We needed something cold to drink to keep us from getting too hot in the summer sunshine.

I gave myself a brain freeze with the first sip, but after that I drank more slowly and was able to enjoy the delicious creaminess of the chocolate shake. The cheese melt was heavenly too, and it calmed the growling of my hungry stomach. We ate at a rustic picnic table, watching the goings-on around us.

At one point a stout, costumed man came stumbling out of the tavern, another actor following on his heels.

"Away, you varlot! You rampallian!" shouted the taller man from the tavern's doorway. "I'll tickle your catastrophe!"

The stout man staggered about as if drunk. "You sodden, contumelious louse!" he yelled before weaving and lurching his way down the grassy walkway that stretched between the two rows of vendors.

I was pretty sure Kiandra had no idea what the insults meant, but she laughed along with me and Shontelle.

As I was finishing up my cheese melt, I caught sight of an attractive dark-haired man dressed in a costume that included black boots, dark trousers, a leather doublet and arm bracers, and a gray cape. He carried a sword at his side, and his hair reached nearly to his shoulders.

"He looks like Aragorn from *The Lord of the Rings*," I said to Shontelle, with a nod in the man's direction.

"He really does," Shontelle agreed. "He's almost Viggo Mortensen's doppelgänger." She watched him walk by. "Very easy on the eyes."

"Don't let him hear you say that," a man's voice cautioned. "It'll go to his head."

I turned to find local man Matt Yanders standing next to our picnic table. Matt owned the Harvest Grill, one of Shady Creek's restaurants. He was also a member of the science fiction and fantasy book club I hosted at my literary pub, the Inkwell.

"You know him?" Shontelle asked Matt, her gaze returning to Aragorn's look-alike.

"As much as it pains me to admit it, he's my brother." Matt's grin softened his words. "Flint, you scobberlotcher, get over here!" he bellowed.

Flint's face broke into a grin when he spotted Matt. "It's my knave of a brother!"

Matt pounded Flint on the back when he reached his side. "Flint, allow me to introduce these three fine ladies, Shontelle and Kiandra Williams, and Sadie Coleman."

Flint bowed. "Ladies, I'm honored to make your acquaintance."

"Is that a real sword?" Kiandra asked him.

"But of course." Flint pulled the blade from its scabbard. "It's a weapon of the finest craftsmanship."

"Cool!" Kiandra said before taking a long sip of her milkshake.

"How are you enjoying your day, ladies?" Flint asked me and Shontelle.

"It's great," I said.

"We're having a blast so far," Shontelle added.

"Excellent! I'm glad to hear it."

A woman wearing several gauzy scarves and many bracelets breezed past him.

"Minerva!" Flint called out.

The woman stopped in her tracks and turned to Flint. She smiled when she saw him.

Flint gestured at her with a flourish. "Have you ladies met our most esteemed soothsayer, Minerva the Mysterious?"

Minerva came closer and addressed us. "If you wish to have your fortune told, I am most happy to oblige."

"For a price." Flint chuckled.

Minerva gave him a sidelong glance. "Worth every penny."

"Undoubtably," Flint said.

"I wouldn't mind having my fortune told," Shontelle said. "It sounds fun," she added to me and Kiandra.

"Then please," Minerva said, "come this way."

"I'll stay with Kiandra," I told Shontelle.

Her daughter waved at her, but most of her focus was on her milkshake.

Shontelle followed Minerva the Mysterious into a small tent across the grassy walkway from our picnic table.

Flint bowed again. "My ladies, I'm afraid I must depart," he said to me and Kiandra. Then he addressed his brother. "You useless knave, we shall meet again."

Flint headed off, with several female fairgoers flitting along behind him, snapping photos with their phones.

Matt laughed before turning his attention to me. "I'll see you at the Inkwell sometime soon, Sadie."

I said goodbye, and he took his leave.

Kiandra finished off her milkshake with a loud slurp.

"All done?" I asked her.

She nodded and jumped up from the table. "Can we go look at the costumes?"

Next door to Minerva the Mysterious's tent was a costume rental shop. While we were eating, I'd seen two women, dressed in regular clothing, go into the store. Now they emerged, fully decked out in Renaissance wear.

"Sure," I said in response to Kiandra's question. "Let's go take a look."

I gathered up all our garbage and tossed it in a nearby bin. Kiandra skipped off ahead of me and disappeared into the shop. I followed after her, then paused one step inside the door so my eyes could adjust to the dim interior.

We browsed the store for a few minutes, until Kiandra lost interest.

"Let's go look at the hats," she said when we emerged from the costume rental shop.

She dashed over to a shop called the Mad Hatter and tried on a pirate's tricorn hat.

"How about this one?" I suggested, holding out a blue velvet hat with a fake peacock sitting on top, the tail feathers cascading down over the back rim.

Kiandra removed the hat she was wearing, and I plunked the peacock one on her head. She checked her reflection in a small mirror set out for that purpose.

She giggled, and I snapped a picture of her with my phone so we could show Shontelle later.

"You try this one," Kiandra said, handing me a gray cavalier hat with a single feather.

As we tried on several other hats, I noticed the curly-haired juggler we'd seen earlier standing nearby, speaking with a raven-haired woman who was texting on her smartphone. The device looked out of place, considering that she was wearing a Renaissance costume.

"I deserve my own show, Rachael," the juggler was saying. "I could draw in as much of a crowd as Ozzie."

Rachael continued to tap away at her phone, not even glancing up. "It's not happening, Toby. How many times do I have to tell you? Ozzie is our biggest draw. And your strength is street busking."

"But—"

Rachael cut him off. "But nothing. That's all I've got to say on the matter."

Toby looked as though he was about to protest again when Rachael squirmed in her costume.

"This bodice is too tight," she complained. "You'd think Patty was trying to suffocate me when she laced me up."

For the second time in the past hour, Ozzie Stone appeared on the scene.

He dipped down in a theatrical bow. "Allow me to assist you, milady."

While she'd talked with Toby, Rachael's expression had been stern, a crease traversing her forehead. Now the crease smoothed out, and she smiled.

"Thank you, Ozzie." She turned her back to him.

Ozzie loosened the laces on the back of her corset and began retying them. As he worked, he spoke quietly into Rachael's ear. She giggled, her dark eyelashes fluttering.

Toby the juggler scowled at them, but they took no notice. He muttered something under his breath that I couldn't quite hear. Ozzie rested his hands on Rachael's shoulders, and she giggled again. Toby's nostrils flared. He stormed away and disappeared into the crowd of fairgoers.